Davidson King
Hug It Out

Hug It Out
Haven Hart Universe
Copyright © 2018 Davidson King

ALL RIGHTS RESERVED
Cover and Interior design by Designs by Morningstar
Editing done by Heidi Ryan of Amour the line Editing
Interior Design and Formatting provided by Flawless Touch Formatting

The unauthorized reproduction or distribution of this copyrighted work is illegal. No part of this book may be reproduced or transmitted in any form or by any means, including electronic or mechanical means, including photocopying, recording, or by any information storage and retrieval systems, without express written permission from the author, Davidson King. The only exception is in the case of brief quotations embodied in reviews.

This book is a work of fiction. While references may be made to actual places and events, the names, characters, places, and incidents either are products of the author's imagination or are used fictitiously. Any resemblance to actual persons, living or dead, events, or locales is entirely coincidental.

Licensed material is being used for illustrative purposes only and any person depicted in the licensed material is a model.

DEDICATION

I'm dedicating this book to my amazing husband.
He's a little bit Teddy and a lot Riordan.
But more than that he's my heart, and the love and support he gives me daily is why I want to hug it out with him for the rest of my life.

Chapter One

Teddy

"On the left, Zach. Left. Other left. How do you not see the health? It's next to the boulder that looks like an elephant."

"Oh, excuse me, Teddy. It's a fucking beta, we've never gone through it," Zach, a fellow gamer, said to me through my headset.

"So, make a note. Though I don't think health is supposed to be obvious in this game." I liked it better when games made it easy to grab, but this one was a bitch.

"And now we're dead," he said with a loud sigh.

"It's cool. I gotta go anyway." I sipped my slushy and started shutting down my console.

"Yeah, you got people to hug." His laugh onlymade me roll my eyes. Whenever I wasn't beta testing games, writing reviews for them on my website, or writing strategy guides, I was running my own business: Teddy Bear Hugs & Companionship. Zach found it hilarious I cuddled people and nurtured them.

"Whatever, Zach. I have to go. Talk later." Without another word, I disconnected and began getting ready for my job.

First, a shower. My client today was a seventy-year-old woman. She'd been diagnosed with breast cancer and lived alone.

Three times a week, I went to her house, would sit and talk with her, and then we would sit on the couch and hug while watching her daily soap operas.

Many people didn't understand how vital it was to have human interaction and touch. I started this business because of my grandmother.

When my father passed away from a sudden heart attack when I was ten, my mother sort of drifted away. She worked more, traveled more, and I saw her less and less. Then I only saw her about twice a year. My grandmother, my father's mother, took me right in and showered me with more love than any boy could handle. She always made sure to hug me and be there when I needed a shoulder.

When I turned twenty-one, she got sick. Cancer. She was a survivor, but it took a lot out of her to fight. When she needed it, I made sure to return all the love she'd given me. It was in that moment when I realized I wanted people to know of this amazing feeling.

When I explained this to my best friend, Delly, she wanted in. My mother gave me some money she had received from my father's life insurance, and with it, I started Teddy Bear Hugs & Companionship. Delly signed on with me and five years later, we were four people strong.

I showered, skipping the aftershave and cologne, and headed out. I had just started the car when my phone vibrated. The number was one I didn't recognize.

"Hello, this is Teddy. Can I help you?"

"Oh, hello, Teddy. My husband gave me your number and I was hoping you could help me out," a female voice said.

I placed the call on speaker and began driving.

"May I ask who your husband is, and then who you are?"

"Yes! His name is Dr. Robert Banks. I'm his wife, Aisling Darcy-Banks."

"Hello, Mrs. Darcy-Banks. I'm aware of who your husband is. He's the head of psychology over at the hospital. I've seen him a few times when I volunteer over there. He's a very nice man. I've also sat in on some of his lectures over at the university a time or two."

Her laughter was soft. "He is. But I'm actually calling for my brother… Is this confusing you?"

"A little, but go on, I'll catch up." I made sure to drive slower to buy this lady some time. She seemed nervous.

Hug It Out

"My brother, his birthday is next month. He has a very stressful job. Sadly, I don't really know what he does. I suspect government special ops or something because he can't talk about it. Anyway. He's going to be thirty-three and I believe something really bad happened on a job recently. He's been withdrawn, depressed, and doesn't come to family dinners. It's very unlike him. So, I wanted to hire a professional cuddler and companion for him for a month."

Typically, when there was a loss of any kind, the person wanted a week at most. "A month? Do you mean in-home?"

"I want someone there every day for one month." Aisling's voice took on a more authoritative tone.

"Live in?" I began thinking of who might be able to invest all that time.

She hummed. "Is that an option?"

"The only issue with that is the fact that all my employees have numerous clients and obligations.

They'd need to be able to come and go as they please to tend to their responsibilities." I had one employee who stayed weekends for a man, but that was the longest up until now.

"Absolutely, I totally understand. I suppose I could leave that up to you." I felt like she was holding something back.

"Before we go any further, Mrs. Darcy-Banks..."

"Aisling, please call me Aisling."

"Sure. Your brother, he is okay with someone living with him?" I'd had family members try to do this before, and poor Delly was met with an angry girlfriend once. Now I made sure to ask.

The silence was telling. "Well, he will be when I tell him this is how it is. Leave that part to me, please."

I could see my client's house coming up, so I needed to end the call.

"Your husband has my email, I'm sure. If you can send me information on your brother, like what sort of companion you're looking for, I can see what I can do." I wouldn't make a decision until I'd read the paperwork.

"Uhm, I was actually hoping it could be you who was his companion. I know you said you have other employees. But I would prefer you."

"Why me?" She didn't even know me.

When I reached my destination with ten minutes to spare, I let myself focus solely on Aisling and was eager to find out why I had to be the one to help her brother.

"My husband tells me he's seen you do amazing things, like you're a miracle worker. My brother needs that. Money is no option. Please, Teddy?"

Damn it! She said please. "Email me everything and I'll see what I can do. When do you need me to start?"

"August first."

"Aisling, I, nor any of my employees, will step foot on your brother's property unless he's okay with this. I hope you understand." I was adamant about that.

I heard her release a breath. "Understood."

I grabbed my messenger bag, and as I approached the front door, a woman stepped out, her eyes red-rimmed. She graced me with a look I had seen too many times before. A dreaded rush of sadness squeezed at my heart. Grief weighed on her.

"Are you Teddy?"

"I am, are you Maureen's neighbor, Helen?"

She nodded. "Yes. I couldn't find your number. Maureen didn't give it to me. But I saw you were on her calendar, so I figured I'd wait for you. Please come in."

This was the hardest part of my job. People thought that what I did was simply hold people and then walk away. That wasn't the case. I volunteered at the hospital and hugged little babies and children who had been abandoned. Or those that craved touch. I'd watched children and babies die. I'd held the hands of patients in hospice as they took their last breath. It never got easier. I knew what Helen would tell me and,

Hug It Out

as much as I wanted to say I needed to go, I knew she needed me to stay.

Maureen's home was silent. Her programs weren't playing in the background. The smell of coffee and cookies didn't linger in the air.

"Maureen passed away last night. I know you were close with her. You meant a great deal to her, actually. Whenever I brought her groceries, she would tell me what she needed to make for your visits." She choked on her words before continuing. "She didn't have anyone." Then she began sobbing.

Her pain was palpable, and I didn't hesitate engulfing her in my arms. Without resistance, she returned the hug. As I swayed back and forth and tenderly rubbed her back, she began to quiet. When my cheek rested on the top of her head, she released a contented sigh. In that moment, we both found our catharsis.

"You're really good at this, Teddy."

"Thanks, Helen."

"I can see why she felt so much love from just

one person."

Helen lifted her head, offering me a small smile. She'd be okay.

"Everyone deserves love. Even the meanest people in the world."

There was a pregnant pause, and when she spoke, it was almost like a whisper. "Would you like to come over to my house? I can explain the arrangements for her funeral. I hope you can attend."

For the next three hours, instead of embracing Maureen and laughing with her, Helen and I made sure she was sent off to the unknown exactly how she wanted to be.

Chapter Two

Riordan

The doorbell pulled me from my afternoon nap. After lunch, I'd decided to catch up on some shows I had on my DVR and ended up passing out on the couch. Judging from the impatient ringing, it could only be one person.

"Good afternoon to you too, Aisling," I said as she pushed inside.

"You changed the locks. Thank god the gate code worked, and I was able to get through your wall of solitude." She slammed a large bag on the table and I watched, slightly amused, as she began taking out potatoes, a roast, carrots, and other things.

"The wall is not for solitude, it's for safety. You live in a gated community. Not any different, sis."

She made herself at home by taking out pots

and pans, which made a symphony of noise. It was a little jarring, but I was used to Aisling's demeanor, so I let her go about her business.

"You missed your third family dinner. You're not eating. Mom and Dad are beside themselves. Are you going to tell me what's going on, or should I resort to plan B?" She faced me, and judging by the scowl on her face and her hand on her hip, she wasn't fucking around.

"What the hell is plan B?" Aisling was probably the only person in this world who terrified me. She was smart, beautiful, and cunning. Sometimes it surprised me that I was the assassin and she wasn't.

"You accept my birthday present, no questions asked." She raised a perfectly sculpted eyebrow. Her no-muss-no-fuss attitude was firmly in place. I was in serious trouble.

"Why would I accept it no questions asked?"

Standing straighter, she pushed her auburn hair up into a sloppy bun and her hazel eyes pinned me with a vicious look. "If you accept this, I will cover your

Hug It Out

ass at family dinner for one month."

Beer. I needed beer. My kitchen was large, but not so big she needed to follow me to the fridge. But that didn't stop her.

"What the hell did you get me for my birthday that would make you deal with Mom's wrath for an entire month?"

"No questions. Either agree or I tell Mom you have the flu and she descends."

Had I mentioned she was evil? This was terrifying. And I'd stood in a room of twenty Japanese bodyguards hell-bent on stopping me from killing their boss. But a whole month free of family dinners? No Mom asking me about a boyfriend or prying for information I couldn't tell her?

"Fine. But." She was about to interrupt when I held up my finger, halting her words. "It has to be something that won't get in the way of my work."

Her smile was like a million bucks and the shiver that crawled up my spine told me I'd made a grave mistake.

"That's no problem at all. Teddy will not get in your way. You can tell him when you're busy and he'll obediently scamper off." She began washing potatoes like her message wasn't cryptic.

"Who or what is Teddy? Did you get me a fucking dog? That absolutely gets in the way!"

Shaking her head, she shut the water off and pulled out my crock-pot. Her refusal to make eye contact left me curious. "Not a dog, a person."

"What, you got me a maid?" That wasn't so bad.

Her laughter was like the music right before the monster lept out of the closet to eat your face.

"No questions. He will be here in two days. I cleared all of it with everyone and when he arrives, you are to listen to him and do as he says." She abruptly stopped cooking, and when she turned to me, knife in hand, the seriousness of her demeanor was chilling. With a low voice, she said, "You fuck this up and I will not only send Mom here, but Dad as well. And I will tell my husband to call in favors to get you to see a doctor. So help me god, Riordan, I will fuck you up."

I knew when I was defeated. "Okay, fine. Just put the knife down, you whack job."

For the next twenty minutes, I drank my beer in peace while Aisling cooked. Watching her work was peaceful. As my older sister, she put up with a lot from me. I was always a menace. Often times, she was forced to babysit when she wanted to go out. I never cut her much slack. But, she knew how to handle me. She would be a force of nature as a mother.

We didn't look alike. Aisling had all the features of our mother, from her fiery auburn hair to her fair skin and light hazel eyes. My father and I were almost identical with our black hair and green eyes. The only thing we Darcys all had in common was our fair skin.

I knew something was coming. I didn't want to see my family because when I had to look them in the eye, my conscience reared its ugly head. The last job I had messed me up but good. Made me feel ashamed for the first time. Nearly broke me.

It had taken Aisling a week, but now she was on me like a tiger with her prey.

"This will cook for a few hours. I made extra so you'll have lunch for tomorrow too. Teddy will be here Wednesday at nine. Be nice to him. He's already been paid."

Teddy? Who was named Teddy these days? "So, I get nothing more about him?"

She shook her head. "I think he's exactly what you need, little brother." Her smile was small and there was that mirthful twinkle in her eye. I wanted to argue further, but she rushed out like a hurricane.

With the tantalizing aroma of my dinner cooking, I surveyed my house. I wasn't a messy person, but I had been neglecting the basic cleaning. I polished the furniture, happy when layers of dust were gone. My mind wandered as the vacuum sucked away the week's detritus.

When I was eighteen, I was a badass. I never wanted to go to college. Thought I was better than everyone. One night, a bar fight broke out and a guy threatened the owner's daughter. A rush of blinding rage came over me, and in that moment, a veil of red covered everything. Even now, I couldn't remember what thoughts had gone through my head, but I remembered the anger. I grabbed the guy from behind, put my arm around his neck, and choked him out. Dead. Staring at him, I waited for what I'd done to hit me. To feel bad about it. But he was a piece of shit. Known to rough up girls and con old people. The owner told me to run off and talk to no one. I was an idiot, so I did just that.

Two days after the bar incident, I got a visit from a guy. All I knew was his name. Black. He handed me a card and told me to meet him at that address at midnight. If I was late, all the evidence the cops would need to prove I killed that guy would be given to them. I didn't want to go to jail, so I went to the location Black had given me.

It was there I found my calling as an assassin. I trained for two years. It was brutal. We were taught more things than we could remember. After the two years ended, Black showed up at my door, handed me a phone, and said my time had come to do my duty.

I killed people for a living. I got a lot of money for it. Mobsters, drug dealers, who knows. I didn't ask. Much. As long as they deserved death, I did it. Sometimes, their deaths were fast, other times slow.

Through the years, I was given the name "The Dullahan." The foreteller of death. The Irish version of the headless horseman. Not because I killed people. No. It was how I did it. My message. Whenever someone found a body, they knew it was the Dullahan that had done it because I always took the head. One way or another. Whether it was cause of death or a week after the body was buried. Quite a few times in the dead of night, I'd visit a morgue, slip in undetected, find my kill in the fridge, and claim the head. Those weren't so much a bother as an inconvenience. It was the ones I had to dig up that were a pain in the ass. Digging into frozen ground to decapitate a corpse was not a fun Friday night. But, I compartmentalized for years and did it. That was how my clients knew the job was done.

On the street, no one knew who I was. None of my clients had ever seen my face. The men who guarded Black knew my identity, as did Black, Mace, Emma, Lee, and Jones. There'd been times multiple assassins had been called in by Black. The five of us worked well together, so we all knew a lot about each other. Well, more than other people did.

I told my family I worked for the government and I couldn't talk about it. For the most part, they were okay with it, but my mother always pried.

Teddy arrived on time Wednesday morning. When I was signaled that someone was at the gate, I curiously watched the monitors. A light-blue 1998 Ford Escort idled at the entrance. When the gate opened, the old car drove up so slowly, I swore I could feel it dying with each rotation of the tires. When he drove around the circular driveway twice, it reminded me of a dog trying to get comfortable before resting. He finally stopped and waited a few minutes before exiting the vehicle. I couldn't help but cringe at the creaking sound the door made when it opened. Unease crept up my spine over this entire situation.

The first thing about him that caught my attention was his mop of brown curls. They bounced when he walked, radiating happiness. The white polo shirt he wore rested over narrow shoulders. His physique became even more noticeable when a breeze pressed the cotton against his frame, accentuating his lankiness. His legs went on for miles, proving he was almost as tall as me, and there was something about his khaki shorts that made my cock twitch. He may be nerdy with those black-rimmed glasses, but he was a looker. As he got closer, I chuckled when the freckles on his nose came into view. This guy was just as adorable as he was sexy. Judging by the frown on Teddy's face, there was no question I had been caught appreciating the view.

"Hi, Mr. Darcy, I'm Teddy from Teddy Bear Hugs and Companionship. I'm going to be your companion for the month. I have my bag in the car, but

Hug It Out

I thought it might be best if we sit and talk first and establish some ground rules." He shifted uncomfortably and his hand quivered when he held it out.

Everything about this guy was long, slender, and neat. Either he got manicures or he was meticulous about clean, shiny nails. Never a disrespectful guy, I shook the proffered hand. I dwarfed him in my grip and when his eyes widened and I could hear the hitch of his breath, I knew he was affected. Whether it was nerves or more, I wasn't one hundred percent sure. When Teddy went to slip his hand from my grip, I realized what he had said.

"Wait, you're from what?"

"Teddy Bear Hugs and Companionship."

My eyes reflexively shifted to his car parked in my driveway. The hilarity of the entire thing had me laughing.

"You're a companion that drives an Escort?" Now I couldn't stop laughing.

"Mr. Darcy. I'm not that type of companion…

Mr. Darcy. If you could please stop laughing, we can discuss this."

Taking a deep breath, I gestured for him to follow me. With my back to him, I couldn't see his face, but the huff he let out told me he was annoyed with my antics. Once in the kitchen, I was finally in control. "You're my birthday gift from my sister?"

He pressed his glasses up with his finger as he nodded. His cheeks tinged pink and I didn't know if it was the summer heat or the fact he was embarrassed about what I had said about his car, either way, it was cute. Papers were placed on the table by Teddy and the clearing of his throat focused my attention. "I'd like to get all the formalities out of the way first, and then maybe you'd like to hug for a while? See if you feel a comfortable compatibility with me. Sometimes we need to choose others that you will mesh with better."

I opted to make coffee as he rambled on. Cute as this guy may be, I wasn't a fan of having him in my space. All this nonsexual mumbo jumbo was bullshit and realizing it felt like cold water being poured on me. The clicking of his pen sent tingles of irritation through me and the fucking questions about allergies and requests about no lotions, colognes, or scented items during cuddling unless I found a certain aroma relaxing almost made me snap.

"Aisling, your sister, filled out all her paperwork. I need you to fill out your papers."

Right, I was doing this for my sister. Closing my eyes, I counted to ten to calm myself so I didn't pick Teddy up and toss him out the front door. The documents were standard privacy paperwork, medical conditions, and my expectations. A questionnaire was four pages long.

"Look, here's the thing, Teddy, is it?" He smiled all sunshine and rainbows. "I did this for my sister. I'm not really the hugging type."

"Understandable. All I ask is for you to try. Your sister has retained me for one month. I am here until September first."

Here? "Wait, living with me in my home?"

Again with the smile. "Actually, not always. I

have other clients and I'm also a strategy guide writer and reviewer for video games. I have other commitments. But your sister has asked I be here as often as possible. I'd like to go over the schedule with you."

My head started to pound.

"How about I go over all this paperwork tomorrow? Put the papers down. I'll give you the tour of my house, show you where you can and can't go. Sound good?"

"Fair enough."

Chapter Three

Teddy

Aisling had promised her brother was okay with this. The somewhat angry and confused expression on his face told me she had likely been as vague as possible. I was hesitant to take him on as a client, but something about all this called to me.

Riordan Darcy was a sexy man and when I laid eyes on him for the first time, my body tingled. He was gorgeous. There was a mysteriousness that intrigued me. I was grateful for summer in that moment simply because it meant less clothes. His tank top and navy shorts clung to every muscle on his tall body. It was easy to see he took pride in his appearance, and while I would have loved to have seen long hair flowing in the breeze, I recognized the buzz cut suited him. But it was his eyes that drew me closer. Green emeralds that twinkled with mischief and danger. He was on full display. Big, strong, and everything I craved in a man.

This was always the hard part about my job. When I felt attracted. Delly had once been so attracted to a client, she had to pass on being their companion, but I really wanted to stick with this. He looked foreboding, but he also looked like he was in need of some serious TLC.

He wasn't rude, so much as annoyed. I was like a fruit fly to him, I could tell. People I worked for tended to want me there. Riordan seemed unsure.

"There are three bathrooms. One is attached to my bedroom, so we'll call that mine. I have one down in the finished basement. And another is next to a guest room. You can claim that room, I guess."

His tour wasn't very detailed. Going on my own observations, it seemed devoid of warmth and that homey feeling. The walls were all mostly beige and white with a few pieces of art. He seemed to favor hard wood floors and area rugs, again all solid and a little boring. The house was larger than any one person would need, which spoke to his financial status. He wasn't taking me into many rooms, he just pointed to doorways. We walked down a dimly lit hallway that was the barest of bare. White walls and dark wood flooring. It felt joyless. Halfway down, Riordan stopped and turned on his heels, facing me.

"This is not an area you ever need to be. That door there," he pointed behind himself, "only opens with a code and thumbprint. Unless you can read my mind and tear off my thumb, you will never get in there. If you try and fail, you'll wish you had heeded my advice."

That was creepy, but of course, being told I couldn't enter made me want to try. I was a professional though, and would stay away.

"These other doors aren't much, but still keep out. That one leads to the garage, and that one leads to a work shed. Neither require hugs or companionship." The sneer he gave me contradicted the twinkle in his eyes, which only confused me further about this man.

"Look, Mr. Darcy, I won't force myself on

people. I can refund the money to your sister if you don't want this. Should I show myself out?" I was used to people laughing at me when they heard my profession, but I was proud of it and would be dammed if someone was going to bully me for an entire month.

He put his hands up in surrender, and I hated my traitorous body for admiring how massive and beautiful they were. I wanted to feel the pads of his fingers to see if they were rough or soft. "Whoa, calm down." He chuckled. "Returning that money would be the worst thing you could do. Aisling would filet me alive. Come back to the kitchen, I'll take it seriously."

When he slipped past me, his scent danced around me, all minty and refreshing. Damn, this was going to be hard.

"Coffee?" he offered, and I happily accepted. He was graceful for a big man, and very quiet. The mugs didn't clang together and when he placed them on the marble countertop, there was a muted thud. He seemed to just be that way.

"How do you take your coffee?"

Hug It Out

"Two sugars and milk or cream, please."

I sat on one of the cushioned stools by the breakfast bar. At least the kitchen was cheery with its yellow walls and white furniture. When he sat beside me, I felt the current of change. I liked him close and that, in turn, made me also hate it.

"I didn't mean to be a jerk, Teddy. I know my family is worried about me and that's a wonderful thing. I'm loved. But even if Aisling didn't do this, I'm just not a cuddler. I sleep on the edge of my bed. My job has made me alert. I can hear a mouse sneeze while I'm in REM. I've trained myself to be like this." He didn't speak again, but his sigh said more than words could. He avoided eye contact and just sipped his coffee, prompting me to do the same.

"I don't know what you do for a living, Mr. Darcy, and I won't pry. But if there's no chance that this will work, then I think it best I contact your sister and let her know. I can't keep the money if you aren't going to use my services." I kept my voice soft because I didn't want to offend him. Some people really didn't like touch.

"No. I won't disrespect my sister like that." He grabbed the papers I'd brought, and with what looked like interest, began reading them. "What services do you offer that keep us vertical?"

Lord knew I wouldn't mind being horizontal with the man, and that, of course, threw up more red flags. Maybe he was right, no cuddling.

"We are also a companionship company. Talking, hanging out, simple human presence. Maybe we can start there. One week. If after that week it isn't working, we can decide what to do with your sister." I let a little laugh out, which was gratefully returned.

"Can't do anything with Aisling. She's a force. But that seems like a fair deal. You said you had a schedule?" I didn't get to respond before he continued. "Let me see if yours works with mine, and we can start this buddy system thing."

It was a start, at least.

Chapter Four

Riordan

I told Black I needed time when in reality, I wanted out. I was under no illusion he suspected I was trying to find a way. I was granted a break, but no timeline had been given. This made organizing my schedule with Teddy tricky. For now, my schedule was wide open, but there was no telling when that would change. When Teddy explained he mostly had evenings free, we both agreed on two things. One, he'd have to calculate the difference in price and refund that to Aisling, and two, since most of his clients were closer to where I lived, he'd spend those nights at my house.

"Are you okay with me working my other job from here?" he asked as he wrote down the schedule.

"What other job?" had he mentioned this

already?

"I write strategy guides and review video games. I have multiple spare consoles. If you're amenable, I can bring them over and set them up in the guest room. That way, I can work when you're busy." He was fidgeting. "If I had them here, it would make it easier, but if you rather I didn't, I can figure—"

Placing a hand on Teddy's shoulder stopped his rambling as if I had unplugged him. I felt the sharp points of his bones and the warmth coming off his body. It wasn't at all unpleasant.

"You can bring whatever you want and put it in your room. I'm cool with that." His smile morphed his face from worried to elated, and calming him like that felt nice.

Aisling was right, Teddy wasn't horrible. He was doing his job and for family peace, for a month, I could do this.

"How about we play weekends by ear?"

"Sure."

He seemed more confidant now and quickly

was all business again, sliding a calendar over to me. "Here's the schedule. During the week, we will keep it perfectly. Since today is August first and a Wednesday, you have me all day. What do you want to do?"

I was about to tell him he could take the day off when the gate buzzed.

"Hang on, Teddy, let me see who that is. Help yourself to more coffee."

A familiar black Audi idled by the front gate. Hitting the button, I spoke into the microphone. "I got company, Mace, what do you need?"

"What kind of company?"

"None you'd be able to talk to."

Mace was silent for a minute, staring at the monitor while I hoped he'd reverse out, knowing he likely wouldn't.

"Let me in. We need to talk."

Shit, that couldn't be good. After I hit the button to open the gate, I rushed back to the kitchen to talk to Teddy.

"Teddy, listen." He offered me a small, expectant smile as he peered over the paperwork in his hands. "Someone is here. It's work. Can you...?"

He nodded in understanding and his smile just got bigger like I had told him hugs around the world was an international holiday. "I can stay in here if that'll help. It's good to have friends, Mr. Darcy."

"Call me Riordan, and uhm... Yeah, okay, stay here."

I got to the door just as the bell rang. My unexpected visitor stood on my front steps looking like a million dollars. And judging by his attire, he probably was estimated at that. Mace wore a black suit and a white shirt with the first three buttons undone, exposing golden skin and sparse hairs. His brown hair was layered to his shoulders and his sunglasses made him look like a Giorgio Armani model. I'd always thought Mace was a stunning man, but seeing the violent things he could do with those hands of his was a real turnoff.

"Lookin' like shit, buddy," he said with a

smile.

"And you're looking like a magazine ad. What's up?"

The second Mace stepped foot into my house, he began assessing the room, probably looking for who else was there. "Where's the company?"

"He's in the kitchen. We can go to my office."

Mace waggled his brows in an uncharacteristic gesture. Mace wasn't a goofball, he was serious, sexy, and lethal. I was glad when he followed me. "Oh, it's that kind of company. Good for you, man." He patted my back and followed me down the hallway. I put the code in and we entered.

"Not that kind of company, Mace."

Taking a seat in one of my office chairs, he didn't press the issue and I was relieved. "Whatever, I'm not here about your love life. Black sent me."

The name sent shivers down my spine. Having Mace come talk to me on Black's behalf couldn't be good.

"Why did he send you? He could have called

or sent one of his android bodyguards."

Mace chuckled. Black had a ridiculous amount of bodyguards. You couldn't get to the man.

"How much time do you think Black is going to give you?" In a flawlessly smooth movement, Mace pulled out an envelope from the inside pocket of his suit jacket. "He knows what happened in Rome fucked you up. He got bad intel. If he knew that woman and kid were the targets, he would have given it to someone else. He thought it was just the husband. Nothing could be done."

I knew there was money in the envelope when he slid it toward me. "Mace, I've been at this for fourteen years. I know how accurate Black's system is. Human error does not compute. I had the green light the whole way. There was plenty of time to call it off. That woman and her child were the targets, I just know it. They wanted it to be me. I don't know why or how or what game Black is playing."

Mace just stared at me, unmoved, as I got madder and madder. "Where are the heads?" The slight flinch when he asked was the only way I knew he didn't want to ask.

"I didn't take them. How was I going to get the heads when the order was an explosion?"

If he was expecting a different response, I couldn't tell by his stoic reaction. "It's your thing. I was wondering if you had them."

"Why?"

"Your mark was Vincent Abano. You got his wife and kid in that blast. He was set to go to the opera that night, alone. Last minute, his wife and child join him, but no one saw them in the car until it was too late. Black's order was to blow up the car outside the opera house. Obviously, it was an order of show. Whoever put the hit out wanted a spectacle. The spotter saw Vincent, or someone who looked a whole lot like him, get in the limo, but never saw his family get in. Did it occur to you that someone is setting up Black? If you had the heads, you'd know if you got him." Mace made sense, but it was farfetched.

"You think someone is targeting Black?" I

settled in my chair and thought on that for a moment. "It was a spectacle, the cops came running. There was no way I was getting near those bodies. I would have never been able to get to the heads until the morgue, if they were there."

Mace steepled his fingers against his lips, and I could tell he was trying to get in the right headspace to help me figure it out. "I'm sure the intention was for you to get the heads. Otherwise, why have you do it? Someone wanted Vincent's head. But when Black got word it was the wife and kid, he told you to stand down. There were a lot of questions being tossed around. A lot about this doesn't make sense."

That call practically broke me. Black called saying there was a fuck up. Felicia and her son were killed instead. I was to go home and await further instructions.

"Lee was the spotter. What does he have to say about it?"

"He stands by what he saw. Vincent Abano got into that car and at no time did he see the wife or kid

Hug It Out

in there." Mace leaned forward and tapped the envelope, giving me a no nonsense look. "Black wants you in his office Monday. That's apology money. You know he never apologizes. He's not happy about the fuck up."

I could feel my head throbbing. "Mace, I'm not ready."

He stood up and adjusted his jacket, sparing his shirt a quick flattening, and then leaned over the desk. This model-looking man was one of the most violent in the world. He'd been coined Without-a-Trace-Mace or Untraceable, because by the time you knew he was there, he'd gone and left nothing behind. He strictly worked for Mafia bosses and was a legend.

"Riordan, if you're thinking of leaving, Black will kill you. I don't want to be the one told to do it. Take the money. I'll tell Black you need a week. I can't guarantee he'll be okay with that, but when I see you again, I'd like it to be friendly." He knocked his knuckles against the desk and stood. "I gotta go."

We stepped out of the office silently. We both

knew there was nothing left to say on this issue right then. We were just passing the kitchen when Mace halted, turned, and walked in. Fucking hell.

"Hello there, I'm Mace." He approached the breakfast bar and held his hand out to Teddy, who smiled and shook it, not in the least bit taken aback by the stranger's intrusion.

"Hello, Mace. I'm Teddy. Nice to meet you." His eyes shifted from Mace to me. "I'm so happy to see Riordan's friends stop by for visits. It's very important."

Mace was amused. The look on his face told me everything.

"I totally agree, Teddy. Are you visiting or are you something more?"

Teddy's eyes widened, clearly not expecting the innuendo. "Riordan and I are only friends. I'm visiting. As a friend. In the guest room. Friend."

Mace laughed loudly and I had to admit a flustered Teddy was a funny Teddy.

"Walk me out, Riordan. Nice to meet you,

Teddy."

Right before I left the kitchen, I saw Teddy's red face and it was obvious he was embarrassed.

Mace turned to me when I opened the front door, seriousness back on his face. "One week."

Mace never looked back as he strode to his car. I knew if I didn't show up in a week's time, the next time I saw Mace would leave one of us dead.

Chapter Five

Teddy

Aisling had said that Riordan was likely in some sort of special ops. Mace didn't look very military-esque but who knew. I was just glad to see Riordan did in fact have friends. Family often didn't know the people in our lives outside of them. I suspected Aisling didn't either.

"Sorry about that," Riordan said as he entered the kitchen, his smile strained.

"Mace seemed like a good guy. Nice to have someone stop by and check on you." I wasn't fishing per se, but more information about a client always helped me understand what was needed.

Riordan's response came in the form of a shrug. His demeanor wasn't telling me much, and with him sitting next to me at the breakfast bar, it was obvious he didn't want to talk about his friend. "He's a work-related friend."

When Riordan finally made eye contact with me, I noticed his eyes sort of changed color when the sun peeked through the curtain. He was scary in a lot of ways and there was no hiding the sharp edges, but behind that gaze was a softness that showed how beautiful he was. "I have three people who work with me. Delly, she's my best friend. She invested in the company. And then two other people we hired. Though they are all work-related friends, we hang out sometimes. Friends are friends."

Riordan had a pained look on his face. His expression was unreadable. Partly pained and a lot uncertain, but as for why, I had no idea. I didn't know what he was thinking, and he didn't seem to want to share with the group.

"What made you decide to hug people for a living?"

That was a question I was asked a lot. Normally, I said because human touch was important and I wanted to help people. That wouldn't work on a man like Riordan Darcy. He wanted the truth.

"I do this because of my grandmother." I wasn't sure if I could or should elaborate. I'd let Riordan decide if that was enough of an explanation or not.

"Has she passed, is this something you do in memory of her?" Having Riordan's undivided attention was a little unnerving, but also nice. With his hands clasped together on the table top, he watched me with interest.

"No, she's alive. She's seventy-three. Doesn't live too far from me. She's a cancer survivor. Best person I know."

Riordan's smile was soft and if I had to venture a guess, I'd say my answer had pleased him. "You do it to make her proud?"

I understood why he'd come to that conclusion and I wanted to clear that up. "No. She raised me after my dad died and my mom walked out."

Riordan looked horrified. "Your mom left you

when you needed her the most?"

Normal reaction. "Not right away, and she isn't a bad person. She loves me. I still see my mom, but it's my grandmother who is my world."

"And because she was good to you, you want to be good for others?" Riordan asked with genuine curiosity.

"When my grandmother was diagnosed, I understood it all from a different perspective. Human touch and love can heal. After she went into remission, I told her I had found my calling and she supported me." It felt like overshare hour or something.

Riordan fingered the corners of the paper on the table either nervously or simply for something to do, and when he glanced up, it was like he was sad for me. "So it's just you and your grandmother. That's it?"

"You could be in a room full of people and feel alone. I have my grandmother and I do see my mother every so often. I have amazing friends. My family is diverse and the love I feel is plentiful."

He didn't say anything for a moment, then like

he was uncomfortable with the depth of our conversation, he stood abruptly and just started walking out of the kitchen. "Let's get your stuff and you can unpack. I won't see you tomorrow, but Friday I will. At around two, you said?"

"If that's okay?"

"Fine by me. Do you need any help moving your consoles or anything?"

It was a sweet question. "No. I'll bring them over Friday. I can set them all up. Is there a TV in the bedroom?"

Riordan opened the front door and as he walked to the car, I noticed he moved with purpose. Nothing he did seemed to be hesitant or undecided.

"There is and it's big, so there shouldn't be a problem."

I'd only brought one bag, so it was ridiculous for us both to be out here. Something told me Riordan needed to do something. All I could do was stand there like a lost puppy as Riordan took the bag and headed back into the house. Being around him made me feel out of sorts and unsure. Not something I typically felt in my line of work.

"I'll give you the code to the front gate. I'll be here most of this week, but just in case, I have a spare key for you to get in and out." He dropped my bag on the bed as soon as we entered the guest room, avoiding eye contact at all costs, it seemed. Making him feel awkward was never my intention and it felt like rabid butterflies were attacking my stomach.

"Do I make you uncomfortable, Riordan? Is giving me access to your space upsetting you? I don't mind buzzing in each time and you letting me in. The code and key are not necessary." Hopefully, that would make him feel better.

Riordan finally looked at me. His eyes were piercing. "I'm not uncomfortable. I admit this is strange and I don't know how well it will work, but it's fine. Really."

"I'll unpack my things then. Are you hungry? Perhaps we can cook together or go out? I'm told you've been holed up in here. Maybe some fresh air?"

The furrowing of his brow was something I began to notice meant he was thinking and contemplating. I didn't know if it was what he was going to say or do. "I'm not a big cooker. I'm not feeling much like going out. I can order something if you want."

"I can cook. But for today, we can order something. If you tell me some of your favorite dishes, we can learn how to make them together. It's a companionship thing to do." The intensity of his gaze made me squirm, so I made myself busy as I spoke by emptying the few things I had into the Cherrywood dresser.

"I have a cookbook somewhere. My mom's recipes. If you're feeling like you can do them justice, you can make something of hers."

I chanced a glance and saw a wicked smile painted on his handsome face.

"Challenge accepted."

His awkward nod before he left made me breathe a little easier. Like seeing the human within the beast. I finished unpacking and went to hang out with the man who was an enigma.

Chapter Six

Riordan

Teddy told me to pick what I wanted and was fine when I suggested Thai. He had no preferences, so I ordered a few dishes. Chicken satay, massaman lamb, beef curry, bamboo fish, and goong pad sataw. Something for all the tastes. He was sure to find something he liked.

"Wow, you'd think you were feeding an army," Teddy said after I laid out all the food.

"I like ordering a lot so I have leftovers. Plus, I figure you'd like something out of all this." I felt stupid now. How had I become so inept around people?

"Thank you, Riordan. It looks amazing and smells even better. I'm sure to gain twenty pounds."

I held back that he could stand to gain the

weight. We filled our plates and I was just taking a forkful of beef curry the same time Teddy was slurping up some noodles. His cheeks hollowed and my dick twitched. Damn, he was hot when he moaned and hummed. Of course, he was loving the food, but my imagination went to the bedroom with him under me, writhing. I snapped out of it the second Teddy began talking.

"So, Riordan, is there anything you can tell me about your job? I know it's super-secret, but do you travel a lot?" Teddy wasn't fishing. He was making small talk. All my training had made me a human lie detector and a professional reader of body language. He was innocent.

"I've worked in my field for almost fifteen years. It's taken me just about everywhere."

"Do you have a favorite place?" When Teddy licked his fingers, I looked away briefly to get my libido under control, but he was giving me his full attention, so I had to hide how affected I was by his existence.

"Unfortunately, my job never took me to many scenic places. I didn't get to enjoy the sites so much. But growing up, my family took us to Colorado one year. Marron Bells. Gorgeous."

His smile showed his genuine happiness for me. "I have never left Haven Hart. My mom is a world traveler, but I've never been anywhere but right here."

He didn't seem sad about it, just matter-of-fact.

"If you could go anywhere, where would you want to go?" I asked.

He bit his lip and I could tell he was really thinking his answer through.

"Either Plitvice Lakes in Croatia or Moraine Lake in Canada." He took a bite of fish.

"Interesting choices. Both water. Any reason?"

Teddy shrugged. "I love the sea. My father used to take me fishing. He had a little boat. Usually, just on Batt's River, but it was great. Water is peaceful to me."

The conversation took a comfortable pause as we finished our meals. Afterward, Teddy offered to do the dishes. I told him I could do them and of course, he recommended we do it together. Another companion thing.

Side-by-side, we scrapped, rinsed, and placed the dishes in the dishwasher. He told me some more stories about his grandmother. Places his mother had sent postcards from. It was a peaceful conversation, not to mention, very domestic.

Teddy wasn't angry when he spoke about his mother, but I sensed it was because he didn't understand what he was missing. If my mother had abandoned me, I'd have hunted her down and made her face the truth. But I was used to taking down dragons. Teddy didn't strike me as a fighter.

"Thank you for dinner, Riordan." He tenderly touched my arm. I felt his words sink into my skin. Maybe he was a wizard.

"No big. I had to eat anyway, right?"

He hung the towel on the hook and smiled, warming some of the ice inside me. "It's not too late. If you'd like me to head home and come back Friday,

I—"

"No, it's fine. You can go in the morning. I'll see you Friday and we can figure out how this will work." I opened a drawer. "This is the house key. The code is 2567. Can you remember that?"

"Easy enough."

"I'll change it next week. Never too safe, right?"

I could feel Teddy trying to read me. I'd mastered lying. Mastered all the sins. No way would he see through me.

"Whatever makes you comfortable, Riordan." He glanced at the clock. "It isn't late. Movie?"

"Since I picked dinner, you pick the movie."

His smile was so freaking wide, I feared his face would split. How was anyone this happy all the time? It couldn't be normal. "Point me to the choices and I think I'll surprise you."

I doubted it. "This way."

All my movies were on Amazon or Netflix. Handing him the remote, I sat on the couch and watched him flip through them. He sped past the rom-coms, which actually shocked me.

"Ah ha! Have you seen this?" The Amazon screen was on the movie poster for Insidious.

"Not yet, but it's a horror. It's gonna scare the shit out of you." I didn't know why I said that. I judged Teddy based on how he looked and what he did. The look of glee he gave me was a little scary.

"Oh, Mr. Darcy, I'm going to enjoy surprising you. I'm not all cuddles and cake." With a twinkle of mischief, he hit play.

No one surprised me anymore. It was near impossible to do so. How this cuddle-loving man was managing it was disturbing.

Chapter Seven

Teddy

Thursday was spent catching up on reviews I'd been neglecting. One of the best parts about my job was getting to play games before everyone else. Of course, it was also the downfall because some needed a lot of work and it felt like wasted time. There were so few to choose from this month, and the lack of excitement in my choices depressed me.

It was a game of eeny, meeny, miny, moe of the most mundane games. The feeling of dejection was wiped away when one caught my eye. I could work on this one at Riordan's. I knew exactly how I would get into character for it, too.

"Knock, knock," Delly said from my doorway.

"Generally, people knock with their knuckles. On the door. From outside." I didn't really care, but I loved hassling her.

"Shouldn't have given me a key then, dork." She ruffled my hair as she passed me and unceremoniously plopped on my bed.

"To what do I owe the pleasure of your company, brat?"

Never to be someone with nothing to do, she flipped through one of my Gamer magazines as she spoke. "I saw you were taking on that Darcy guy."

Delly and I had talked about me taking on this client for hours. I was on the fence. She never talked me out of anything, she just gave me a different perspective. It was how we got along so well.

"I met with him yesterday. He was hesitant, but Delly, he's hurting." This was one of those conversations where it took every part of my focus to talk about, so I abandoned my console packing and sat on the bed beside her.

"Sweetie, your empathy is what makes you so good at your job but remember, you can't fix everyone. Don't let it get to you if you can't." Wrapping her arms around me, she squeezed in a silent show of support.

"I have a week to convince him to complete the month. I know I can't change him, but I really believe I can make him see things differently." Her blue eyes were filled with worry.

"He doesn't even realize how much he craves something."

"Craves what?"

"I don't know. I need time."

She nodded indulgently. "Did you even take any time off after Maureen's death?"

I knew that was where she was going with this. Typically speaking, there was a mandatory two week period after the loss of a client.

"His sister needed help, Del. She is worried about her brother. I'm telling you, whatever he does for a living, he has seen shit. A lot of it. I couldn't say no."

Delly was a lot like me and expressed herself through touch, so when she pressed her lips to my forehead, the warmth of her love calmed me. "You

Hug It Out

know yourself, but remember that pushing yourself isn't healthy. Be careful. If it gets to be too hard, call me. Let me help you."

Delly was by far the best friend anyone could ever have. Only time she ever gave her opinion was when you asked for it or you were headed for disaster.

"What are you doing today?" I asked her, desperate to change the subject.

"I'm headed to the hospital to hug babies. Want to come?"

She knew exactly how to perk me up. There was nothing more peaceful in this world than holding tiny bundles of the future and loving them.

"Absolutely. Help me get my stuff in this bag."

Hart's Hope Hospital was the biggest and by far the best hospital in all of Haven Hart. I didn't know much about the Hart family, but they clearly had fingers in all the pies. It was a great hospital and I loved volunteering at it.

"Hey, Teddy." The nurse behind the counter greeted us with a bright smile as we entered.

"Hi, Lois. How are you today?" I went through the standard signing in and Delly and I took our visitor badges, clipping them to our shirts.

"It was a rough night but I'm off in an hour and I can't wait to soak my feet, eat ice cream, and cry in the tub." An odd thing to say, one might have thought, but Lois was refreshingly honest. She'd do all those things. She needed to decompress and recognized how to do it.

"Call me if you need me." I said it to everyone. Hugs weren't the only way to make people feel good.

"Thanks. You both headed upstairs?" Her question was rhetorical. The way Delly was vibrating with excitement told Lois all she needed to know about why we were there.

"Yes. I heard there were triplets!" Delly answered excitedly.

Lois and I laughed. Delly loved the newborns, but she had a hard time with the abandoned ones. We usually went our separate ways when we hit the floor.

We said farewell to Lois and headed toward the

elevator. Delly and I would go in separate directions when the doors opened. Delly went to the nursery of newborns while my heart tugged me toward the ones who needed love the most.

The process to even get next to these babies was important. Hands and fingers had to be washed, hair was put in a cap. It was all so impersonal. While I understood the science behind it, I wished I could truly hug these babies as me, not another person in scrubs. Each baby I was seeing today was in the purple room, as I called it. We all did, really. No one wanted to call it the room of unwanted babies. These were babies that had been found at firehouses, emergency rooms, and in dumpsters. Babies that came from neglectful parents, or mothers who were in prison and couldn't be with them. It was never overcrowded, thank god. But there were always at least five at any given time.

"Hello, tiny dancer," I cooed when I lifted up a wailing and flailing little one. She was adorable with her pink hat and a blonde curl pressed against her forehead. "Aren't you pretty. Want to dance with me?"

In order to calm her, she needed to know she was safe and protected. Sometimes, I needed these moments just as much as they did. Feeling her little head pressed against my chest as I swayed and hummed relaxed me just as much as it did her. Relief came for both of us when she fell asleep. Often, we took for granted feeling warm and safe. This tiny dancer had a rough start. I hoped she would find a loving family and always feel safe.

Chapter Eight

Riordan

Aisling called on Thursday. "Hey, Sis. What can I do for you?"

"Yeah, yeah, yeah, how'd it go with Teddy? Is he great? Did you talk? What's happening there?" She spoke so quickly, I almost missed some of it.

"We met. We'll figure it out. He isn't too terrible."

"Yes!" she shouted. "I know you two will be great friends."

I really didn't want to talk about it. So I asked the question I didn't want to. "How's Mom?"

Aisling was silent for a minute. I heard the intake of air before she spoke. "She isn't great. She's worried about you. A lot. But I told her about Teddy and she was so happy you recognized you needed help and were getting it. Yes, I gave you the credit. You're welcome."

"You told her I'm being hugged?" I could absolutely see her doing that.

This made Aisling break out in loud, and if I was being honest, annoying, laughter.

"No, you ass. No one would believe that anyway. A live-in companion. Therapy." She sighed. "Riordan, I wish you'd tell me what happened. Maybe you'll tell Teddy. Maybe you can't. But either way, we just want you back and we will wait. We love you."

"I know. I love you too. Look, I have to go. I have things to sort out."

"Okay. Talk later."

After we disconnected, I went to my office. As I settled into my chair, I was once again face to face with a puzzle of files strewn across my desk. I'd gone over them a million times since I had returned from Rome. How had this gotten so fucked up? Where was Vincent?

Felicia Abano wasn't a great mother. She often

Hug It Out

left her son in the care of nannies and sitters. Their son, Steven, was ten. Now dead. Along with Felicia. Were they even dead? I couldn't get to the bodies. This was a fucked up situation that ate me from the inside out.

Steven Abano, ten. He was a cute kid and was top of his class in school. Had a love for music. Probably why he had gone to the opera with his mother. It would certainly entice him.

I spent the next few hours digging into Vincent Abano's life. Was he in financial trouble? Would the death of a wife and kid get him back on top? I swore if that was the case, I'd spend the rest of my life tracking him down and I'd pop his head off with my bare fucking hands.

Why would he put a hit out on himself, though? Pounding my fists on the desk in frustration didn't help at all, but this whole thing was a clusterfuck.

When my other phone vibrated, I didn't need to wonder who it was.

"Why are you digging into Vincent Abano's

past?" Black's voice was deep. I imagined if the devil was to speak to the world, it would sound a lot like Black's voice. I admit there was a whisky rasp to it that was sexy, but it also demanded attention and no matter how big you were, you felt the threat in every syllable.

"You mean to tell me you haven't been trying to figure out what went wrong?" Questioning Black wasn't wise. Trying to get him to relate or see it from your side was the best bet.

"What makes you think I haven't been?" I could hear clinking on the other end. Likely, Black was pouring himself a drink.

"It's not your conscience, Black. Their blood is on my hands. Mine."

"Hmm. I told you that heart of yours would be your downfall, Dullahan."

Whenever Black felt I needed a reminder of who I was and what I did, he made it a point to call me Dullahan. In our training, we were told that we were no longer one person, but two. We must never forget the beast who lies dormant, ready to strike when

Hug It Out

called.

"You knew when you approached me I wasn't your typical hit man. I didn't even want to be one. I was a stupid kid. Don't act shocked when killing the innocent gets to me." My voice started to rise, so I got ahold of myself. Black had zero tolerance.

I heard him swallow, and his pleased exhale. "I like you, Riordan. Because you have so much to lose, I tend to keep a closer eye on you and yours. But my walls of protection aren't impenetrable."

What the… "What are you talking about?"

"Mace said you were coming into the office next week. Wednesday. We will talk then. Stop looking into Abano's life. Let it rest for now. That's not a suggestion." At that, he hung up.

I knew defying Black wasn't an option, so I abandoned my research for the time being and decided on a shower, some food, and maybe a movie to unwind. I wondered what horror movies were on Amazon that I hadn't seen yet.

The shower felt amazing. I closed my eyes and

tried to let go, but I couldn't. Every time I shut my eyes, flashes of that night invaded my thoughts. The explosion that satisfied me for just a moment only to tear me apart when I heard Black's voice in my ear. "Abort. Target unconfirmed. Fuck, it was the wife and kid. Get out of there, Dullahan." I wasn't a person who killed innocent people. My conscience wouldn't allow it, and my heart was having a difficult time accepting it.

It was eating me up. Aisling was right to worry. People like me didn't grow old. They were taken out or died by their own hand. I needed to get out of this life. I didn't know how, but I did know I wouldn't take anyone down with me. If getting out and keeping my family safe meant I disappeared, then that was what I'd do.

I didn't know how Teddy thought he was gonna fix me.

Chapter Nine

Teddy

"Cupcakes?" Riordan asked. I'd been unable to sleep the night before and found myself in the kitchen at 3:00 A.M. baking.

"Yep. Chocolate vanilla swirl. The frosting is blue because it's what I had left over after Delly's birthday cake." I placed them on the kitchen table and searched for plates.

"I see. But why cupcakes?" He sat at the table and I laughed when he poked at the cupcakes like they were foreign objects.

"It's a birthday present. Birthdays are best when there's cake of some sort. I like cupcakes better than cake because they portion my intake."

Riordan chuckled. "I imagine sugar would have you climbing the walls."

"I don't eat a lot of sugar for many reasons, but I always make exceptions for birthdays." Riordan watched with interest as I plated the cupcakes.

When his was in front of him, he dipped his finger in the frosting and sucked. Sweet mama mia.

"You okay, Teddy? You froze there for a minute. You also didn't answer my question."

Question? Oh. "I'm good. Just tired. What's your question?" Sitting down, I began nibbling my cupcake, desperate for something to occupy my thoughts other than Riordan's lips, tongue, and sucking.

"I said it's not my birthday today so whose are we celebrating?" Riordan devoured half the cupcake in one bite.

"Yours. I realized I didn't know exactly what day your birthday was on, so I thought I'd celebrate it today."

He nodded as he ate the rest of the cupcake. "You could have just asked me."

The blue frosting on Riordan's lips taunted me.

Hug It Out

I wanted to kiss them clean. I had to stop. "I could have, but where's the fun in that?"

His smile was mischievous. "So, you don't want to know?"

I wasn't sure what he was up to. I had quickly come to realize he could be sneaky at times. "I like mystery. I think it's…"

"August tenth," he interrupted.

"God dammit!" I slapped the table in mock frustration. "Now I'll have to make more cupcakes on your birthday."

Seeing Riordan laugh made me happy. I could tell he didn't do it a lot. Or he hadn't done it in a while.

"You're off the hook, Teddy. Thank you for the cupcakes." He gestured toward the door where I knew the box I had brought was sitting. "Are those your consoles?"

"Yeah. Let me take them up to the guest room. It won't take long to set them up. I had a great idea for after."

Riordan didn't look like this was exciting

news, but I imagined most of his life was balanced between being paranoid and being cautious. "What sort of idea?"

"A surprise, of course."

"You and your surprises," he grumbled, but I didn't think he minded.

It didn't take me long to set up my PS4 and I wanted to hurry so I could return to Riordan. A quick once-over showed everything was connected correctly. The bag I needed for the surprise sat on my comforter and when I grabbed it, I silently hoped he was going to be okay with this. Downstairs, Riordan was sitting on the couch watching CNN. Anderson Cooper was talking about some attack in Rome a few weeks ago, killing a family. Depressing, and that wasn't a state I wanted Riordan in.

"Ready for your surprise?" I asked as I wiggled the bag in front of him.

He eyed the little black bag skeptically. "Depends, what are you going to do to me?"

It was funny seeing him nervous. Without

answering, I grabbed the large afghan from the back of the couch and laid it on the floor.

"If you'd be so kind as to remove your shirt and lie on the floor. I'm going to massage your back." It looked like he was about to protest. "It's not hugging or cuddling. It's touch therapy, and who doesn't love a massage?"

He assessed everything from the bag to the afghan, even me. He was always on guard, and I really wanted to make him drop it. "What's in the bag?"

So paranoid. "Lotions, oils, that sort of thing. You can choose. There's a non-perfumed one if you'd prefer. Your paperwork said no allergies, so pick what you like." He caught the bag effortlessly when I tossed it, and swiftly opened it and went through it.

He sniffed a couple, made a few disgusted faces, then settled on a brown bottle. "I like this one."

I gestured to the blanket. "Sandalwood and pine. I love this one. Lie down. Shirt off."

Watching Riordan remove his shirt was better than the time I mastered threading the needle in Sniper

Elite. The man was ripped.

My mouth went dry when he laid on his stomach. His back was a work of art. Literally. I took in the massive tattoo that covered his back in awe.

"Holy tattoo," I whispered, but he must have heard me because he peeked over his shoulder.

"Ahh, I forget it's there sometimes." He didn't say more about it, just rested his head on his arms.

"It's beautiful." Sitting beside him, I popped the oil bottle open.

"Thanks." He didn't seem willing to talk about it, so of course, it piqued my curiosity.

We were both quiet as I squeezed the oil on his back and slid my hands over his warm skin. When I applied pressure, Riordan groaned, sending a shiver through my body. I quickly got lost in the outstanding ink beneath my fingers and desperately drank it all in.

I recognized it. Everyone had heard of the headless horseman. He carried a pumpkin and rode a horse as dark as night. And while the horseman in this particular tattoo wasn't holding a pumpkin, it was easy to tell what it was. I wanted to ask so many questions, but I didn't want to offend him.

Gliding my fingers along the lines and curves of the ink, I fell into the art with each slide and push on his silky flesh. There were small details that pulled me in like a story in a book. The saddle on the horse held knives. The horseman had a gun in his hand and a sword hanging from his belt, and dangling from the hand that gripped the reins was what looked like a garrote. This was a modern creature, but legendary all the same. It was terrifying and enchanting.

I couldn't help wondering why he had this particular tattoo.

The massage lasted an hour. We barely spoke, but I felt Riordan fall deeper and deeper into the relaxation I hoped he'd find. The slur in Riordan's words told me he was exactly how I wanted him to be, like jelly. I took a moment to admire his dark lashes resting on fair skin. It was a delicate peek into a rough and rigid man.

Some clients shared why they were depressed

and needed another human being in their life to hold or talk to. Others gave away little details I eventually pieced together. I felt like Riordan wanted to speak about it, but was bound by something or someone. I wasn't familiar with government procedures, so I didn't know how much he was allowed to say. He was a tricky puzzle.

My fingers were beginning to cramp, so I sat back. Riordan moved slightly, then settled. His breathing indicated he was asleep, so I quietly stood. It wasn't too cold with the central air on but the pebbling of his skin told me a blanket wouldn't hurt. His face was so peaceful and when he didn't have those stress lines and a permanent scowl, he was even more gorgeous. A thin blanket was on the ottoman, and when I rested it over his fair skin, he opened his eyes and looked at me without seeing me. A moment later, he slipped back into his sleep.

Chapter Ten

Riordan

Something woke me. I couldn't place what it was, but it made me leap up from the floor. I was on the floor, why? Right, Teddy, massage. Scanning the room quickly, he was nowhere to be found. Had he gone home?

The lights in the kitchen were dimmed and the hallway where my office was, was dark. No way would he try to get in there. He was either in his room or he had left. I felt groggy and couldn't remember ever falling into such a deep sleep before.

Quietly, I walked up the stairs and as I got closer to the guest room, the faint sound of music and cursing drew me near. I was sure there was no threat, but I could admit my curiosity was what had me pressing my ear against the door.

"There are bubbles everywhere, Zach. This game is not for easily annoyed people."

Who was Zach? Had he invited someone over?

"Fucking hell. Is that a cotton candy troll? Jump on his back and stab him with a lollipop."

What in the…? I had to know, so I knocked.

"No!" he shouted, followed by, "Come in."

Nothing could have prepared me for what I was greeted with when I opened the door. Maybe I hadn't woken up yet and Teddy wasn't sitting there dressed as a gigantic rabbit.

"What the hell are you wearing?" I asked, taking in the huge ears that flopped forward and backward and the big feet, currently resting on the ottoman. And it wasn't just that he was a bunny, he was pink.

"What?" He barely looked at me before his attention was back onto his game. "Love shrooms, Zach, crouch down."

I hadn't noticed the headphones he was wearing when I first looked at him, and I soon realized

Hug It Out

he was talking to someone named Zach.

"I'm dead. Thanks a lot, asshole." He angrily slammed his controller down and ripped his headphones off. Whatever videogame disaster I had just witnessed was over and Teddy angled his head to give me his undivided attention.

"I didn't meant to make you lose your game." He looked ridiculous. It took everything in me not to laugh at him.

"I wasn't calling you an asshole. I was talking to Zach. He's my partner when we have co-ops. He loves leaving me to die. Real jerk." His smile proved he wasn't really mad.

"Okay, you're gaming, but what's with the music and the bunny suit? Where did you even find a costume like that to fit you?" It was like I had walked into the twilight zone. Umbrella by Rihanna was playing softly in the background and he was dressed up ready to trick-or-treat.

"Yeah. I like to be in character." He smiled so brightly, and the whole situation seemed surreal.

"In character?"

He nodded. "Yes, I'm playing a beta game, Fluffy Fairy Bunny Bubbles. I'm the Fluffy Fairy Bunny. I need to stop the bubble army before they…"

Nope. I couldn't let him finish. "Okay. Yeah. I'm going to make dinner. Come down when you're defluffed."

What the hell was Aisling thinking? Teddy was a project. Fluffy Fairy Bunny Bubbles? Shaking my head and hoping to forget what I saw, I went down to the kitchen and began preparing dinner. It felt like a stir fry night and with my brain clearly trying to figure out what the fuck it had just witnessed, I didn't debate it.

Twenty minutes later when Teddy walked in, I was relieved to see he'd abandoned the bunny slippers and floppy ears in favor of a form-fitting white t-shirt and pajama pants.

"Whatcha making? Need help?" He leaned over the wok, his arm brushing slightly against me, and sniffed.

Hug It Out

"Chicken stir-fry. Is that okay? Do you have any allergies?" His touch had the hairs on my arm standing and the zip that went through my veins startled me. Teddy lived for touching and I wondered if he knew the affect he was having on me.

"I love stir-fry and no, I'm only allergic to penicillin." He pointed to the wok, and with a deadpan expression, asked, "Is there any of that in there?"

Funny guy. "No, this is the penicillin-free version."

I was a very aware person. Years of training had made it as easy as breathing. With Teddy moving around behind me as I chopped the chicken, it felt like an itch I needed to scratch, like I could physically feel him breathing, for Christ's sake. He set the table and hummed, unaware of my internal struggle.

"I heard that song in your room. Rihanna, right?"

He chuckled. "'Umbrella'. Sorry, I like that song, but I'm sorry if what you saw made you uncomfortable. I can stop. This is your home and you should never feel weirded out here."

Even though he wasn't upset, it bothered me that he felt like he couldn't be himself. Fucking two days with this guy and I was turning into mush.

"It's fine, Teddy. I just wasn't prepared, is all. Now I am. You won't be able to shock me anymore." It was good to know your opponent. I knew Teddy wasn't an adversary, but in some ways, he was. I needed to convince him I was fine so he could convince my sister.

The sound of his feet shuffling on the floor slowly told me Teddy was attempting to sneak up behind me. He whispered in my ear, "I guarantee I will surprise you many times while I'm here, Riordan."

Shivers danced over my entire body. I wanted his surprises. Why?

"Dinner will be ready in a half hour. There's wine in the cellar. Did you want to pick a bottle?"

Teddy was still so close. I felt his eyes boring into my skin. After a few seconds, he agreed.

"It's the door over there." I pointed to the only

other door in the kitchen, and watched as Teddy headed down. When he was out of sight, I took a deep breath.

What was he doing to me?

Chapter Eleven

Teddy

I wasn't a drinker, but I needed space. Riordan was affecting me more than I was used to and I wasn't helping matters when I encouraged the pull to be near him. Seeing a hot guy jog past and admiring him was one thing. If said hottie was my client, it would be wrong on so many levels.

The basement, or wine cellar, was stocked with hundreds of bottles. I didn't want Riordan to think I was going through his stuff, so I quickly took in the room. There wasn't a lot; a picnic basket, an old bike, and a small area with tools. Staring at the wall of wines was like trying to figure out a rubix cube in the dark. I knew nothing about wine except that red was the worst. I had some once, and then threw up for hours. My mom favored Pinot Grigio, so I snagged a bottle of that.

I took a moment before ascending the steps to collect myself. I had to remember Riordan was a client, he was going through tough times, and he needed a friend, not some guy his sister had hired acting like a wanton whore. The smells as I entered the kitchen were heavenly.

"Not long now. Have a seat and I'll plate it for you when it's done," Riordan said, his back to me. His shirt was still off and it was like the tattoo came alive. My eyes roamed all the way down his amazing body. Damn, that man's ass... No. Stop it, Teddy.

Riordan worked in silence. Years in special ops must have helped him master small movements and quiet. I chuckled when I caught a trace of the scowl on his face.

"What's so funny?" he asked as he came over with the wok and plated our food.

"You get a serious look of concentration when you cook. Did you know that?"

"My mind is always going. I like structure and

order in all things and that takes concentration. Keeping my mind on task prevents chaos and mistakes."

Riordan's voice cracked when he said mistakes. I desperately wanted to ask, but instead, I tried to get him to see it differently.

"Or you get an undiscovered masterpiece. I am sure there have been many dishes that were invented due to a mistake or taking a chance."

The small smile it earned made me feel successful.

"This is delicious, Riordan. Where'd you learn to cook?"

He scoffed. "I can't cook. My mom always tried to teach me but alas, that sorcery went to Aisling. I learned enough to survive."

"Well, you're good at it."

After we finished, I told Riordan to let me clean up and he could go relax.

I didn't feel like I was being much of a companion to him. I felt like I was being humored for

Hug It Out

his sister's sake. I needed to try and get Riordan to open up. The massage was a first step, but maybe he'd allow a cuddle or something.

"Did you want to watch a movie?"

I went into the living room and the expectant look on his face made him look like a little kid.

"Movie?" he asked again.

"Riordan, I want to ask you a question."

"Oh, for fuck's sake," he grumbled. He'd put on a tank top while I had cleaned up the kitchen, thank God.

"No attitude please. I need you to allow me to do my job."

"You massaged me. Which was amazing, by the way. We talk and eat and all the other companion stuff," he answered with conviction.

"Yes, true, but I feel you would benefit from cuddling." I held my hand up when he tried to protest. "You're not a cuddler, I know. You told me a few hundred times."

"If you know that, why are you pushing?" Now

he sounded angry. I didn't want him mad.

"Hear me out. I'm not asking you to strip and do a lap dance for me. I am asking you to allow me to cuddle you."

His eyes widened comically. "You want to big spoon me?"

Big spoon, what? I burst out laughing. "Oh my god. That's hilarious. I'm using that for another one of my clients. He's a comedian. He'll love it."

Riordan stood and tossed the remote on the vacant cushion. "Fuck this."

"Wait." I followed after him as he angrily stormed down the hallway toward his office. "Please. I'm sorry. It took me by surprise. You're a really funny guy."

"I'm going to do some work. Stay or go, it's up to you." He turned, his expression was emotionless. "I don't want to cuddle, Teddy. Don't ask me again. As of right now, Wednesday will be our last day. Want to make it to the end of the month, you'll stop pushing the issue."

Hug It Out

I was at a loss for words. He unlocked his door with a bunch of beeps and as it shut in my face, hope dimmed. Fuck.

I felt hurt, but also like an idiot. Was it possible Riordan was touch adverse? I doubted it because he had allowed me to massage him. Maybe touching with purpose. It needed to be for a reason? I didn't feel like I was pushing the issue, but I did laugh at him so his anger was warranted.

I was sure Riordan expected me to leave, but I had no intention of doing so. I'd wait until morning and hopefully after tempers calmed, we could talk about it.

Chapter Twelve

Riordan

I ended up sleeping in my office on my couch. It was the only place in my entire house Teddy wouldn't follow me into.

I was hard on the guy last night, and I knew it. The thought of being close to Teddy was a need as much as a fear. I knew I'd love pressing up against him. His smell was so fresh and he radiated happiness, all things my life was lacking. He probably could have convinced me to try, but then he laughed at me and I reacted… like a three year old. I had a tantrum and locked myself away.

There were cameras all over the house, so like a creeper, I watched him get ready for bed and stared at his still form as he slept. Why didn't he leave? I stayed awake for a while wondering about that.

Hug It Out

Shutting off the camera to Teddy's room was the only way to finally pass out.

When the sun rose the next morning, I wasn't looking forward to the awkwardness. Recognizing I needed to man up, I decided I'd go fix us both breakfast and apologize.

In the kitchen, I was greeted with amazing smells and a humming Teddy. My hope of apologizing through food was dashed as he happily went about making a terrific breakfast.

"Morning, Riordan." His smile was sweet as he handed me a mug of coffee.

"Morning. Thanks."

A long moment passed with neither of us speaking and when he went to return to his cooking, I had to say something.

"Teddy?"

He didn't answer, just gave me a hopeful look. No doubt, he wanted this strangeness between us to go away.

"I'm sorry I snapped at you last night. You

were trying to help and I acted like an ass. Not to say you aren't being pushy about the cuddling, I'm just saying I could have handled it better." There. Done.

He cocked his head to the side and regarded me for a moment through narrowed eyes. "I accept your back-handed apology and raise you an apology of my own. I shouldn't have laughed at you or pushed. Had you not locked yourself away in your office, we could have had a lovely evening. Since that was stolen from me last night, I will be spending today with you. I'll leave around five and return Monday afternoon as the schedule states."

How was that an apology? "You're punishing me?" I couldn't believe it.

He didn't answer right away, but the exasperated sigh told me I wasn't following what he was saying. He placed a plate filled with scrambled eggs, bacon, and French toast in front of me. Wow.

"I'm sorry you feel like hanging out with me is a punishment." There was certainly an air of hurt to his words and when he ate without looking at me, I was positive I had, in fact, fucked up… again.

"Sorry again. Okay. Fine. What did you have in mind for today?" I took a moment to savor the delicious breakfast, loving the cheese added to the eggs.

He wiped his mouth and excitedly began talking. "Well, it's actually a nice day today. A little hot but not humid. I was thinking a picnic in the park. Then we can maybe go down to the river to cool off. That would likely be the end of our day, but what do you say?"

"A picnic. In the park?" He couldn't be serious.

"Yes. I'll make it, you just have to show up. By show up, I mean meet me by the front door at eleven thirty."

Fuck it. "Sure. Okay."

Teddy practically bounced in his seat. Why did a picnic in the park with me excite him so much?

As promised, I met Teddy at the door at eleven thirty. He was carrying a picnic basket I recognized and had tried to forget I had. One Valentine's Day, my mother bought me a picnic set for two. She said one day, I'd meet someone I wanted to woo and it would come in handy. She'd be happy to see I was using it.

"I saw this basket last night when I was in the basement. It's what gave me the idea."

I didn't feel like explaining why I owned one, so without responding, I opened the door for him and gestured him to go first. My truck stood imposing next to Teddy's little powder-blue Escort in the driveway.

"I'm driving." I reached the passenger side before him and reflexively opened it for him, garnering a smile.

"Okay. I'd like to go to Fredrick's Park, if that's good with you?"

"Fine."

I couldn't help but notice how my truck dwarfed Teddy as he sat in his seat. When I hopped in, he was beaming.

"This is an impressive truck." He tapped the glove compartment, over the car logo. "GMC is good, right?"

Hug It Out

I loved my truck. I loved my car and motorcycle too, but my truck was everything. I bought it before it hit the dealers' floors. Black and silver exterior, leather seats that were as soft as silk, and of course, it was fully loaded and so much more.

"This is a great truck. Best out there in my opinion." Turning the ignition was a small reward. The hum sent a vibration through my body and I couldn't stop my smile as I revved the engine. When Teddy chuckled, things began feeling right again.

With the music on, I pulled out of the driveway and headed toward the park. About a mile into our drive, I suspected we had a tail. Teddy was going on about how he loved the park and did meditation there every weekend. I tried to pay attention, but when turned onto Fifth Avenue and the car followed, I realized I was right.

"I met some wonderful people in the meditation group. We may see some of them there. A few months ago, we had a lovely man join us. Stunning, really. He's so sweet and smart. Whitest hair

I've ever seen on a person that was natural. You'll never guess his name." Teddy was going on and on.

"What side of the park are we going to?"

"North side is best. That way, we aren't too close to the playground. It's quieter."

When the car followed us to the north side, I knew I had to think fast. Fuck.

"I'm going to drop you off and then find a spot. It looks busy." It wasn't busy at all, and Teddy looked at me like I was nuts, but he didn't argue.

After Teddy hopped out, I drove toward the south side, happy to see the car had followed me. When I cut the engine, I didn't hesitate to grab my SIG P226 out of my glove box and slipped it in my waist band. I wasn't sure who was following me, but I was sure as shit about to find out.

The windows of the black BMW were tinted and there was no way to see who was inside. When the driver and passenger side doors opened, I was coiled to strike. The two men who exited I'd know anywhere. Black's drones all had a certain look about them.

Placid expressions, dark clothes, slicked back hair, and sunglasses regardless if they were required.

"Why the fuck does Black have you guys following me? He said Wednesday. It's not Wednesday. Fuck off." My voice was thunderous. I was so sick of this shit.

"Calm down, Dullahan," Drone One said. "He has you under surveillance for your safety. We were coming to your home to inform you, but you were leaving. So we followed you to let you know. I think we can all agree had we not informed you that you were being watched, all of us would have been met with a bullet to the head."

He wasn't wrong. "Why do I need surveillance? He afraid I'm gonna run?"

Drone One's lip quirked just enough to tell me I was at least partially right.

"We don't question Black. Just know we are near. If you run into trouble, we won't be far away."

Protesting the order would have been futile, so I stood at the ready as they got back in their car. It wasn't until they had driven out of sight that I returned to my truck and drove back to the north side of the park.

My phone vibrating didn't shock me.

"Tell your drones to fuck off, Black."

The deep timbre of his laugh sent unpleasant chills through my body. "You will tolerate what I tell you to. They aren't there to spy on you. When I see you, we will discuss things. Until then, pretend they aren't there and stop being so disrespectful."

He hung up and I wanted to smash the phone against the dashboard. He was infuriating.

When I pulled into the parking spot, I saw Teddy setting up the lunch he'd made with his telltale smile in place. With a deep breath, I went to get this happy fucking lunch over.

Chapter Thirteen

Teddy

I wasn't stupid. Something was up with Riordan. Dropping me off in front of the north side of the park wasn't necessary. He was distracted. The door to the truck wasn't shut but a second before he sped off like he was chasing something. The man was fickle.

Setting up the picnic didn't take too long and by the time the last of the food was set out, Riordan was walking toward me, scowl in place.

"Find a parking spot?" I asked, knowing full well there were plenty.

"Yeah," he grunted and sat on the checkered blanket, his eyes scanning the layout. "What's for lunch?"

He clearly wasn't going to say more, so I

joined him on the blanket. "I made chicken salad sandwiches, a fresh salad, some grapes and cheese, and for dessert, I brought a couple of those cupcakes I made. If you're thirsty, I have iced tea."

"Sounds good." He grabbed a sandwich, gave it a sniff that I found amusing, and proceeded to shovel it into his mouth. I wanted to tell him to slow down, there was no rush, but he was seriously distracted. He didn't engage in conversation. His answers were monosyllabic, and he kept scanning the park like something was going to jump out and steal his grapes.

I was about to call it a wash when I saw two familiar people walking my way. Both had their blankets and water bottles.

"Oh, Riordan, let me introduce you to a couple of my friends." I stood and did my best to ignore Riordan's sigh.

As soon as my friends were close enough, we hugged in greeting. They were such great people and I felt myself relax.

"Teddy, glad to see you came today."

"I didn't. Not to meditate, that is. I'll likely come tomorrow. I'm having lunch with a friend." Gesturing to Riordan, I rolled my eyes at his half-assed wave. "This is Riordan. Riordan, these are my friends, Poe and Snow."

"Poe and Snow, that's funny, are you twins? Wait a sec." Riordan stood and pointed. "I know you."

"Name is Snow Manos, I don't believe we've met." Snow held out his hand, his eyes never leaving Riordan's face, a face that happened to be sporting a scowl.

"Manos," Riordan whispered. When he looked at me, there was such a look of surprise I wasn't expecting. "You're friends with Snow Manos, Christopher Manos' husband?"

Status meant nothing to me. Rich, poor, powerful, weak. People were people. So, I shrugged and answered, "I guess. I don't know his husband. Snow, Poe, and I all met a couple months ago in our meditation group."

"I see," was all Riordan said before slowly

backing up and leaning against a tree.

Snow watched Riordan with a look of amusement on his face.

"Are you both coming tomorrow as well?" I asked.

"I am," Poe said. "Been a stressful week. I need some peace."

Poe was an artist. Funny enough, he was also colorblind. He was only able to see the world in black and white. I once told him there were a lot of people who were colorblind. This turned into a huge conversation about the rarity of his condition. I was shocked to find out that only about one in 40,000 people have achromatopsia. He wore very dark glasses when he was outside and generally stayed in the shade because of the light sensitivity. His whole life, he had struggled. I asked him once if seeing was such a struggle, why would he choose to be an artist. He felt the world would benefit from seeing things through his eyes. I never knew there were so many shades of white, gray, and even black. He was truly talented and brave.

"Great. I'll be around tomorrow then. Have a great session."

Riordan watched as Snow and Poe walked toward the pagoda where the meditation sessions were held. When he didn't look away from them, a pang of jealously hit me. Anyone could see they were stunning. Snow's alabaster skin and hair and his fire blue eyes made his beauty unique. Poe was almost his opposite, but exquisite all the same. His long, raven hair and midnight eyes against his fair skin made him seem enchanting. Each had feminine qualities, and I wondered if that was the type of person Riordan liked.

"How long did you say you have known Snow Manos?" Riordan asked, eyes never leaving where my friends had gone. Though Riordan never came out and said he was gay, I saw the looks he gave me and my friends. It was a silent proclamation.

"Few months." Not being one for interrogation, I went back to eating.

"You make it a point to have powerful

friends?" Riordan's question was almost accusatory. Like I was hiding something.

"Do you make a habit of being paranoid all the time?"

The corner of Riordan's mouth curled up and he chuckled dryly. I couldn't tell what that meant, but I was sure he'd explain it to me.

"Being paranoid has kept me alive more times than I can count." Joining me back on the blanket, Riordan finished his lunch, not elaborating further about his paranoia. We were silent and I found myself tilting my face toward the sun and breathing in the pleasant breeze.

When I opened my eyes, Riordan was watching me. He looked away quickly, but not fast enough. What did he see when he looked at me? A goofy gamer who loved to hug? Did he see the man behind the bunny suit? Maybe he wished I looked more like my friends and less like a nerd.

Odd that this was bothering me. Normally, I didn't give a shit what people thought. Riordan was a

Hug It Out

client and I needed to remember that.

"I didn't mean to be insulting, Teddy, or accusatory. It's not every day I find out the man hired to keep me company is friends with Christopher Manos' husband, a man who happens to be a well-known crime boss." When he lifted his sunglasses and exposed his eyes, I felt better. The barrier was unnerving and reading people was better this way. "In my line of work, people are judged by those they associate with. Too many times, I've been right. Hang out with shit and you start to smell."

Now it was my turn to react. "Snow is not shit. He's an amazing guy. He may be married to a crime boss, but he's not like that. He's my friend because he treats me with respect. Now, I think I will be ending this lunch. You can put it all away. I'll call a cab to take me home."

Riordan jumped up when I did. His hands were inches from my arms, yet I could feel them as if they were on me. "Whoa, calm down. I wasn't calling him shit. Wow." He chuckled. "You're a spitfire, huh?" He rubbed his hand over his buzzed head almost like he was nervous. "Here I thought you were all marshmallows and rainbows. It's nice to see there's a fire in your belly."

"Look," I said as I began putting the food away since it was obvious Riordan wasn't going to do it. "I want to help you. Aisling hired me, and I know we said we'd give it a week, but I'm not sure it's going to work. Perhaps you'd be more comfortable with someone else."

I'd guessed Riordan was gay and called him paranoid. Both assumptions I would have never made with any other client. I also didn't fight with clients. I was breaking all my own rules and cutting this short would be wise.

"You want to quit because we had a little spat?"

"It's not a spat." I tugged the blanket until he got the hint and moved off it. "I work for people who want me there. You don't. This isn't about you being a jerk about my friends or dropping me off to park." I was mid-fold when I turned to give Riordan a sardonic look. "You do realize you pulled into a spot to let me out to find a spot, right?"

I could practically hear Riordan counting to ten as he closed his eyes and pinched the bridge of his nose. "I know. I had to deal with something. I can't tell you, but…" He inched closer to me, eyes soft and sincere. "I don't think you're horrible. Our company is strange, but I like it. Let's just do the whole month, it'll be fine, I'm sure. I don't want to start over with someone else."

In a gesture almost too sweet, Riordan brushed a curl from my forehead and smiled. "I need you to not ask me about the things I do. I can't tell you. Ever. But I promise I will relax more and stop being such a jerk."

I could see the truth in his eyes. I knew calling it quits was probably the right thing to do. We were clashing left and right. He'd try to see things my way, but we'd argue again. But I was a fool sometimes and I really believed I could help him. "Okay. We can stick to the schedule for the month as planned. But if it doesn't work, if we're fighting or it's stressful, we need to break the contract. Agreed?"

"Agreed."

Chapter Fourteen

Riordan

I didn't see Teddy until Tuesday. He was supposed to come by Monday, but had called to inform me that his grandmother was sick and he needed to care for her. Aisling asked me to try hugging and I was going to tell Teddy I'd give it a try. I hated it, but if I didn't, she'd never let me hear the end of it.

The sound of the key turning announced his arrival. Glancing at my reflection in the glass cabinet showed a scowling man and that wasn't how I wanted Teddy to see me. So, when I stepped out of the kitchen, I gave him the biggest smile I could muster.

"Oh, sweet god, did you murder someone?" That was how he greeted me. I guessed my face betrayed me.

"Not today," I joked, and it was true.

Teddy watched me through narrowed eyes. "Why are you greeting me like the opening scene of a Leave It to Beaver episode? What's happening?" Suddenly, his eyes were darting all over the room.

"I'm trying to be friendlier, remember?"

He didn't look at all convinced. "I see. Well, it's freaking me out. Stop it."

I couldn't help but laugh. I wasn't lying when I said I enjoyed his company. He was full of surprises, had so much energy, and made things feel brighter.

"I thought since it's in the high nineties today, we could swim in the pool." I pointed in the direction of the backyard.

Teddy's brows rose. "That would be nice. My car died this morning, so I had to stand at the bus stop. I'm roasting."

That bothered me. Why didn't he call for a ride? "You should have phoned. I would have come and got you. You're an hour from here and the nearest stop is a mile down the road." Now that I really took notice, I saw Teddy was covered in sweat. His curls looked like limp noodles on the top of his head.

"It's fine. My friend, Delly, said she would get me in the morning. I had it towed to Axel's Automotive. It's not too far from here."

"That place is still running?" The owner up and disappeared one day. Underground rumblings spoke of Christopher Manos' involvement. I wasn't asking questions, but it was shut down for a while.

"Yeah. New management." He pushed his damp hair off his forehead and sighed. "Let me get my suit on and I'll meet you outside."

"Great. Mine's on, so I'll just grab some towels and meet you out there."

It was almost unbreathable outside. The humidity was high and when I thought about Teddy walking in this, it upset me. He should have felt comfortable enough to call me and ask me for a ride, or at least to contact Lyft. This was my fault and I was going to try to make him feel more welcomed.

The sound of sliding glass doors drew my attention. He wore bright red swim trunks that made his fair skin pop. His hair was still droopy, but the rest of him was a sight that had my body reacting.

"I managed to get everywhere but my back. Could you help me?" he asked as he held a bottle of suntan lotion out to me.

"Oh, uhm, sure."

Taking the bottle, I squeezed some onto my palm and pressed my hand against his back. There were adorable freckles over both of his shoulders, but his back was pristine. Not a blemish or hair, and I wondered for a moment what his skin tasted like. He was pasty but his skin was soft, and painting his back with the lotion wasn't a hard task. My cock certainly loved the contact.

"I don't need a gallon, Riordan. Just one coat." Teddy laughed and I realized I was slathering it all over him.

"Right." With slippery hands, I shut the bottle and hastily handed it back to him. "Sorry. You're so pale, I was being careful."

Teddy smiled softly. "Thanks. You want

some?"

I was glad when I refused, he didn't go on and on about the dangers of the sun and exactly what cancer would do to my body like my mother often did.

"That water looks amazing." He was quick to reach the ladder, but paused when his foot hovered over the water. It was a little chilly, but I liked the shock of cold on hot days like today. I also had a hidden practical joker inside me. So when Teddy had his back turned, I did what any man-child would do. I cannonballed, covering Teddy in a wave of chilly water.

When I surfaced, I caught the tail end of a stream of well-worded cursing.

"Was that necessary?" he asked with amusement.

"Yep."

"You're in a good mood today, so I'm going to let it slide… this time." He took the steps one at a time and hissed when the water lapped right above his navel. "Cold, but nice."

I could tell Teddy needed the cool down and was appreciative of the water and chill time. When he seemed calm and relaxed, I called his name, and the blissed-out expression I was greeted with made what I was about to say a little easier.

"I've been thinking," I began. "I want to give the hugging a go. Not the cuddling, but I think it's only fair."

He pursed his lips and gave me an odd look. "Only fair?"

"It's what you do, and I'm not letting you at least try." Opening my arms, I was surprised when Teddy didn't move.

"Riordan, I love that you're willing to try, but I'm not in the business of making people feel uncomfortable. It's okay. We can pal around. Company is important and seeing you so happy today reinforces that sometimes people only need a friend."

He didn't want to hug me? What the fuck?

"But I want a hug, dammit. I want to try." I slapped my hand against the water, splashing Teddy in

Hug It Out

the face.

"Don't throw a tantrum."

"A tantrum?" Was he serious?

He chuckled. "People who hire me for hugging and cuddling do it for comfort." He wiped some droplets from his face. "Did you know platonic human touch releases oxytocin? It's a chemical in our brains. Touch can lower blood pressure, stress, reduce social anxiety, and pain. It also helps people with PTSD. I think it's why Aisling wanted this to work."

PTSD. I didn't think I had that, but no question I had high blood pressure and mad amounts of stress.

"Teddy. You obviously know a lot about this. I wish you had laid it out like that to begin with." Risking rejection once more, I opened my arms. "I want to try."

I saw a glimmer of skepticism on Teddy's face, but it was short-lived. As he made his way to me, I was actually excited. I wanted his hug to wash away the stress that had been eating away at me. I wanted it to make me stop worrying about my meeting with Black tomorrow. I wanted it to erase the mistake that killed a woman and her son.

"Okay, Riordan, let's hug it out."

Chapter Fifteen

Teddy

People like Riordan didn't open themselves up often. Asking for things never came easily. I often suspected it was because so much was demanded from them. In Riordan's case, it was likely the fact that his job put him in a position of power. He had to make hard decisions on the spot. Made choices that either saved or destroyed lives. To see him standing there, arms wide, asking for a hug, was gifting me with his trust and I knew it wasn't easy for him.

When I was a couple of inches from him and could feel the heat of his body, it was like I was a magnet and he was the metal. Resisting the pull was hard, but I wanted this to be perfect. I concentrated on the details of the massive man in front of me. I loved how he was only slightly taller than me and I didn't have to look up at him. But it was the broad shoulders and muscles that covered his body that gave him a dangerous look. I was nervous and excited all wrapped into one.

Trust was a huge part of what I required. That went both ways. Riordan was trusting I could help him and I was trusting him not to grind my bones to dust.

"When I hug you, try not to speak. I want you to close your eyes and try to melt into me. Feel the positivity I'm pushing into you. Think about all the things that make you happy. Evict the darkness from your mind and vanquish it from your heart. There's no room for it there. The longer you allow it to reside, the more crowded everything will become. Can you try this for me, Riordan?"

The sun was brightening one side of his face, playing with the flecks of colors in his eyes, and the committed look was all I needed to convince me he was willing to try this. He didn't speak, he just nodded, and I was okay accepting that as an answer.

Our chests, stomach, and arms all came

Hug It Out

together at the same time. My embrace was deliberate while Riordan's was reflex. I didn't need to ask him to know that he was reacting and not feeling. I needed to get him to feel. That was why most hugs turned into cuddles. There was no time limit on pain. It washed away when it was ready. This was the part of myself and my job I was good at. While it was physical and my body loved feeling him pressed against me, the louder part, the one that genuinely cared, was in control.

Being only slightly shorter, I comfortably rested the side of my face against Riordan's neck. One of my arms was around his waist and the other was around his shoulder. My hand rested by the nape of his neck. There was so much pressure there. Gently, I kneaded the base of his skull and along his neck. I noticed he immediately began relaxing. Each hug was different for each person, and while somewhat technical, emotion had to play its part.

I brushed soft caresses against his skin and very slowly swayed. I thought that would be difficult, but Riordan was truly allowing me to give him the best hug I could and I wasn't going to disappoint him.

He smelled like chlorine and I caught a whiff of his shampoo or body wash. He truly was prepared for this. I suspected he used aftershave, but today that scent was absent. He was following the contract. All skepticism faded away in that moment and I focused on happy thoughts.

Riordan's arms felt wonderful wrapped around me. I felt so safe and protected, and that made it easy to help him feel happiness, comfort, and even love.

Long minutes passed, and I wanted to check in with Riordan and make sure he was okay. Pulling back slowly, I felt a little resistance, which was good. Riordan's eyes were closed, and I could tell he was in a perfect daydream.

"How do you feel?"

The breath Riordan released was felt even by me. When his eyes opened, his pupils were blown wide and for the first time, I saw a man allowing himself to feel bliss.

Hug It Out

"I feel relaxed, Teddy. I'm glad we did this. I—" He seemed to want to say something, but was struggling with the words.

"What is it? Just spit it out."

His chuckle was so carefree. "I think we should do more of this."

That must have been so hard to admit. Smiling at him, I said, "There's a fine line between hugging and cuddling. We hugged for about twenty minutes."

I could almost see the gears in his head working. "Maybe later we can hug while we watch a movie or something?"

He wouldn't say cuddle. Whether he was fine with that or not, he wouldn't surrender yet.

"That sounds like a fantastic idea."

We splashed around for another hour like we didn't have a care in the world. When the water had my teeth chattering, we got out and rested on lounge chairs. The sun kissed my skin and it felt wonderful. Glancing at Riordan every couple of minutes, I saw he was the most relaxed I'd ever seen him. Most of the time, he was like a coiled snake ready to strike. Now he was like a sloth hanging in a tree. The visual made me laugh.

"What's so funny?" Riordan asked. He'd put sunglasses on and I missed looking into his green eyes.

"I thought of something funny, is all."

He pulled his glasses down and stared at me. "You have to tell me now. I feel like you're building up the suspense."

I didn't want to tell him. What if he got upset?

Riordan huffed and turned so he was sitting on the lounger. His no nonsense gaze was boring into me and I knew he wouldn't give up.

"Whatever it is, tell me. I won't get upset. I apologize for making you fear my reactions." He gave me a come-at-me gesture. "So, let's hear it."

"It's not going to be funny now."

"Let me decide."

I decided to just blurt it out. "I was just thinking you looked relaxed like a sloth. Hanging in a tree."

Hug It Out

As predicted, Riordan didn't laugh and I admit after saying it out loud, it sounded stupid.

"A sloth?"

I didn't want to see anger or whatever he was feeling at that moment. So, I settled on watching the glittery water in the pool.

He didn't say anything. I heard the squeak of the lounger and assumed he had lain back down or was getting up to leave. I was about to apologize when I was suddenly hoisted in the air.

"What the balls, man?" I shouted.

His boisterous laugh almost distracted me from the direction he was taking me.

"No. Don't. I just got warm."

Riordan's eyes darted between me and the pool. I thought he was going to let me down, but his wicked smile told a different story.

"That's what showers are for." I barely got a squawk out before he tossed me in the pool.

By the time I emerged, Riordan was gone. I swept the property for any sign of him, but he was nowhere to be seen. Had he gone back inside?

"What's wrong?" Riordan's voice came from behind me, but I didn't see him at first until I looked up. There he was ridiculously hanging from a tree.

"What the hell are you doing?"

"I'm hanging out… like a sloth." He smiled, and I couldn't even pretend to be angry. I just laughed.

Later that evening as we hugged on the couch watching some horrific B horror movie, I suggested having a barbeque in his backyard for his birthday on the eleventh.

"But my birthday is the tenth," he answered.

"I know, but maybe we can have a few people over to celebrate. Like that guy Mace who stopped by. And your sister."

When Riordan didn't respond, I lifted my head from his chest and by the undecipherable expression on his face, I feared I had pushed too hard, again.

"If you'd rather not, it's okay. I was just thinking out loud." Before I could rest my head back on his chest, his hand tenderly gripped my chin.

Hug It Out

"If you invited Aisling, you'd have to invite my mother and father too." I couldn't tell if he was phrasing that in a way that said no or not.

"I'm sure if I spoke with your sister, she'd take care of that."

Again, silence.

"Fine," he said, and then his hand slid to the back of my head and he guided me back to his chest.

I didn't want to push it much further. He had said fine. I was sure he was battling inside his head, but part of recovering from a mental block, whether it be depression, anxiety, or whatever, was to figure out why, if there was a why, and try to mend the broken fences. He was willing to try, and that was all I asked.

Chapter Sixteen

Riordan

When I woke Wednesday morning, it felt like I was about to attend a funeral. The bleak weather, the suffocating ache that made you feel like any minute you were going to start crying inconsolably. The crushing anger because you couldn't alter anything. The guilt for breathing air while the one in the box was in forever darkness exploring the unknown.

Black had to talk to me. He had news, I knew he did, but for the first time since I had met him, he had serious issues and didn't feel safe talking about them other than at his place. Well, his headquarters. It was rare that any of his team ever met Black in other places than our homes or somewhere designated by him. He was a very careful man. A dangerous man. One that didn't believe the word "mistake" was a

Hug It Out

viable excuse for anything.

Teddy's friend, Delly, had picked him up as promised, and though I wanted to meet a friend of Teddy's, I was also not in a good place mentally. I told him I had a very important meeting. He wished me luck and gave me an all-encompassing hug. I was becoming addicted to those hugs.

A couple of hours later, I was in my truck, idling in front of the parking garage attached to Black's headquarters. It was smack in the middle of the city. One of hundreds of buildings. No one would know there were dangerous killing machines associated with this place. "Hiding in plain sight," Mace always said.

Inside, the lobby looked like a regular corporate building. White marble floors, black couches and chairs. A desk where a couple of security officers, Black's drones, stood. Nothing suspicious. They waved me in, knowing who I was and why I was there.

As I took the elevator to the top floor, I

replayed that fateful day in my head. I'd missed something, clearly. But what?

Black's office took up most of the floor, with only a few cubicles for his secretaries. Most people require one, he required several.

Lana Davis, Black's personal assistant, greeted me. She was what I dubbed the girl next door, right down to the pearls and sensible shoes. The fact she worked in this organization was sort of funny. "Hello, Mr. Darcy. Mr. Black will be with you shortly. Can I get you coffee?"

"No, thank you."

I didn't have to wait long. Within a few minutes, Lana called me in, and after taking a deep breath to calm my chaotic thoughts, I opened the door.

First thought that entered my mind each time I entered Black's office was that there was a lot of leather and wood. It reminded me of an old-fashioned gentleman's club. I expected a bunch of men sitting around on leather couches, smoking pipes and talking about politics and the stock exchange. At first, I didn't think it suited the man himself. But after a while, I realized it did.

Black's appearance was what you'd assume any typical rich business man would look like. He was always impeccably dressed in the most expensive suits, had an air of calm, and a hum of intimidation. He charmed people closer with his long, blond hair, steel-gray eyes, and killer smile. If you weren't hypnotized by him within a minute, all he had to do was speak and you'd be his the second his whisky sex voice hit your ears. He could lull a baby to sleep if he wanted or strip a person of all their clothes. I'd heard him raise his voice once and gone was the seduction and born was the thunder. Black was not a man to be trifled with.

"Good to see you, Riordan." His voice danced over my body. He called me Riordan, which was a good sign.

"No offense, Black, but I wasn't given a choice."

"True." He gestured for me to sit and I took a

seat on the couch across from him. He had a glass of bourbon in his hand and his wingback chair seemed more like a throne.

"Would you like a drink?" He wouldn't get it for me, no. Black waited on nobody and I wasn't feeling like being played with today.

"I'm fine."

After a sip, Black placed his tumbler down and regarded me in his stoic way with his crossed legs and steely gaze. It used to terrify me, now it just made me confused. "We have a serious issue."

"No shit, Black. You said you had answers for me. You told me to stop looking into Vincent Abano's past. I've been waiting for an explanation and you wouldn't give me one until I was here. So?"

His clenched jaw and flared nostrils were as close as I'd get to seeing the man lose control. "Don't speak to me that way again. I'm going to let it slide because of the clusterfuck this hit was. Watch yourself."

Warnings were few and far between with

Black. I knew when I was close to pushing too far, so I didn't press.

"I've talked with Lee. His story hasn't changed. He says he watched Vincent get into his limo, then he followed him to the opera house. And from a distance, he saw the car explode. He never took his eyes off the car." He uncrossed his legs and reached for his drink.

"I wired that car to blow. I saw it pull up and I hit the button. I too saw it go up. If Lee didn't take his eyes off that car, then at some point, Vincent slipped out."

"That was my thought, or it was something else."

He didn't elaborate, he simply walked over to his desk, opened the top drawer and took out a large manila envelope. There was no way Black couldn't see the questions written on my face, but the only response I got was the envelope slapped down in front of me.

Without hesitation, I opened it. Vincent Abano on a beach. A blonde-haired, big breasted woman beside him.

"When were these pictures taken?"

"The day of the bombing. I received them this morning."

I had a million questions. I started with the most obvious.

"Then who did Lee see getting into the car?"

Black hummed as he took a sip of his bourbon, whether to buy time or show that he was in charge of the pacing of this conversation. "I suspect Vincent was the one who hired the hit on himself. He hired someone who looked like him to be a decoy just so we'd think he was in that car. I am certain if we'd checked the morgue, we'd find all three there, but perhaps we wouldn't now. Maybe just the wife and kid." He scratched his chin. "That wouldn't explain the decoy's body though." He shook his head. "I'm missing something."

This was crazy. "How did you know it was the wife and kid? And so quickly?"

"Right before the explosion, the doors opened.

Lee saw the wife and little boy step out. The car went up and Lee called in."

This wasn't right. "But Lee saw Vincent get in, or someone who looked like him."

"It's clear Lee figured he fucked up somehow. He saw them and reacted. Either way, they weren't the target you were being paid for."

"So Vincent was trying to fake his own death, or make someone watching think that?" I tapped the photos. "Who gave you these?"

"As you know, Riordan, not all clients are known. I ask few questions. Vincent set up for his wife, child, and some other person to be killed. I want to say he's in hiding, but with him out in the open like this, I suspect something different."

He still hadn't answered the question. "Where'd you get these pictures, though?"

He wasn't going to give me a definitive answer. I was a fool if I thought he would. "I have eyes everywhere. Vincent is a recognizable man. When word got out he was suspected dead, these came to me.

Obviously to show me there was no way he was dead."

"And what is it you suspect?"

For a moment, there was a flicker of genuine fear in Black's expression. "The reason we needed to speak here is because it's one of the only places I trust that doesn't have extra ears. Someone in my organization is a mole. Working against me. The last twenty-four hours have proved that Vincent Abano is trying to push me out and create his own organization. I don't know if he knows we are aware he's alive, but this morning, he checked himself into a hospital in Switzerland."

"For what?"

"Plastic surgery. He's giving himself a new face."

This was something out of a James Bond movie.

"He's an influential man. He doesn't need more money, so why do this?"

Black retrieved another envelope from his jacket pocket and handed it over. Inside was what looked like Vincent's bank records. He was deep in the red.

"He's not doing well. With the death of his wife and son, he stands to gain a hefty sum. Good start up money, and if he has a partner, they would gain a lot." He pointed at the papers in my hand. "If he's dead, he gets nothing. Which makes me think the decoy was for us to think he's dead. That information would trickle down to anyone looking to beat what's owed out of him. We say he's dead, he's dead." The exhaustion was starting to show on Black's face. "He'd need someone to alter papers and then convince the insurance company he's not dead while keeping us in the dark about him getting the money. A mole in my organization would have those capabilities."

This was all wrong. "Black, your clients won't go anywhere. They are loyal. People know your name."

Black smiled one of those wicked smiles that said he wasn't stupid and he knew how this game was played. "If I'm out of the picture, then there's no one else to turn to for the dirty jobs other than Abano."

"You think Vincent is going to take you out?"

Black let out a long laugh. "Good god, no. I'm nearly untouchable. Whoever this mole is will try and wipe out each of my hitters until none are left." His expression turned furious. "We need to find the mole, eradicate him, find Abano, and end this."

"How?"

"You, Mace, Emma, Jones, and Lee. Meet at the coffee house around the corner in one hour." Black was already texting. "You are the team on this. Find the defector, find Abano, and end it."

"Black? How do you know the mole isn't one of the five of us?"

He slipped his phone in his pocket. "I don't."

CHAPTER SEVENTEEN

Teddy

After spending time with another client, I returned to my apartment to wash some clothes, clean up, and make that phone call to Aisling about Riordan's birthday barbeque.

"Hello?" she answered on the second ring.

"Hello, Aisling. It's Teddy from Teddy Bear—"

She cut me off. "What has my ass of a brother done? Are you calling to cancel the arrangement? Did a hug turn into an assault?"

I wanted to laugh at the last part, but I chose to ease her mind. "No, he's fine. I was actually calling you at his suggestion."

"So why are you calling me, Teddy?"

"I told Riordan I wanted to have a barbeque for

his birthday. Now, I realize his birthday falls on the tenth, which is a Friday, so I suggested that Saturday. The eleventh." She was so quiet, I thought I had been disconnected until she hummed, so I continued. "He suggested I call you. I think because it's his birthday and you all being his family, he wants you to be there but he won't call his mother. But you would make sure she's there."

Aisling cleared her throat. "I see. And he actually wants all of us to be there?"

"Honestly, yes. I really think he does, but he doesn't know how to ask or make it right." I didn't want to break confidentiality, so I was very careful when talking about Riordan to his family. "Whatever Riordan has experienced has affected him a great deal. But I see so much progress with him. He actually hugs me and likes it. He's laughing more and even joking."

"I haven't heard Riordan really laugh recently." She sounded so sad.

"I'm planning to start the barbeque at one. It's not too early that it will interfere with people sleeping in on the weekend. Can I expect you to come?"

"Yes, my husband and I will be there. I'll call my mom and ask her. Uhm, Teddy?"

"Yes, Aisling?"

"Whatever it is you're doing, thank you."

Thank yous were never necessary when it came to my work. I loved what I did and I recognized these people needed me.

"You're welcome."

By the time all my laundry was done and my place was cleaned, it was close to four in the afternoon and I had to go into the city to meet a new client. I called a cab, as my car still wasn't out of the shop and it was too hot for the bus, plus I was too tired to walk.

I liked living outside of the city. I wasn't in the expensive part of Haven Hart where Riordan or Snow lived, but it was safe. I didn't like chaos and noise when I wanted to relax, so the city wasn't an option. Being an hour away was a good distance and made me enjoy going there when I had to.

Even though there were quite a few coffee

shops in the city, everyone in Haven Hart or Hart City knew Quirks and Perks had the best coffee ever. Family-owned, a bakery on the premises, and a small bookstore? Yes, please. When I suggested to my perspective new client we meet there, she was happy.

I arrived ten minutes early, so I ordered myself a muffin and a coffee. People watching was one of my favorite things to do, so I snagged a booth by the window and did exactly that. Being it was so hot outside, everyone I glanced at was dripping or fanning themselves with the nearest flat object. Why they subjected themselves to that heat when there was a perfectly air-conditioned room not three feet from them was beyond me. I was just about to go grab a book in the store to pass the time when a familiar face caught my eye.

Riordan was sitting at a round top at the very edge of the café with four other people. I recognized Mace, but the others I'd never seen. One guy appeared to be Japanese-American. He had styled black hair and one look at his clothes made me think he was perhaps

Hug It Out

a student or professor. A little geeky but stylish and very much out of place in that group. Next to him was a radiant redhead if I didn't know any better, I'd say she was Jessica Rabbit in a black business suit. The woman had amazing style and even though her shoes would give me a nose bleed, I could admit she had good taste. The last guy scared me just by looking at him. He had an expression that screamed "stay away". He had a goatee, was bald, and wore denim and leather despite the heat. He watched everything around him and even when the others laughed, he never did. He gave me the creeps. All five of them were so out of place. If you saw them separately, you'd never think they were friends. Like The Breakfast Club or something.

I thought about going over to say hi or even just wave, but before I could decide what to do, my client arrived. Her dog had passed away a few weeks ago and she was feeling lost. She missed the cuddling they used to do. She suffered from high blood pressure and her dog was the one who kept her calm. She didn't want to just go out and adopt another. She didn't feel ready, but she longed for a connection. I knew working with her would be easy.

When we said our goodbyes, I glanced back toward Riordan's group and saw they were still talking. An idea struck me, and I grabbed my coffee and decided to execute my plan.

Chapter Eighteen

Riordan

"You're telling me Black wants us to team up and figure out who this mole is? Then what, kill them?" Emma sat across from me drinking her sugary stupid latte. She felt this mission to be beneath her. Like me, she had a call sign. Hers was Hemlock. Her specialty was poison. She'd often debate that what she did was harder. It was more personal and intimate. To be able to get close enough to slip a drop of death into a bottle of beer or be able to know how to lace your lipstick with a killer concoction and kiss a grotesque man in order to get the job done.

What Black was suggesting would get her eight hundred dollar Louboutin's dirty and she wanted no part of that.

"That's what he said, and if you want to tell

him no, then go right ahead." She scoffed when I offered her my phone.

"Where are we even supposed to begin?" Lee asked, looking around the table. "It could be one of us."

Lee, aka Whisper, got his name because he was quiet. You didn't know he was there. He'd ninja anything you had that was technical and when you went to watch your evening programs, it would be the last thing you'd do. He was able to rig a remote to shoot enough electricity into your body, you'd die in seconds. One time, he was able to make the steam from a teapot exude a concoction that killed a guy in under a minute. And you never heard him. He was also an excellent lookout, and that was why Black used him.

"That's the tricky part. We're going to have to start from the beginning," Mace said. He was completely unfazed by any of this, like he knew what Black was going to make us do.

"Maybe we should be looking around us. Anything different going on? Let's use our fucking heads here." Jones. The scariest-looking motherfucker of all. But probably the smartest. Like me, his kills were known and brutal. To the dark circles, he was known as Hangman. His victims were always found hanging from something. He made headlines in Chicago a few years back. A hit to kill an entire mob family came through. Jones killed them all two days apart. Each was found hanging from a tree near a famous monument. The words "serial killer" were used. Jones said if they suspected a serial killer, then they'd be looking the wrong direction. He was right.

"I was thinking maybe it's a past case. Somewhere Black fucked up," I suggested, earning wide-eyed looks. "Don't give me those looks. We only know as much about Black as he will allow us to know. Obviously, whoever is doing this with Abano wants to destroy Black. Let's look there."

"And what makes you think Black will let us go looking through those files?" Emma quirked a sculpted eyebrow and her bitchy attitude was out in full force today.

"I think he may allow us a little leeway here." Mace smirked and shot Emma a wink, which she ignored. "He can't expect us to solve this by walking around the globe calling out Abano's name."

I was about to respond, but the sight of Teddy walking toward our table made me freeze up. Oh fucking Christ, no.

"Is that—?" The rest of Mace's sentence was cut off by Teddy's arrival.

"Hey, Riordan, so great bumping into you here." He was giving each of us that award winning smile that made a person feel like a million bucks.

"Not really bumping into someone when you walk over and butt into their conversation," Jones said with a look of disdain.

Teddy laughed, completely unaffected by Jones' jab. "Good point. I never did understand why people said that." He shrugged and when his eyes fell on Emma, he held out his hand. "I'm Teddy, a friend of Riordan's."

Teddy had this effect on people, I'd noticed.

Hug It Out

They didn't know if he was real and therefore, he must be mental or something. Emma had that look going on right then, but she did end up shaking his hand.

"Pleasure. I'm Emma, also a friend of Riordan's."

Teddy went all around the table greeting everyone happily. Mace was the only one to be genuinely nice to him.

"Since you're all friends of Riordan's, I want to take a moment to invite you all to a birthday barbeque we're having, well, I'm having for him this Saturday. It's at one o'clock at his house."

This was a nightmare. These guys weren't my friends. We barely tolerated each other. I knew he had invited Aisling, and that meant my mother. These people and my family. Together.

"Teddy, I'm sure they're busy." I tried to stop what I knew was inevitable. One thing we all knew was information was power and the more you knew, the more you had. Getting a chance to see my family and my personal life was too good a thing to pass up.

Most of these guys had no one. It was why being assassins worked for them. I was the only one who had everything to lose.

"Don't be silly, Riordan, we'd be delighted," Emma said gleefully. "Can't wait to get to know you better, Teddy."

Collective nods from around the table confirmed they would all be in attendance. Mace at least had the decency to give me an apologetic smile. He knew the price I'd pay.

"Great." Teddy practically bounced with excitement. "I look forward to seeing you all there. Bring something if you'd like, but it's not necessary."

"I make a killer Bundt cake." Emma winked at Teddy.

"Then I can't wait to taste it," he said, oblivious to whom he was speaking.

"I'm not bringing anything," Jones grunted.

"That's fine too. Well, I won't keep you all. See you Saturday." With a wave over his shoulder, he was gone and I had four sets of eyes on me.

"Wasn't he delightful?" Emma's smile was wicked.

"Look, don't come to my barbeque. Leave it be."

That made everyone laugh and Lee, who'd been pretty quiet, spoke up. "Is Teddy a friend, or more?"

"A friend. We just met a few days ago. Last week, to be exact. He's a happy guy and likes doing nice things. Don't worry about it." I tried to brush it off, but something I said must have struck a chord.

"You just met him a week ago?" Jones asked as his eyes darted in the direction Teddy had left.

"Yeah."

"Isn't that a little suspicious?" Emma pushed her coffee aside and I wasn't in love with where she was going with this. "Weren't we just saying someone entering our lives recently would be suspicious?"

This was absolutely ridiculous. The thought of Teddy being an evil assassin was comical.

"He's not a vicious murderer."

"If he's not the mole, maybe he's working for them. The best assassins are the ones you don't expect, Riordan. You should know this." Jones slapped my arm. "Have you checked him out?"

"He works with my sister's husband. He's not a killer." No way was I going to tell them what he did for a living.

"Okay, here's what we do." Mace spoke up, silencing everyone. "I'll run surveillance on Teddy. Riordan, you can even be with me when I do it. When he's not with you, we can track him. See what he's up to." He looked at Lee. "You need to start hacking, dude. Talk to Black about getting access to files and see if anything pops out." To Emma, he said, "Bake a non-murderous Bundt cake for Saturday and see what you can find out about the plastic surgeon Abano is using."

"I know what I'm doing," Jones grumbled before Mace could give him a job.

"What's that?" Mace asked.

"I'm going to interrogate Black's drones. No

one is closer to Black then his bodyguards. You want close, that's it. I'll clear it with Black, but I'm doing it."

It was a good idea, so no one argued. Mace said he would follow Teddy by car and video until Saturday. Then he and I would see what his day-to-day entailed. I knew I was going to have to tell Mace who Teddy was and why he was staying at my place. I had to do it before the birthday party, for fear it would get out. I'd also have to ask Teddy not to tell anyone what or who he was.

Chapter Nineteen

Teddy

My grandmother's house never changed. She never put new pictures of me over old pictures, she simply bought more frames. Needless to say, her walls were covered with my face. There were also some of my father and a few of my mother. With my mother always gone, it was near impossible to have new pictures of her, and my father dying sixteen years ago meant there were no new photos of him. One simply had to look around her house to know how much she loved me.

"Teddy, I'm fine. Feeling much better, so there's no need to check up on me. Don't you have a client today?" Anne Harris was a seventy-three year old firecracker. With not even one wrinkle on her face and very little gray in her hair, she looked fifty. Her

Hug It Out

carefree, sometimes careless, behavior made her seem twenty. You wouldn't know she was the age she was. She was also my world and I wasn't ready for her to leave it, so I doted on her.

"I will be with this client for three straight days, so hush and let me make sure you have all you need." Opening her cabinets and fridge, I was happy to see the weekly grocery delivery had arrived. "Do they put your things away, or are you stubborn and push them out to overexert yourself doing it your way?"

I practically heard her eyes rolling. "If you weren't so big, I'd throw you over my knee and tan your hide." She chuckled. She wasn't a violent woman and had never hit me a day in my life.

"You're avoiding the question, Grandma."

She huffed. "I used to, but last week I realized my bones won't let me, so the nice delivery boy does it." There was a weird lilt to her voice and when I turned to confirm it, she waggled her brows.

"Why are you doing that?" I asked, crossing

my arms.

"He's a looker, Teddy. Single, too. He goes to college a couple hours away but works all summer and the weekends here." I knew where she was going with this.

"How lovely for him." I refused to entertain her match making and immediately returned taking inventory.

"He's twenty-two."

"Good for him." Why did she have so many olives?

"He's graduating this year and hoping to open his own tattoo parlor."

Okay, that was enough.

"Grandma, what's your point? Just say it."

As much as I wanted this conversation to end, I didn't rush her. I knew the lecture was coming, so I leaned against the counter and let her say her piece.

"I love you, Teddy." I knew she did. I never doubted that, no matter how meddlesome she was. "He saw your pictures and commented on what a beautiful smile you had."

With my picture everywhere in this house, it would almost be rude not to comment.

"I'm not lonely, Grandma. I don't need you trying to set me up with people."

She sighed and fingered the knitted tablecloth. "I won't be around forever and your mother isn't reliable. I just want you to have everyday love in your life."

She always worried about me. I was twenty-six, but to her I was still that ten-year-old boy who had lost his hero. I was sure when she looked at me, she saw me standing over my dad's fresh grave, weeping.

I didn't like to see her upset and I knew she needed reassurance I was okay. Her fierce grip when I took her hand in mine told me she'd be around for a long time. I didn't want her spending it searching for my happiness.

"I have so much love in my life, Grandma. When my prince comes, I will simply welcome a little bit more." She chuckled when I gave her hand some butterfly kisses.

"You're so much like your father." Her eyes were soft with love and she gave me a sad smile.

"That's the best compliment ever. Now, let me make you some of your favorite hot chocolate before I go."

"Fine, I'll humor you."

I fixed her hot chocolate and sat with her awhile, talking about my new clients without giving too much away. When a Golden Girls Marathon began, I left her to it and started my trek to the bus stop.

Riordan had asked me to call him to pick me up, but I didn't feel comfortable with that. Delly was with a client, so the bus it was.

It wasn't terribly hot, so walking the mile from the bus stop to Riordan's wasn't a nightmare. The code had changed, so I took out my phone to pull up the new one and let myself in. I wasn't sure what I expected when I opened the front door, but it wasn't the silence that greeted me.

"Riordan?" My voice echoed through the

house. It seemed no one was home.

I was an hour late, so perhaps he had to get somewhere. I wanted to make myself useful, so after I dropped my stuff in the guest room, I intended to start dinner. The crockpot was cooking but it looked like it had only been turned on a short time ago. No aroma had filled the house yet, so wherever Riordan was, he hadn't been gone long ago.

I was about to text him when I heard the front door. By the time I had made it to the kitchen table, Riordan appeared in the doorway.

"Hey," I said with a smile that immediately faltered when I saw the scowl on his face.

"Why on earth would you invite them to the barbeque?" His voice was all gravelly and I could tell he was angry, but it was also sexy. His words finally got through to my brain.

"Who? Oh, your friends?" Why was he angry when he said I could invite people?

"Why did you assume they were my friends?" He lowered his quickly rising voice and seemed to calm himself. "They aren't my friends, they are colleagues."

"But you were all hanging out at Quirks and Perks like friends. I assumed…"

Riordan's thunderous voice cut me off. "Exactly, Teddy, you assumed!"

He was genuinely mad and, if I had to guess, afraid.

"Oh, Riordan, I'm so sorry. I didn't mean to overstep. I saw your friend Mace there and the others. I was so happy you were out and hanging with them, I reacted."

Riordan slammed his fist against the doorway. He didn't make a move toward me, but the anger radiating off of him was palpable. While I didn't think he'd hurt me, to ignore that kind of rage would be foolish of me.

"Mace is not my friend either. He's the closest of all of them, but still." He took a deep breath and I was glad he was trying to settle. "We were having a meeting when you saw us." He shook his head. "When

Hug It Out

you mix work and personal, you blur the lines. I don't like blurring the lines."

"How can I fix this?"

"You can't. If I cancel or tell them not to come, it seems deliberate. But Teddy, you can't tell them who you are or why you're here. That's not their business."

I felt so guilty, I'd do anything to reassure Riordan that he could trust me. "I'll tell them anything you'd like. Who shall I say I am?"

"I don't play video games, so we can't say we met that way." I could see Riordan was trying to play scenarios in his head. "I told them you worked with my brother-in-law. We can go with that."

What was he suggesting? "Are you saying we tell people we're a couple?" That might work. A new boyfriend who wanted to fit in. That would work, right?

Riordan's expression was pained. "Honestly, Teddy, anything we tell them will seem strange. Not to mention, if my parents and sister are there."

This whole thing was a mess of my own

making. I had to think fast. I could just say I was a friend, but what weirdo friend asked strangers to their other friend's birthday? None, that was who. The overzealous boyfriend would be the only thing believable at this point.

"I'll contact Aisling and have her explain to your mother and father that they are not to mention why I was hired. I will tell them you have colleagues that will be at the barbeque and they believe we are newly dating. The lack of touching won't seem too odd if we are new. Plus, I have no doubt your family will want to make this comfortable for you."

I didn't know when Riordan ended up so close to me, but suddenly, he was a few inches from my body and it made the hairs on my arms stand at attention… not to mention other things. "I'm not a touchy-feely guy. The lack of contact wouldn't surprise anyone."

"That's good, and I'll be sure to tell them all I'm some video game programmer or something."

The corner of Riordan's mouth curled yp and

damn, he was so sexy. "I'd leave out the bunny suit."

That made me laugh. "I won't mention it."

Any anger Riordan had a few minutes ago seemed to have left his body, and the tenderness I felt when he touched my arm was wonderful.

"My colleagues will ask you a million questions about me. Answer none of them truthfully and tell me each one they ask."

It was an odd request, but I still felt guilty so I agreed.

Riordan released my arm and pointed to the crockpot. "I made chili. It will take a few hours, so how about we take a swim and relax for a while?"

I made quick work of getting into my suit and meeting Riordan by the pool. We spent the next few hours relaxing by the pool and talking about whatever sprang to mind. I told him about my grandmother and he told me all about his parents, Sioban and Hagen Darcy. I made a mental note to have some Irish dishes for the barbeque that would hopefully lessen the blow of what had happened with him and his family. I knew he hadn't seen them in a few weeks and his mother was worried.

By the time the evening ended, I was happy Riordan and I were on good terms again.

Chapter Twenty

Riordan

The morning of my birthday started amazingly with Teddy making me breakfast of scrambled eggs, bacon, sausage, hash browns, toast, and orange juice. We sat on the deck enjoying the unusually cool morning.

"Do you usually spend your birthdays with your family?" he asked, tucking his leg under his butt and angling toward me.

"Not always. Sometimes, I was away for my birthday, so we'd do something when I returned." My mother would celebrate a month later if she had to.

"Your mother asked Aisling if it was okay to make your birthday cake for tomorrow. I didn't have any issue with it and something tells me she needed to do this."

That woman loved to bake and often times, she managed to make the cake look like whatever I was into at the time. Transformers one year, Monster Trucks another. Whatever I wanted, she made.

"I'm sure it will be delicious."

There were a few moments of silence before Teddy was jumping up and pulling on my arm, trying to get me to stand.

"Okay, go get dressed. Since tomorrow everyone will be wanting all your attention, I get you for the whole day. I have plans."

Teddy's plans made me worried. Even though the picnic was nice, I'd seen this man in action. Between bunny suits and inviting people to my home, I felt a little nervous.

"Don't look so scared," Teddy chuckled. "It will be fun."

It wasn't until I had been driving for a half hour, Teddy told me we were going to the convention center. Asking why was futile. Teddy could keep a secret like it was nobody's business.

Hug It Out

Pulling off at the exit, I saw the huge billboard declaring the Horrorfest Convention was in town. I felt like a little kid as excitement had me practically vibrating in my seat. I'd always wanted to go to Horrorfest, and of course Teddy loved scary movies just as much as I did.

We spent almost four hours there. We saw Jason, Freddie, and Michael Myers lookalikes. We got pictures and autographs. We watched an amazing show on stage makeup and one on how they did gruesome kills on screen. Teddy won movie tickets for a year and as he went on about all the movies that would be coming out that year, I found myself wanting to go see them with him.

I didn't even think about Black's drones following us around until I pulled down my quiet street and they passed by my house, likely to turn around and park.

"I didn't make you a cake since I knew your mom had one coming tomorrow, and we already had the cupcakes, so…" I watched in amusement as Teddy ran to the freezer the second we entered the kitchen and pulled out two tubs of ice cream.

"We're having ice cream?" He held two of my favorite flavors in his hands, mint chocolate chip and peanut butter crunch. I must have told Teddy I liked those because there was no way he'd know. He always seemed to remember things I told him.

"No. We are having ice cream sundaes." He went through my cabinets pulling out sprinkles, sauce, nuts, whipped cream, all the fixings.

He was so excited, his happiness became infectious. We laughed when we piled our sundaes so high they toppled over, and the carefree feeling that filled me felt wonderful.

I couldn't remember the last time I sat with someone and just laughed about silly things. Teddy and I came up with names for ice cream flavors that didn't exist and even though my family had made all my birthdays special, I couldn't remember one being so perfect. I wanted Teddy to know how special the day was.

Hug It Out

"Today was just what I needed, thank you."

"I'm so glad you had fun." He reached for me and immediately, I grabbed his wrist. His eyes widened. "Sorry. I didn't mean to scare you. You have some chocolate sauce on your lip. I was just going to wipe it off."

Teddy was wearing his black-rimmed glasses today and they made his eyes bigger and brighter. It was like they shined with possibility. Before I could second guess myself, I pulled him closer.

"You better wipe it off then." Pressing my lips to Teddy's felt like a reprieve from all the darkness swirling in my mind. It was everything I thought it would be and more.

I swallowed his surprised yelp and pushed aside the voice telling me this was a bad idea and instead, lightly nibbled his bottom lip. When he opened his mouth and my tongue slid inside, it was a battle of hot and cold, and when he lightly suckled my tongue, I growled with so much want.

I still held his wrist in my hand and I shivered

as I felt his other hand grip my shirt as if to stop me from fleeing or anchor him from his own drift.

He tasted like peanut butter and sunshine. His body was warm against mine and his tongue dancing with my own sent pure joy through my body. My cock was painfully hard and when I pushed even more against him, I felt his hardness. To know he was just as affected as me solidified kissing him was right.

Teddy pulled away first, gasping for air. His hand was still fisted my shirt and his other was in my grasp. Our ragged breaths were all that was heard in the kitchen for a few seconds.

When his eyes locked with mine, there was only a sliver of color around his blown pupils. His lips were swollen, and he look completely debauched. It was a fucking hot look on him and I wanted to see all the reactions I could get out of him, but he pulled away suddenly.

"Riordan, no, we can't."

Can't? "Oh, I assure you, we can." My wicked grin affected Teddy for a moment and I thought he'd give in.

"I want to. We can't, though. You're my client."

His client. Right. "I could fire you."

Shaking his head, he chuckled. "If you fire me, I'd simply have to find someone else to fill the calendar. At least proving we are compatible tomorrow won't be difficult."

"So you're saying we can't fuck?"

Teddy winced, but quickly recovered. "Riordan, I'm not sleeping with you. I won't deny I'm attracted to you and when the contract ends, if we still want to explore this, I'd like that."

I was having a real hard time with the rejection. "I wanted to fuck you, not marry you, Teddy." I released Teddy's wrist like it was on fire and stepped back.

I could hear Teddy's protests as I escaped to my bedroom. I didn't care what he had to say, I felt rejected and it was the last thing I needed. He'd fucked with my head like so many others, and I just wanted to forget Teddy Harris for one goddamned night. When I opened my bedroom door, there was a rectangular, thin gift, wrapped and lying on my bed, and the anger and embarrassment that festered inside me disappeared and confusion took its place.

I knew who it was from and I knew I'd feel like shit when I opened it. I was right. The card read: You're an amazing person with an amazing heart. Happy birthday, from Teddy.

The gift was the most thoughtful thing I'd ever been given. I'd told Teddy that first day by the pool when we were talking about grandparents that one of my favorite things to do was sit on the rocking chair with my grandfather while he read me Winnie the Pooh books. After he died, I was never able to bring myself to read them.

The gift was a black and white painting of an old man sitting on a rocking chair with a little boy clutching a Pooh doll. The bear was the only thing in color. Honey yellow. There was a quote from A.A. Milne written in the clouds. "You are braver than you

Hug It Out

believe, stronger than you seem, smarter than you think, and loved more than you know." I tried to collect myself when I heard Teddy by the door.

"My friend Poe is a painter. Only paints in black and white. He made an exception when I asked for the bear. He works fast, so I knew I'd be able to get this to you for your birthday." Teddy's voice startled me. I didn't turn around for fear I'd cry.

"Thank you, Teddy," I whispered.

"Happy birthday, Riordan."

I heard the whisper of the door being closed, and waited until I heard the shower turn on and was sure Teddy couldn't hear me. Then I wept for the first time in years. For Felicia and her little boy, for my family I had been avoiding, for the fear of what was going on with Black and his organization, and for the unwavering kindness Teddy had shown me.

Chapter Twenty-One

Teddy

Sleeping hadn't come easy for me last night and I was dragging ass in the morning. Riordan's kiss lingered on my lips even now. I knew I should contact Delly and tell her to either get someone else over here or terminate the contract, but I couldn't. It was like I physically had to stay there.

Part of me wondered if it wasn't my cock that had taken over all thought, but then I'd get this little tickle in my brain. It would tell me to stay, that he needed me. I just had to try and not let Riordan push over that line again. I didn't think I was strong enough to walk away again.

When he'd rushed off to his room and I'd followed in his wake, I knew he was seconds from breaking down, so I left. My gift was something I wanted him to look at and remember that he was an incredible person that had love all his life. I took a memory and made it something he could always see. I prayed I hadn't overstepped.

When I went downstairs in the morning, it was clear that Riordan was still in bed by the lack of coffee and the deafening silence.

I had a long day ahead of me, so instead of twiddling my thumbs, I made coffee, grabbed a granola bar I found in the pantry, and nibbled on it as I willed the coffee to finish dripping. As I sat at the kitchen table, all too aware that Riordan still hadn't emerged, I started making a list of what to make for the barbeque today.

I called Aisling the other day and asked her about some Irish recipes I could use for the barbeque, and she was very helpful. She went on about some Macguire barbeque sauce recipe written in the seventeenth century and how it was thought to be lost. Recently, it had been discovered and she offered the recipe to me to mix in with burgers and ribs. I jumped at the chance. Who wouldn't?

As I began pulling out ingredients and following the recipe to a T, my nerves got the better of me and I realized how much I didn't want to disappoint Riordan or the Darcys with a family dish.

"Morning," Riordan grumbled as he avoided all eye contact with me and went straight to the coffee pot.

"Morning."

The clock read nine thirty and with everyone arriving in three and a half hours, I wanted to make sure he and I were okay.

"Riordan, can we talk for a minute?"

He didn't answer me right away as he was currently chugging a scolding hot cup of coffee down his throat. When he finished, the myriad of emotions dancing across his face made me regret bringing it up, but it had to be done.

"Teddy, I don't want to talk about it. I made a mistake. I'm sorry. You've been a great friend and I overstepped. Won't happen again."

It felt like a hammer to the heart. I didn't know

what to expect, but it wasn't that.

"I'm sorry too if I led you to do that or…"

He cut me off. "Let's just move past this." He looked at the large white bowl with the sauce in it and took a good sniff, smiling gleefully as he asked, "Is that what I think it is?"

"I got it from your sister."

Riordan absently rubbed his stomach. "Oh, I can't wait to taste it. I'm going to shower and get ready, and then I'll help with whatever you need."

When Riordan was done, we swapped and I got ready. By the time one o'clock came, we were ready for the guests.

Aisling and Robert arrived first and it was the best case scenario. Aisling was on good terms with her brother and I really liked Robert. We never ran out of things to talk about.

One at a time, Riordan's colleagues arrived and I knew I needed to make this as stressfree for Riordan as possible. We had a story and we would stick with it. Each came with a dish or in Jones' case, beer.

"Is this your Bundt cake?" I asked Emma as she arrived.

"It is indeed. I hope you enjoy it."

It smelled like cinnamon and I was very much looking forward to trying it. I went to take it, but Riordan appeared at my side and snatched it out of Emma's hands. She rolled her eyes at his antics while I stood there confused at the glare he shot her.

Riordan went inside with the cake I had a funny feeling I'd never see again, and then sat beside his sister. He was smiling and joking with her and it made me feel wonderful. He really needed this. The last guests arrived and there was no question they were Riordan's parents. Since Riordan didn't see them arrive, I went right over to them.

"Hello, you must be Mr. and Mrs. Darcy. It's so great to meet you. I'm Teddy." I took the cake from Riordan's mother and shook both their hands, trying desperately not to embarrass myself or ramble.

"Please, call us Hagen and Sioban. It's a real

pleasure to meet you," Hagen said with a firm handshake. "We can't thank you enough for helping out our boy like you have."

I hoped Riordan realized how much the people around him wanted the best for him.

"Well, he's a little rough around the edges, but I'll smooth him out." Hagen returned my smile, but Sioban couldn't take her eyes off her son.

She was twisting her hands together nervously and it didn't take a rocket scientist to know how badly she wanted to hug him.

"Riordan," I shouted across the yard. His eyes shifted from me to his parents, and the wide smile he was sporting faltered slightly. He handed Aisling his beer and walked over like a man with a purpose and didn't stop until he was fully embraced in his mother's arms.

"I missed you," she whispered.

I wanted them to have their moment, so I took the opportunity to join Riordan's colleagues, who had made a circle with the lawn chairs and were having their own little conversation.

"Can I get any of you anything?" I asked.

"Nah. We're good. Have a seat." Mace patted the empty chair next to him. Not one to be rude, I sat.

"So, tell us a little about yourself, Teddy," Emma asked. The tan shorts and black tank top gave her a softer appearance than the last time I saw her and with her fiery red hair in a simply ponytail, she looked like America's sweetheart. The only thing that felt off was the sarcastic smirk she seemed to be wearing as an accessory.

"I'm a video game programmer and I write strategy guides." That was what I told Riordan I'd say. When Riordan told me he'd explained how I also worked with his brother-in-law, I added that I helped Robert out sometimes, but didn't go into too much detail.

"I am a huge gamer. It relaxes me. Uhm, do you have any favorites?" The quietest of the group, Lee, I believed his name was, asked me.

"I do, it's hard but I always like MMO's the

best."

Lee's eyes widened like mine always did when I met someone who shared my passion. "Like World of Warcraft? What's your handle? I love that game."

I didn't see the harm in telling him. "It's GrizzlyBear11. But the E in bear is a three. Friend me."

Lee smiled and I immediately thought I could be friends with him. He didn't seem like the others.

"Video games aren't really my thing, so what sort of things do you do when you're not stopping wizards from ending the world?" As Emma sipped her wine cooler through a straw, she kept her cool gaze on me. There was an air of discontent about her.

"Oh, just what everyone else does, I suppose. Go to the movies, meditate, stuff like that."

Mace laughed. "Meditate? I can't sit in one place for too long or I start to itch." This got everyone to laugh and that caught Riordan's attention and he came over.

"What's so funny?" he asked.

"Teddy boy here likes to be one with shit," Jones, the gruffest of them all, rumbled.

"It's called meditation, and it really calms you. You should try it sometime. Jones, was it?"

"What makes you think we are the meditating type?" Emma pulled her glasses down her nose, piercing me with her black eyes.

"There's no type, Emma. It's for everyone." When I saw the look of disbelief on all their faces, I got an idea. "How about you all try it. I'll help you."

"Uh, Teddy, that's a bad idea," Riordan whispered in my ear but not soft enough to stop Emma from hearing.

"Oh relax, Riordan. I'm sure it will be illuminating." Emma winked and practically slinked over the small patch of grass near the pool "Come on then, turn me into jelly."

I could tell Riordan wasn't happy but with his family looking on, I didn't want to make a scene. Mace joined me and Emma, and while I knew Jones wouldn't try, I was a little sad Lee had no desire.

Hug It Out

"Okay, let's begin."

Chapter Twenty-Two

Riordan

I knew Mace was joining Teddy and Emma for the meditation because I was able to inform him about who Teddy was. He wasn't totally convinced Teddy wasn't a plant, but he didn't argue about helping me keep an eye on him today.

"Teddy is lovely." My mom squeezed my arm as she stood beside me. "You seem to like him."

"How can you tell?" I answered her, but kept my eyes on the three of them the entire time. They were sitting in a small circle and talking softly. Too softly, because I couldn't hear.

"You have a softness in your eyes when you look at him. You also seem quite a bit protective of him." She chuckled. "Maybe he's more than just a companion?"

I thought Aisling was going to tell my mother

about the plan Teddy and I had concocted. But by her hopeful words, she either wasn't told or was having wishful thinking.

"Mom, I'm glad you said that." Her eyes widened in what was pleasant surprise, but she didn't understand. "Teddy and I are telling my friends that we are newly dating. I really don't want anyone knowing why Teddy is here. Can you go along with that?"

She flinched, and although there was some disappointment there, she also seemed determined to help us pull it off.

"Of course. Aisling said something about that. I guess I just forgot, you know, with seeing the two of you connecting so well."

A short time later, Emma stood, brushed grass from her shorts, and went to the cooler, seemingly done with the meditating. It was a perfect opportunity to corner her.

"Just what the fuck do you think you're doing?" I hissed in her ear.

"Don't you get all growly on me. Your new

boyfriend is actually a sweetheart." She popped the cap from a beer and took a few sips.

"So you agree he isn't a mole?"

She shook her head. "I think more than ever he just might be." Her gaze landed on Teddy, who was talking with Mace. "The timing is what gets me. And no one is that sweet."

Two weeks ago, I would have agreed with her. No one was that sweet. But Teddy was special. He rocked people's worlds with love and affection. I'd never met someone so selfless.

"It's Teddy's heart that drew me to him." By the look of astonishment on Emma's face, I realized I had said that out loud.

"Well look at you, Casanova." Her joking demeanor only lasted a moment, then she got serious. "Be careful. I've seen the worst of men and I know how convincing they can be. I've seen them fool people into thinking they are loved only to crush them into a million pieces, take everything they value, and leave them barren and alone."

Hug It Out

I was taken aback by the venomous way she spoke of men. I had no idea Emma hated them—us—so much. I didn't want to dig deeper into her hate at that moment, so I promised I'd watch my back.

"Maguire Sauce!" The sound of my father's boisterous voice distracted me from Emma's hateful diatribe. "Good on ya, Teddy. Do you know about the World Cup Barbeque Tournament in Lisdoonvarna every September?"

Even from the distance I was standing away, I saw the blush creep over Teddy's face as he joined my father by the grill. He listened intently as my father broke into a story that engaged everyone enough that I was able to get Mace's attention.

"What's up?" he asked, and we slipped inside while everyone's attention was drawn to the story.

"What happened with the meditation? What sorts of questions are you all drilling Teddy with?"

Mace held up his hands and chuckled. "Calm down. Acting like that, I'd think you really cared for the face hugger."

I knew a part of me did care for Teddy, but I had to be careful around these guys. They were sharks, and the first scent of blood in the water would have them attacking. I wanted them to think he meant little to me. Just a new boyfriend who wouldn't last long.

"I just don't want him getting suspicious. He's a companion and they think he's my new boyfriend, but if Teddy is a plant, I don't want him knowing we are on to him. The wrong questions could have him running." I knew Teddy was innocent, but I had to be careful.

Mace pulled a face that screamed disbelief. "I don't think he's the mole. But I'm still going to track him for a while longer." His smile was predatory. "And if you don't care about him, then when your time with him is over, you won't mind if I ask the cub out to dinner?"

The thought of Mace, or any of these fuckers, touching or going near Teddy enraged me. Grabbing Mace by his shirt, I pushed him against the wall. "You stay the fuck away from him."

Hug It Out

Mace laughed. "That reaction, my friend, is what will cost Teddy his life. If someone wants to hurt you, they will strike at your heart." Shaking me off, he took a moment to right himself. "A lot of people think it's the parents or siblings that garner the most reaction out of someone. It's not. It's the other half of a person." He pointed toward the backyard where everyone was laughing at something my father said. "If they get that reaction out of you by saying something like I did about Teddy, you'll show your hand and the game will be over."

"When I first joined the organization, I heard about Dullahan. Didn't know it was you at the time. You were a legend. In training, we heard of the man who snuck into a mansion of forty guys undetected, snuck into a bedroom and waited hours until his mark showed. When he did, Dullahan was there. Sliced him from throat to groin, took his head, and disappeared into the night." Mace shook his head, a wistful smile on his face. "I wanted to be like that. I wanted to be known and feared. So I worked my ass off to be like you. I've done things even nightmares fear and so have you."

I knew Mace was right. Mace had done things even I couldn't do. I didn't know if he had a conscience, but I knew he was the best at what he did. He knew how to twist people and leave his mark. He didn't talk much about it, but there was a reason why after only five years of working for Black, he was his number one.

"You need to be Dullahan sometimes. Put that mask on and don't show anyone the man behind it."

"Fine, but stay away from Teddy."

"Fine."

By the time we went back outside, everyone was filling their plates. Teddy smiled at me when I moaned over the ribs. They were amazing and the comments from everyone else, my parents included, made Teddy duck his head in embarrassment. I was starting to get addicted to that blush.

I was glad the rest of the evening was uneventful. My mother made a giant cookie for my cake that had everyone laughing.

With a promise to my mother that I would make Sunday dinner soon, she, my dad, sister, and Robert left. Jones wasn't far behind, exclaiming he'd had enough family time and was going to the bar. He asked if anyone wanted to go, and Lee hopped to it. I wondered if Jones realized how Lee watched him.

While Teddy and I cleaned the dishes, I noticed in my periphery that he was glancing my way. Again, he blushed when I caught him doing it. After the kiss and his reaction, I most certainly wasn't laying a hand on him. So I tried to think of other things, but working closely beside him and the humming he was doing made it difficult to concentrate.

"I'm exhausted," Teddy said with a yawn, which in turn made me yawn. "It was a really great day. Everyone seemed to believe we were dating and no one butted heads."

He was tapping his fingers on the counter and when he bit his lip, there was no doubt in my mind he was anxious.

"Are you nervous?" I asked. Gently cupping his chin, I pulled his abused lip from his teeth's grasp.

"I, uhm." He was looking everywhere but at me.

"Just spit it out, Teddy."

"I can't stop thinking about the kiss. I know it's unprofessional and I will have to find a replacement companion for you and I'm blurring the lines, I get that, but I was wondering if maybe…"

It was all I needed or wanted to hear. I hoisted Teddy onto the counter and devoured those plump pink lips like I had daydreamed about doing all day.

Teddy wrapped his arms around my neck and gave as good as he got. When his legs wrapped around my waist, it was like we were fused together. I slid my hands under his pert ass and carried him to the living room.

Even though I knew my house like the back of my hand, I still liked seeing where I was going. I pulled Teddy's face back, making Teddy moan with so much need, I was about to say fuck it and drop to the

Hug It Out

floor and devour him right there. But he latched onto my neck, licking and sucking it like I was his favorite flavored lollipop. By the time we made it to the sofa, my dick was ramrod straight.

"If you need me to stop, say it now, Teddy. You need to tell me to stop."

His lips were wet, the freckles on his nose seemed brighter, his cheeks were pink, and his eyes were filled with so much lust, I thought they'd explode.

"Don't stop, Riordan. I don't want to go backwards with you."

I didn't want to go backwards either.

Chapter Twenty-Three

Teddy

I was going against everything I believed. I was a goddamned professional. But as I watched Riordan with his family, heard his dad tell me amazing tales about Riordan as a boy and teenager, and when I saw him get all growly and protective when his friends spoke with me, it lit something inside me. There was no way I was going to be able to touch this man, talk with him, know him, without getting more attached.

I meant when I said I would get him a new companion if he wanted. I'd hate it, but I was compromised. I couldn't segregate professional and personal. I didn't want to.

He placed me gently on the large couch and hovered over me, his eyes piercing me with so much lust, it left me speechless. He really wanted me and it wasn't a look I was familiar with. I'd slept with a few guys in my life, but none ever craved me the way Riordan seemed to.

His fingers glided down my chest almost too softly to feel, but it was like an electric current that sparked when he touched me. I lifted my arms when he began pulling my shirt off. A moment of vulnerability was all I got before he was removing his own shirt. I drank in every glorious inch of him. He was a work of art with his sculpted muscles, curves, and darkness that seemed to seep out of him.

There was an unrushed chaos brewing between us. Like we were on the edge but wanted it to last forever. He licked and sucked my skin, eliciting moans and hums from me that were out of my control. He was owning every inch of my flesh and all of my reactions.

"Riordan, god, I can't..." I felt like I was on fire, ready to burst if he didn't get even closer to me.

"I got you." He pressed his lips against my neck, tattooing his promise into my skin. When his hand found my zipper, I wanted to weep for the relief I knew was coming.

He was killing me, I was sure of it. Did anything ever feel as good as all the sensations Riordan was giving me? I couldn't think of a single thing.

When we had to pull away to strip our shorts off, it was like a rush of cold and I was about to pull Riordan back down to me but it was like he had read my mind, and his breathtaking body was covering mine a moment later.

"God you feel so—" he mumbled.

At the same time, I said, "I need you."

Feeling his dick rub against mine released something inside me and I pushed Riordan's chest until he sat up. The confused look would have seemed cute if I wasn't desperate to taste him.

"My turn," I said before straddling him.

"Fuck yeah," he chuckled.

His scent and taste were intoxicating and only fed the crazy lust burning through my body. I licked over his Adam's apple, down to his nipples. I gave each a suck and a nip. The rumble of his chest with each ministration made me feel powerful and I wanted to take my time, but at the same time, I wanted to know every inch of him. By the time I slipped off his lap and my lips grazed his cock, I was hungry for him.

When I looked at his face, I gasped. He had a salacious smile and a glint in his eyes. I felt like I was dancing with the devil and embracing every sin.

His green eyes never left mine as I slowly worked my tongue down his shaft. When the tip was in my mouth, I couldn't help the hum that escaped when his pre-come hit my tongue. He tasted like addiction and like a junky, I sucked it all the way down. Riordan's rough grunts and moans possessed me.

His fingers ran through my hair and the sweetness, while nice, wasn't what I wanted. He must have noticed because a second later, he gripped my curls and I reveled in the sting as he pulled my head up, grabbed his cock, and slapped it against my lips. "Suck it."

Fucking hell. I couldn't deny his order even if

I wanted to, so I sucked him, letting his hands guide me up and down. I loved when he shouted my name as his come released down my throat.

"Get up here." His voice was raw, I'd done that, and I relished in the thought. When my legs straddled him, his face turned wicked and I nearly lost my balance before he was hoisting me up so my dick was against his face. His tongue teased the slit and between pleasuring him and the feel of his mouth, I knew I wasn't going to last. When I came, it was like a dormant part of me was finally freed.

When I could no longer hold myself up, he guided me back down to his lap. Our breathing was the only sound in the room. I wanted to ask him if it was good or he was all right. He must have sensed it because before I had a chance to say anything, he spoke.

"Not tonight, Teddy. We'll talk tomorrow." Sedated and happy, there was no way I was ruining it by arguing. We rested side by side on the couch, his arms and a blanket he had pulled from the couch wrapped around me. I was asleep in seconds.

The morning sun streaming into the living room woke me and I realized something was off.

I was no longer in the warmth and safety of Riordan's arms... Hell, Riordan wasn't even there. When I turned my head, I heard more than felt the crinkle of paper and realized it was a note.

Riordan had thoughtfully placed my glasses beside me, so I wasted no time slipping them on and read the note.

Teddy,

I didn't run away. I got a call while you were sleeping and had to run out. I don't know when I'll be back. I'll call you when I'm home. Please don't try to call me. I will explain what I can when I see you.

Please be careful.

~R

Oh God, what happened? Was it family? Something else? Why was he telling me to be safe? I suspected it had something to do with his job. The one he couldn't talk about.

I couldn't sit there and wait and was relieved to see it was only 9:00 A.M. It left me plenty of time to make it to meditation. Still without my car, I called Delly and she offered to drop me at the park since she had a client to meet at eleven.

No matter how hard I tried, I couldn't stop worrying that something was horribly wrong with Riordan.

Chapter Twenty-Four

Riordan

The vibration of my phone startled me awake, the clock on the mantle read two in the morning, so I knew it couldn't be good news. I was comfortable and warm with Teddy cradled against me and I wanted to ignore it, but it was my work phone, so I couldn't. Carefully and regretfully, I extracted myself from underneath Teddy.

The text message simply said: The cave in thirty minutes.

The cave was a secure location of Black's that only Mace, Emma, Jones, Lee and myself knew about. He had locations for many of his people. This one was ours. It was only ever used to organize a group operation or if something was up. With everything going wrong with this mole and Vincent Abano, I figured it was the latter.

The twenty-minute drive to the house dubbed "the cave" was filled with a million internal questions. Did they find something? How bad was it? Was it all over? When I arrived, I saw several cars were outside—Mace's, Emma's, Lee's, and what I believed was Black's. I didn't even knock before one of Black's drones opened the door.

"About time you made it," Emma said from the couch, and judging from her somewhat unkempt appearance, she too had been woken up.

I knew I was only one minute late and she was just being picky. "I wasn't near my phone. Why were we called in?"

"Jones is in the wind," Mace answered.

Black appeared in the doorway, coffee in hand. "After your little barbeque yesterday…" Black raised a sarcastic brow. "He went out to a bar. Lee was with him. They had a few drinks and Jones got a call. Lee said he rushed out of there like he was on fire. Of course, Lee followed him."

Lee sat in one of the chairs, giving very little

away. The obvious worry was evident but nothing more.

"He followed him to an alley. There, a black van was waiting. Jones spoke to the driver for a minute or two and then got in the passenger seat," Black continued.

"And because of that, we were called in?" There could have been a million different reasons. Maybe it was a friend. Maybe it was a lead.

"I've been trying to reach him since Lee reported it and he's not answering me. ME." Black was furious.

"Was he in the middle of a mission? Maybe this was part of it." There had to be an explanation.

"No. You were all off mission. That's why I had you grouped together to locate the mole." When Black sat beside Emma on the couch, she immediately stood and moved away, garnering a scowl from Black.

"I think it's likely that Jones is the mole." Emma snagged the beer from Mace's hand and drank it down. If Mace was upset, he didn't show it.

"Because he got into a van?" Their faces told me that was exactly what they thought. "You're serious?"

Mace simply shrugged. "You know he and Lee are best friends. He'd never abandon Lee without a word."

Lee had been silent since I arrived and the only sign of him taking in any of what we were saying was the fact that his eyes darted to whomever was talking.

"Do you think he'd do this, Lee?" I asked, but Emma interrupted before I got my answer.

"We aren't dealing with amateurs, Riordan. Jones knows how to trick a room. It's not easy to pull the wool over our eyes. He'd probably been working Lee and all of us over for years to pull this off." The slamming of the beer bottle drove home how angry she was. "How did you not see this, Black?"

Black narrowed his eyes and flared his nostrils, showing the monster inside for a mere moment. All his attention was on Emma and if they were alone, I'd fear he'd end her. "Do you know how many of you I have

Hug It Out

working for me? I vet you all when you first start out, study you for years. Jones has worked for the organization for twenty years. No red flags have gone up with him in all that time. I don't follow every little thing you all do, but recently I've found myself checking up on past missions. Time changes people. I'm not fool enough to think otherwise." He stood and stalked over to Emma. He stopped when they were toe to toe, dwarfing her. She showed no sign of backing down or even a flicker of fear. "Tell me exactly what it is you think he's been trying to pull off."

"The mole, whoever it is—and you have to admit it looks real good that it's Jones—is working with Abano. Why, I don't know. All our digging turned up nothing." The intimidation stare down ended when she looked away first. That was how it usually went down. Black wasn't anything but one hundred percent alpha and would have stood there until she submitted.

"Lee." He had been watching Emma and Black the entire time, but his eyes shot right to me when I called to him. "You know Jones better than any of us.

What're your thoughts?"

Lee clutched his messenger bag and stared at the carpet as he spoke softly. "It's not like him. Like, Jones is gruff and rude and he's arrogant and all, but with me," He shrugged, a doleful look on his face showed how truly affected he was by Jones' disappearance, "he tells me things and he's nice to me. He'd never leave me in a seedy bar alone even knowing I could kill everyone in there in under a minute. He's... protective."

"So him going off like that was not typical?" Mace asked as he took a seat beside Lee.

He shook his head as he just stared at the carpet, maybe wishing for it to conjure up an explanation.

"Why are you all acting like he's some victim here?" Emma shouted. "Maybe it was his job to get close to Lee. He's the tech guy, after all. Lord only knows how much info you've dumped on him."

Lee's face turned red and he sneered at Emma. It was in that moment where he showed his ability to destroy and kill. "We never spoke of what we do. It wasn't like that."

Emma scoffed. "How about instead of thinking Jones is in trouble, we realize he is trouble?"

"We don't know what's going on, but we should be on guard. If Jones is the mole and realizes we figured it out, he may come gunning for all of us," Black said.

"My family." It was all I could think of to say. "Do you think Jones would go after them to get to me?"

"If Jones wanted to get to you, he'd just get to you. He isn't some newbie that needs to tear down walls to get in the room. He walks through those walls," Mace answered.

"Do we know if Teddy is a plant yet?" Black asked, and that surprised me. I didn't realize Black was informed about that possibility.

"We haven't had a lot of time to trace him or anything," Lee said. "He seems average, but I couldn't find much in his background. Doesn't mean a lot though. If anyone looked in our backgrounds, they wouldn't find much either." Lee gave me a look that said he was well aware of what Teddy's other occupation was. If he looked in his files, he knew.

"No way is Teddy in on this." I couldn't believe it. It didn't connect with anything.

"You don't want to see it." Emma languidly crossed her arms. "You're thinking with your dick. Typical."

"No, I'm not. I've been doing this a hell of a long time. Don't tell me I don't know what to look for." Raising my voice only managed to upset me further. "I've slit the throats of family men who tucked their little girls in bed at night, then went off to torture and rape people sold into slavery. I've stared down four serial killers in my day who had convinced the world they were school teachers, lawyers, and doctors. In the end, they all fell and I stood."

"I've been here longer than all of you," Emma shouted, pointing her finger at everyone except Black. A wild-eyed expression on her face made me wonder how unhinged was she becoming. "Maybe realize that."

"Okay, everyone calm down." Black stood in the middle of us. "Mace, take point on this. Track Teddy. If he's in on this, then we'll know fairly quickly."

"Mace is on point?" Emma asked as red creeped up her neck and her expression pinched.

"Yes." Black didn't leave room for argument.

"What do I do?" Lee asked.

"If Jones is going to contact someone, it's going to be you. Keep trying to get ahold of him and see what your interwebs are weaving," Mace ordered.

"And me, your holiness?" Sarcastic Emma wasn't out of the ordinary, spiteful Emma was. Lately, she'd been more vicious, more outspoken. I was sure I wasn't the only one who noticed.

"Go down to that bar, talk to some of the men there. Do what you do best and get some answers. Maybe someone saw something."

Emma left the house without a passing glance

at anyone. Lee followed, quieter and more reserved.

"I'm going home. Teddy will start to worry." It was past four. If he was still sleeping, I could slip in, remove the note, and Teddy would be none the wiser.

"Not yet," Black said. "We talked about this. You're the only one with something to lose. My guys are parked in front of your house right now. Teddy is safe. We need to go over a plan for your fucking family if Jones or whoever is involved decides to do something. Have a seat."

It took hours. After it was finalized, I was grilled about Teddy. I told them what I knew without giving away anything too personal. Following Teddy and suspecting him at all was stupid. I trusted my gut.

By the time I got home, I was upset to see Teddy was gone. In the kitchen, I saw a note on the fridge. He was meditating in the park, then picking up his car. He wanted me to call him when I got home to talk, but I wasn't sure what I could say to him. Our night had been perfect and maybe I was delusional to think any more than fucking could come out of it. I had

Hug It Out

to figure shit out before talking to him.

Chapter Twenty-Five

Teddy

When I arrived at the park, Poe and Snow were already there. I noticed someone else who I'd never seen before was lying on the grass. Obviously, they knew him, or he wouldn't be with them, so I felt confident approaching. The stranger was easy on the eyes, that was for sure. With his dark-blond hair and five o'clock shadow, he gave off a rugged appearance. His long legs were stretched out on the blanket and while he wasn't as muscular as Riordan, he was certainly built.

"Hey, Teddy," Snow greeted as he waved me over with a beatific smile on his face. "I'm glad we both picked the same day this week. I feel like I haven't seen you in forever." He looked behind me, and then his blue eyes crinkled with amusement. "Where's your hot bodyguard?"

Hug It Out

Poe snickered, making the stranger scoff and I think glare, I couldn't tell for sure through the dark glasses he had on.

"Riordan had to go somewhere, I guess. Uhm, can I sit with you guys?" My eyes lingered on the stranger, hoping it clued them in to introduce me.

"Teddy, this is Bill. He works for Chris, but he's also a friend. He is having some anger issues and Chris thought it would be a good idea if he tried some meditation." Snow smiled at Bill fondly. Bill just grunted and playfully pushed Snow.

"Good to meet you." At least when I offered him my hand, he shook it. His grip was strong and precise.

"You okay?" Poe asked after I got situated.

"I dunno. Just some stuff going on in my head." I tried closing my eyes to center myself before our session began, but I kept seeing Riordan when I did.

"I know that look," Snow said. There was mischief in his expression.

"What look is that?"

Snow placed his hands over his heart, comically let out a sigh, and in a singsong voice, he said, "That's the look of troubled love."

This time, I shoved him playfully, making him laugh and lightening my spirits momentarily.

"Trouble in Riordan paradise?" Poe asked as he tied his long hair up in a ponytail.

I wasn't sure what to say. I knew Snow would understand the dark side of things, but I wondered if I wasn't being paranoid. Perhaps Riordan was telling me to be safe like a mother told her kid to be safe before they left the house.

"Wow, something is really bothering you." Snow's joking demeanor changed to one of worry when he realized how serious I was. "What's up?"

"Okay, but please don't say anything." Everyone agreed. Bill paid me no mind, his head on the blanket, eyes to the sky. So I gave Poe and Snow my attention and began to tell them what had happened.

Hug It Out

"Riordan and I, we're getting closer. But last night, he left while I slept. Wouldn't say where. He left me a note and... okay, I know this sounds like I'm paranoid, but he told me to be safe." Poe looked worried, and Snow had his ever-present thinking face on.

"Maybe he wanted you to be safe because he cares about you and the world is scary?" Poe was clearly trying to be the calm one. Leave it to Snow to be the devil on my shoulder.

"How much do you know about what he does for a living?"

"I don't. I think it's some special ops thing. That's what his sister told me when she..." I didn't want to embarrass Riordan, but I trusted these guys.

"What is it, Teddy?" Snow asked as he put his hand on my arm in comfort.

"I was hired as a companion for Riordan. He was really depressed and it's something that I do. Not sexual. Well, it wasn't until last night and..." Waving my hand in front of my face, I dismissed the unimportant information. "No one knows what he does is all I'm getting at."

Snow and Poe shared an equally worrisome look I was about to question, but Bill caught my eye. His glasses were pulled down on the bridge of his nose and suddenly he seemed very interested in my conversation.

"You ever see any American flags on his wall, pictures of soldiers in the sand, or medals hanging somewhere?" Bill asked.

"No."

"Dude is in the dark then."

"The dark?" I didn't know what that meant.

"Special ops, secret or no, they all start somewhere. If he really was military of some sort, he'd have pics of his buddies up from past missions before he was sucked into the keep-your-fucking-mouth-shut club. If for no other reason than to convince his family. How none of them picked up on it is beyond me." He plucked a piece of grass and put it in his mouth. It was dangling there and he went back to staring at the sky.

Hug It Out

All interest in the conversation was gone once again.

"But what's the dark?" I didn't understand.

"Teddy." Snow grabbed my attention. "Bill's saying that whatever Riordan is doing, it's probably not for the government, and if it is, then it's not legit. The dark is… well, let's just say it's not where the decorated soldiers linger."

"Like CIA?" Poe was clearly just as confused as me.

"No, when I say 'dark,' I half mean what Snow said. I mostly mean the dark because you won't find him. You don't find people like that. He's Riordan to you, but something completely different to others." Bill had only turned his head slightly to talk to me. He seemed annoyed by the questions but answered anyway.

The silence was loud. I no longer felt paranoid. Now I felt afraid.

"Teddy, when Riordan said to be safe, I think he meant that literally. If he's in the dark like Bill says, than there may be trouble coming his way." Snow leaned closer, his hand gripping mine tighter. "If you're in trouble, Teddy, believe me, I can help."

"How?" I never asked much about Snow and I certainly never spoke about his husband, but I had a feeling whoever Snow's heart belonged to was a powerful man. Snow knew life in love with a man in the dark. It was how I knew he'd likely understand.

"He has a Chris." Bill chuckled, solidifying my thoughts.

"Call me. Any time, you understand?" Snow released his grip, but gave me a stern look.

"Promise."

The instructor got our attention and I tried to stay calm the entire hour, but it was impossible. I needed to talk to Riordan.

Chapter Twenty-Six

Riordan

I was second guessing everything when I returned home to an empty house. I had to talk to Teddy but as the hours ticked by, it felt like a bad idea. I was so fucked up in my head. I didn't call Teddy on Sunday. Or on Monday or Tuesday. On Wednesday, Mace ordered me to come with him so we could tail Teddy. I didn't want to. Sure. The urge to touch, taste, and be near him was strong and there was a slight ache in my heart that bothered me a little. A part of me wondered if staying away until after the operation would be better. I had no chance of getting out of this life while there was a mole in the organization.

My phone buzzed while I was in the car with Mace running surveillance on Teddy. I knew before I looked at it, it was Teddy. He was directly in front of us sitting outside Quirks and Perks, his posture screamed dejected. I had done that.

"You haven't called him, have you?" Mace asked.

"What am I going to say? Sorry, I need to disappear from your life because I'm fairly certain if we stick this out, you'll end up dead?"

"I don't know what you should say. I'm not exactly the relationship type. But he has a key to your place, he has his shit at your place, and you said you were the one who mentioned there was something to talk about. Now he can't get his stuff and you're not answering his calls. He's one stressed out shiver away from calling the cops to do a wellness check on you."

Shit. He was right. "Fine. I'll text him that I've just been busy and… I dunno, I'll start there."

We watched as Teddy urgently grabbed his phone to read the text I'd just sent. The look of relief that passed over his face as he read my message made the moment bearable.

"He's got it bad for you, bud." Mace chuckled. "If I'm not mistaken, you got it bad for him too." Mace shook his head. "How'd you get here? Remember that hit two years ago, Diego D?"

I remembered that hit clearly. Order came from a distraught father. His only daughter had been raped and tortured for weeks. When they caught Diego D, it was all over the papers. But he ended up getting off on a technicality. Black hesitated giving me the hit because the father wanted Diego to die by inches. Slowly, and the body was never to be found.

"You looked at that picture of that guy's daughter and took it without a second thought. Diego suffered horribly. You peeled his skin in strips, cauterized his junk, and ripped his eyes from his sockets. Damn, you put Jones to shame on that kill." He gestured to where Teddy was sitting across the street. "Now you can't even call the face hugger because you're afraid? He likes your sorry ass a lot and you like his."

"He can't, we only met two weeks ago. He's just a really caring person. Too good for my sorry ass." I mumbled the last part, but Mace had heard it.

"Heard you wanted out of this life, that true?" I didn't take my eyes off Teddy and my silence must have answered his question. "I'll see if I can help after this operation is over." That got my attention and I whipped my head around to see if Mace was serious. "I promise nothing. But I'll try."

"Thanks, man."

We didn't talk much as we watched Teddy finish his coffee and snack. Mace drove slowly as Teddy walked to his destination. The entire time his nose was in his phone. He bumped into about seven people, never phased.

"Thought he had a car?" Mace asked as we watched Teddy help a woman pick up apples he'd knocked over when he slammed into her.

"He does, but he probably has a client up this way so he parked it somewhere."

At the pedestrian crossing, Teddy didn't even stop to see if he could cross the street. A car swerved to avoid hitting him and around about the time Teddy waved obliviously at the angry driver, I knew he was more of a threat to himself than others.

"Jesus fucking Christ. He has no self-preservation skills at all!" Mace was gripping the steering wheel, obviously just as on edge as I was.

"Yeah, real badass deep undercover mole we got there." To think Teddy was anything sinister pissed me off. "We're wasting our time."

When Teddy finally entered an apartment building, we felt better about his chances of survival, so we went back to Quirks and Perks for coffee.

"Jones said he was going to interrogate Black's drones, remember?" I asked Mace. He offered an answering nod. "What if he got one of them to sing and he got a lead, and that's what the sudden disappearance was all about?"

"But why not tell us, or at least Lee?" Mace sipped his coffee, eyes constantly scanning our surroundings. That was our life, always watching.

"Maybe he couldn't." Mace was about to say something, but I wasn't done. "Hear me out. Jones is an asshole, we all agree with that, but he's not disloyal."

"You're saying he found out who the mole was?"

"I'm thinking if he didn't, then he's close."

"So either he didn't tell Lee to keep him safe or…"

I finished his thought, even though I hated it. "Or Lee is the mole and he had to get away from him."

The thought made me sick, and by the look on Mace's face, he was with me.

"I think it's safe to say we can't share this information with the group. I'll contact Black." He released a frustrated sigh. "If Jones got info from a drone, then it's not just this mole we have to worry about. It goes deeper. The mole and Abano have gotten to others. Black isn't safe, none of us are."

"How the fuck are we supposed to get to the bottom of this if we can't trust anyone?" We were fucked.

"Riordan, we keep what we find to ourselves. I'll contact Black, but we need to figure out some outside help. Someone not attached to the organization."

I knew Mace was right, and I only hoped Black had an idea of where we could go to get that kind of help.

We followed Teddy until he returned to his apartment, and then went our separate ways. Mace was going to talk to Black and I was going through all the files on all the agents. If Lee was the mole, like him or not, I would end him. I needed to get this figured out. I was a walking target, and so was everyone else I cared about.

I was home at my desk sifting through tons of papers when my phone buzzed with a message from Mace letting me know Black was informed Jones had hopped a plane to Switzerland. That was where Abano was last seen.

What the fuck was going on?

Chapter Twenty-Seven

Teddy

I was minutes away from calling Snow to ask him to help. I was so worried about Riordan. Then he texted me. It wasn't much, but it was enough to make breathing easier.

The last few days had been filled with so many thoughts. Was Riordan the man that Bill said he was? Maybe he didn't have pictures around his place because the memories hurt. There were so many scenarios in which a person would tell someone to be safe. I was overthinking. Poe was probably closer to the truth. Riordan cared, so he told me to be careful.

I was done worrying. I spent my time working with other clients, finishing up a few video games, and getting my notes and reviews out. It was a good thing I had multiple consoles.

On Thursday, I decided it was time to get

Riordan to talk, so I drove over to his place. I was tired and sweaty by the time I arrived. I really had to consider getting a new car. Air conditioning was a must.

At his gate, I pressed the code in and... nothing. I tried again and still nothing. He changed the code?

"Mr. Harris?" A tall and very broad man approached my car.

"Who's asking?"

"I was asked to give you these should you show up."

It was then I looked down at the giant's feet. It began to feel like there were bricks sitting on my chest as I saw my duffle bag filled with games and my consoles resting at his feet.

"Where's Riordan?" I didn't like any of this. Riordan was a lot of things, but not a coward.

"I don't know." Whatever kindness this man had originally was officially gone. "Take it or don't, that's all I was asked to do. I'd get away from the gate before the cops are called." He didn't spare me another though and stalked to his car, driving off before I could say another word.

Fuck you, Riordan. "Fine," I mumbled, got out of the car, and retrieved my belongings. At first, I kept my eyes focused on the ground, avoiding the cameras that pointed at my car. "Maybe not a coward, but a fucking asshole for sure." The whirring sound of the camera rotating made me snap. I was so beyond livid at this point.

"You watching me, you asshole?" I didn't care in that moment if neighbors or passersby saw me. "I gave you a lot of credit you didn't deserve. What you do deserve is everything you get. Push the world away and you are alone. Maybe that's what you want. Fine."

Sweat was pouring down my face, and I was glad because I didn't want him seeing the tears falling. I couldn't believe I had been so fucking stupid. I really thought Riordan was different. I'd never read someone so wrong in my whole life.

I couldn't give a shit anymore. Peeling out of

Hug It Out

the driveway, I hit the gas, desperate to get as far away from Riordan as possible. People had walked all over me my whole life. I always made excuses when they treated me like shit. Done. I was done.

The traffic was just as bad on the way back home. I was still over an hour from my place, but I needed a drink so I pulled into the first bar I saw.

The cool air that hit my burning, sweaty skin felt heavenly. I may have cheered, couldn't be sure. The place was completely empty and judging by the fact it was only two in the afternoon, this would explain that.

"What can I get you?" the bartender asked.

"Something strong. Not tequila, but strong like that."

The man gave me a placating smile. I knew what I looked like. Sweaty, nerdy, and out of my element. I didn't care. I was hurting. I could recognize my emotions. I could even admit to them. Unlike a certain Mr. Darcy Ass. Darsehole! That thought made me laugh.

"You alright there?" the bartender asked as he placed two shots and a beer in front of me.

"I'm about to be."

Shot after shot, hour after hour, by the time the sun set, I was three sheets to the wind. I knew I was sloshed, but I also knew I didn't want to be sober.

"You've had enough," the bartender said. "I've called you a cab."

I wanted to argue, but every time I tried to speak, my words got all garbled. I admitted defeat, handed him my card, and waited until he gave it back and informed me my cab was there.

There was no way I was paying for him to take me all the way home, so I asked him to take me to the nearest hotel.

My eyes scanned the landscape as it whizzed by and when I saw a sign saying north on it, I realized he was going the wrong way. "No, south. Take me to a hotel closer the place where I live area." Oh fucking hell, I couldn't speak. I didn't care as long as I could sleep.

Hug It Out

"We're here, buddy." I tried scanning my card in the little payment console, but when I couldn't, I tossed it at the driver. Everything felt blurry and I just wanted to sleep. My hope of resting my head on a soft pillow was short-lived when I saw no hotel in front of me.

"No!" I was about to get back into the cab, but it drove off. "Fuck." Squinting, I tried to search the street name, but I couldn't see shit. Even with my glasses on, things were fuzzy. Where the fuck was I?

"You look like a rabid squirrel."

The sound of the booming voice made me jump and spin around in search of the direction it had come from, but everything was dark.

"Who said that?"

"Wow, you are trashed," the voice chuckled.

I heard footsteps and when the person stepped under the streetlight, I wanted to punch his face and run away.

"Get away from me." When he was nearly an inch in front of me, I put all my strength into trying to push him away. "I hate you. You're a horrible man. Piece of…"

"Shit, yeah, I know. I watched your video. Impressive." His grin only angered me more. Was he seriously laughing at me?

"Am I amusing you?" My attempt to fold my arms over my chest was a complete failure. It was like my body was against me. It didn't help that Riordan was witnessing me at my most inebriated.

"You're amusing the hell out of me." When he reached for me, I jumped back. "Don't move, Teddy, you'll fall."

"I'm steady." Of course, that was when I slipped on a rock, nearly falling on my ass, but Riordan caught me.

"Come inside."

"No!" I wiggled and flailed my arms, desperate to get out of his grip. So much so, Riordan finally lifted me over his shoulder. "I will throw up down your pants if you don't put me down right now, Mr. Darsehole."

Riordan laughed so hard, he had to stop

walking. "Darsehole? Oh, drunk Teddy is the best."

I tried my hardest to beat Riordan's back and butt, but... his ass was really amazing and suddenly I was caressing it and humming. Riordan chuckled.

He set me on the couch gently as soon as we were inside. Neither of us spoke. The room was spinning and I wasn't sure I could form coherent words, but he was finally in front of me.

"I'm so mad at you."

"I know." Riordan practically whispered, but I heard him. "I'm so sorry and I am going to explain what I can... when you're sober."

I never wanted to leave and stay at the same time before, but that was how I felt.

"I have to get my car and go home. I can't be here, Riordan, I... can't."

I felt the dip and knew he was beside me. When I chanced a glance at him, I saw regret.

"Teddy, stay tonight. I will talk to you in the morning. I'll try to explain. If you want to walk away after that, I—" He released a sigh. "I'm sure you'll hate me more when I'm done, but right now you need to sleep."

I couldn't argue. I was exhausted. When I stood, Riordan tried to steady me but I pushed him away. I didn't want him near me. I couldn't handle all the conflicting messages. When I finally made it up to the guest room, I tripped over something. On the ground was my consoles, games, and duffle bag. How did they get here?

"Your car is in my garage. No one knows you're here but me." He spun me around slowly so I was almost touching noses with him. His green eyes were dark and full of so much emotion, I almost pulled him to me. "Tell no one you're here. Wait till we talk in the morning."

My brain was too sloshy to get lost in my thoughts and questions, so I face-planted on the mattress and within seconds, I was fast asleep.

Chapter Twenty-Eight

Riordan

After getting word that Jones was off to Switzerland, everything spiraled out of control. Mace spoke with Black and we came to the conclusion that we couldn't trust even one of his drones. Mace, Black, and I agreed to only converse with each other. I didn't like giving Lee and Emma half stories, but we had no choice.

My main concern was Teddy. With all of his stuff at my house, I knew Mace was right that he'd eventually come for it. I had to make it look like I was kicking Teddy to the curb to keep him safe. I knew enough about Teddy to know it would hurt him. Especially after the text telling him I was ready to talk.

I hated packing all his things and giving it to one of Black's drones. I explained that Teddy and I were over, he was causing me issues. Asked them if they saw his car to give him his stuff. I knew word would get out that Teddy Harris was no longer linked to anyone in the organization.

Watching as Teddy screamed at the camera wasn't easy. He was sweaty, angry, and gorgeous. When he sped away faster than any normal person should, I asked Mace to do me a solid and follow him for me.

Black called off his drones for the night, which made it easier to get Teddy back to my house. With Teddy drinking his sorrows away in the seedy shithole bar for seven hours, we were able to get his car and belongings back to my place without a problem. Mace stayed at the bar until the cab was called and paid the driver off to send Teddy to me.

I hated to do it, but I locked the house so no one could get in or out. If Teddy tried to leave, he wouldn't be able. I wasn't sure exactly how I was going to explain everything, but him hating me was something I'd live with to keep him safe.

My evening was spent sleeping on the couch,

Hug It Out

so I could be at the ready if Teddy tried to sneak out. He'd hopefully find the water and pills on the nightstand when he woke, and enough of his hangover headache would be gone before he faced me. Knowing hangovers well, I made a greasy breakfast for him. Partly for the hangover, mostly as an olive branch of peace.

"That smells both good and nauseating at the same time." Teddy ambled in, washed and changed, but looking miserable.

"Greasy food helps a hangover better than anything else, in my opinion."

I placed the full plate in front of Teddy and watched as he poked his eggs and bacon. I never wanted to know what someone was thinking more in my life than I did in that moment. I gave him silence while he ate, and chose to wait until he gave me a sign that he was ready to talk.

"I feel better." He pushed his dish to the side, and when he met my eyes, there was a lot of emotion there. Anger for sure, but what hurt was the closed off nature of his posture. "You going to explain your insane behavior yesterday or can I go and move on from this?"

I was out of time. I sat across from Teddy, hoping it was less imposing. He was so unsure of me and it felt like we were back where we had started, and in a way, we were. I could tell he was unsure about me. I hated that he was, but I had put him through hell yesterday.

"I'm going to tell you as much as I can, but there's a catch." Teddy rolled his eyes, but I ignored it. He wasn't going to blindly agree to anything, so I pushed forward. "You can't leave this house."

"You're going to hold me prisoner?" Teddy was baleful and while I expected an argument, the pure bitterness in his tone surprised me.

"No. But you're going to have to trust me when I say that if you step out those doors after the spectacle of you leaving yesterday, a lot of flags will go up and someone may try to kill you."

That got Teddy's attention. Gone was his

anger, replaced by fear. I didn't want him to be afraid, but I knew if I wanted him to stay alive, I needed him to understand.

"What's going on, Riordan, are you in...?" He dropped his voice to a whisper.

"No one can hear you or see you in here, Teddy. Say what you want."

He nodded, but there was still disbelief in his eyes. "Are you in the dark?"

I'd heard that in my line of work a lot, but hearing Teddy ask it made the hairs on the back of my neck stand.

"Why ask me that? Where'd you even hear that?"

Teddy was warring with himself, I could see it on his face. "I was concerned when you left me the note telling me to be safe. Stupid to panic, but something felt off, so I talked to some friends and one guy overheard and said you were likely in the dark."

"Who? What guy?" Had Teddy been approached?

"I just met him, he was a friend of Snow's. Bob—no, Bill. I didn't get a last name. He works for Snow's husband."

In that moment, the biggest roadblock Mace, Black, and I were facing began to crumble.

"Snow's husband? Christopher Manos?" Teddy nodded. "You're good friends with Snow?" I knew they were friends, but I wasn't sure how close until now.

"Yes, but that's not the point. Your story is."

"Right, but we are coming back to this."

For the next ten minutes, I explained to Teddy what was going on. I told him I worked for an organization that was filled with unscrupulous people. He flinched when I said assassins and looked positively ill when I told him I was one. He asked me for details, but I just couldn't tell him the things I'd done. I didn't want it to touch him any more than it already had.

I told him everything I could, and why the show I had put on yesterday was so important.

"Why not let me stay away then? Why bring me back?"

"I never wanted you to go. I knew all along, I'd have to bring you back. If there was just one drone, or if this mole wanted to make sure I was affected, they wouldn't hesitate to put a bullet through your eyes."

Teddy fidgeted with his napkin left over from breakfast, then he looked at the tabletop like visions of explanations would appear. All I could do was watch the emotions on his face. They shifted from anger, sadness, worry, and finally to nothing.

"Your family has no idea?"

"No."

He chuckled humorlessly. "You kill people for a living. Your sister unknowingly got me involved. I have to stay here, but not be here." He was stating facts, not asking. "How is your family not in danger and I am?"

"They are, but not as much as you. Family is important, but when you have someone—a partner, spouse, whatever—they're far more valuable assets.

My parents are being watched by a few people Mace knows. Aisling and Robert leave tomorrow for a surprise cruise. They are safe. But I'm out of people. Mace, Black, and I are the only ones in the know."

Teddy waved his hand dismissively and sneered. "Wait, so the people at the barbeque were all mass murderers? They did meditation with me, but could have killed me." His eyes widened and there was the realization. "There were assassins here and no one knew. Oh my god, Riordan!"

It looked like the gravity of the situation was finally hitting him.

"Teddy, please. I know this is a lot to take in. You've only known me for a couple weeks and… I blame myself, but…"

Teddy whipped his head up, then he pointed right at me and shouted louder than I thought possible, "I blame you too. You made me tell them we were a couple."

Okay, I wasn't even going to argue. "I fucked up. You threw me off my game. I'm sorry."

Teddy laughed. I couldn't tell if he was laughing because he was amused, or more manically. "You're blaming me? I threw you off? Ha."

Maniacally it was.

"Teddy, I can't trust anyone but Black, Mace, and you. So for me to keep you safe, you need to stay here and do as I say."

He narrowed his eyes and all the light that filled me with happiness when I looked at Teddy was gone.

"You said earlier you wanted to get back to Snow. Why is that?"

He realized I wanted to use his friend, and I deserved his distrust.

"I need your help, Teddy."

He scoffed. "No, you need Christopher Manos' help and you want me to ask Snow to arrange that."

No sense in beating around the bush. "Yes."

With shaky hands, he pulled out his cellphone. "When this is all over, I never want to see you again, Riordan Darcy."

I didn't get a chance to respond because the second I tried, he stormed out of the room. I could hear his voice, but couldn't make out his words. But that didn't matter. I never want to see you again, Riordan Darcy, played on a loop in my head, a stabbing pain in my heart accompanying it each time. After a few minutes, he came back in. His posture screamed stay the fuck away.

"You're gonna have to use your ninja magic. If you want an audience with Christopher Manos, you, Mace, and whoever need to get to his place tomorrow evening by seven."

"Thank you, Teddy."

"Don't thank me. Don't anything with me."

Chapter Twenty-Nine

Teddy

I holed up in the guest room all night, only leaving to grab food. I could feel Riordan's eyes on me whenever I passed by, but he didn't try to talk to me and I was grateful. I didn't care that I was acting like a teenager. I was so confused. I felt angry, sad, trapped, and then there was the fact that my heart was a traitor. I knew he was an assassin who killed people for money, and that was all sorts of wrong. My heart, however, whispered about how I didn't know why he did it. Give him a chance.

Saturday morning, I was up before the sun. I snuck downstairs and forced down some dry toast, barely tasting it. Coffee didn't even give me the morning thrill it normally did. Around nine when Riordan entered the kitchen, I didn't even return his good morning. I went right back into my room.

Delly texted me, asking why I cancelled my clients for next week, and I told her Riordan was sick. She bought it, but I felt guilty for lying.

Zach messaged me on my PS4 account, asking why I hadn't logged in for a few days. I told him I had the flu. All the lies were bothering me. It must have been agony for Riordan. Or maybe he liked lying. Liked killing people.

My restless hiding was interrupted at around two in the afternoon by a knock on the door.

"What?"

"I need you to come to the living room. Mace and Black will be here soon and I need you to know what's going to go down tonight."

Go down? He was meeting Christopher Manos. I'd done some research on the man. Surprisingly, there wasn't a whole lot to find, which was scarier than I thought. He was dubbed a Clean Criminal. Never arrested or anything. One piece said Christopher Manos had a presence about him. You felt fear no matter how hard you tried not to.

Hug It Out

I'd smiled when I came to an article on Chris and Snow's wedding. A small one, since it was a private affair, but they looked so happy and in love.

"Teddy, you hear me?"

"Fine. I'll be down in a minute."

I'd showered already, but I wanted to look presentable in front of Riordan's boss. Not because I cared what he thought of me, but because... Okay, I didn't want him to think I was the geeky, video gaming, hug-loving nerd that I was.

I opted for a plain t-shirt and jeans. I tried to calm down my curls as much as possible even though it was futile. When I was happy with how I looked, I went downstairs. Mace was there with a drink in hand. He offered me a smile I did not return.

"Oh, so it's like that?" Mace asked, seemingly amused with the situation. At least Riordan had the decency to look upset.

"Why am I here? I'm not involved. When we get there, I'll likely go sit somewhere with Snow while you all do your weird assassin shit."

Mace chuckled. "'Weird assassin shit'?"

"Teddy, you need to know as much as possible. Knowledge will keep you alive." Riordan was scaring me a little, but I refused to show it.

"I'm aware that real life isn't the movies, but I do feel it's safe to say that too much knowledge could also get me killed."

"Kid has a point," Mace mumbled into his drink.

"Kid? You're what, ten minutes older than me?" I snapped, but was proud I'd stood up for myself. Even if it was in front of a murderer.

"Wow. You need to calm the fuck down." When Mace stood and began walking toward me, Riordan intercepted.

"Mace, sit. Teddy, you're right and wrong." He gave me his undivided attention. "In this case, you knowing doesn't hurt you anymore than not knowing. Whoever is involved will already assume you know everything since you've been staying here. So you might as well know."

Hug It Out

I had no comeback for that. Somewhat appeased by his answer, I sat on the furthest cushion away from everyone. Mace and Riordan spoke quietly to one another while I waited for whatever was next. The doorbell ringing made me jump.

"Black's here." Mace went to answer the door, and try as I might, I couldn't see anything since Riordan was blocking my line of sight, but I heard him. His voice was like liquid sex. Like you could drink it and just come right there.

Then I saw him.

There was so much to take in at once. My eyes went to the long, blond braid that seemed to fall down his back. His body was very impressive with his muscles and the bajillion dollar suit. It was his silver eyes that caught my attention the most. It was like they glowed when he looked at you. He had a dangerous-but-sexy presence. But still, my eyes slid to Riordan, who was watching my every reaction.

He rolled his eyes in response to me ogling his boss. I was unapologetic, after all, I was human and I had eyes and a dick. Sue me.

"This must be your Teddy bear," Black said as he sat beside me.

"Just Teddy. Maybe Theodore to you, because I don't like you very much." Where the fuck did that come from?

Black let out a boisterous laugh. "Oh, he's spunky. I see why you like him."

That got my attention and for the first time, I saw Riordan embarrassed. He liked me.

"How about we go over tonight. We are entering Christopher Manos' house. He invites, he never accepts." Mace pointed to me. "Teddy has an in, Christopher's husband, Snow. If there's weakness in his armor, it's his husband. So, having Teddy there will make this go smoother and maybe we'll get out alive."

"Why wouldn't we get out alive?" I asked in shock.

"If Christopher Manos thinks we are a threat to his family or anyone he cares about, we won't walk out of there alive." Riordan sat on the other side of me

Hug It Out

and if we weren't in a life or death situation, I'd be loving the sex sandwich I was currently a part of. "This is why we need his help. Mace and I have training and we'd put up a hell of a fight, but Christopher will be prepared for that."

"This isn't filling me with confidence. Snow is my friend, he wouldn't let his husband kill me." This was ridiculous.

"How much you know about Snow's past?" Black asked me.

"Just what he's told me."

The three of them exchanged looks, clearly something I wasn't privy too.

"Listen," Riordan said. "Christopher is almost as good as Black's entire organization, but I can tell you this much. Last year, the head of the Sokolov family, his son, and his brother went missing. Poof, out of nowhere. Never seen them again."

"Okay, what's that got to do with Snow?"

Black hummed and if I didn't know better, I'd say he growled like a threatened animal. He tilted his head in my direction. "I don't like when huge names disappear, so I did some digging. Ray, or Roman as he is known by his family, had a thing for Snow. Heard he tried to kill Snow."

"Oh my god!"

"In a matter of hours, Christopher Manos made the entire Sokolov Empire crumble and absorbed all its profits. There's no trail or trace or anything. You don't mess with Christopher's family and live to tell the tale." Mace sounded matter-of-fact about it, while inside, I was shaking.

"Maybe I shouldn't go."

Black chuckled. "No, you go. You're the wild card. If we stand any chance of walking out of there alive, it's you who will get us there."

I didn't like any of this, not even a little bit, but I listened as they told me what their plan was. I knew I was to stick by Snow if at all possible. At about six-thirty, Black made a call for his "drones," as Riordan called them, to investigate suspicious activity at some location, giving us the time we needed to get out. We

Hug It Out

all went to Riordan's garage and got into a sleek sedan that fit us comfortably.

"Okay, let's get this done." The sound of the car starting felt like the last march of a dead man.

Chapter Thirty

Riordan

Christopher Manos' house was designed in such a way that you knew he wanted you to feel the power of the man the second the gates opened. I could tell Teddy was feeling the house's intentions. I'd seen far scarier and had faced the worst of the worst. This was just another house owned by just another monster.

My attention was drawn to the front door as it opened. My eyes darted to Teddy quickly, making sure he wasn't near whoever was coming for us. When I was convinced, I stood at the ready as three men walked toward us. None of them were Snow or Christopher, but that didn't surprise me.

"Good evening," Black said, taking the lead.

"Evening," one guy said. "I'm Frank. Understand this isn't a social visit, therefore, we are going to have to pat you down. No weapons inside. If you got any on you, you'll get 'em back when you leave."

"Fair enough," Black answered as he lifted his arms. I knew he wasn't happy about it, but we didn't need weapons to kill, they were just nice to have. Mace and I followed Black's lead and lifted our arms as well. Teddy leaned against the car, arms folded.

"Teddy, you need to be patted down," I told him.

"Why? I've never even held a gun. I'm here because I'm how you got here. Is Snow home?" he asked Frank, who didn't look amused.

"Arms up."

"This is ridiculous, like I'm in some dramatic movie." He raised his arms and tried not to laugh as Frank glided his hands along the inside of his legs.

"All clear," another guy said after checking us out.

"Donny, take them to the study."

I did a reflexive sweep of the foyer as we entered. There weren't any noticeable threats, so I took a moment to appreciate the house. It was extravagant with its sweeping staircase, wine colored carpeting, and carved wooden hand rail. A few large statues stood at either side of it and many pieces of art adorned the walls. But there were little touches that convinced me it was a home. A skateboard leaning against the stairs, a coat on the floor, and echoing laughter from deeper inside.

"This way," Donny gestured.

The study wasn't very extravagant at all. Aside from being large, there was a huge oak desk on one side, a well-stocked bar on the other, two very comfortable looking couches, and a wingback chair. The table that was between the couches and chair was plain wood. I supposed if you made it this far into his home, he didn't want to scare you too much more.

"Have a seat. Maggie will bring you beverages and Mr. Manos will be in shortly." Frank left, but the other two guys stayed, both standing guard by the exits. Teddy was talking with one of them and I wanted to ask who he was.

"Hello, gentlemen. I have coffee and tea. If you wish for something stronger, I'm sure Mr. Manos will offer it to you," a small woman, Maggie I assumed, said.

"Thank you." Mace smiled, ever the charmer, and stood to help her. The action made the man who was talking to Teddy react and he was at Mace's side in a flash, gripping his arm.

"Have a seat," the guy said.

Mace rounded on him, ripping from his grasp. "I was helping the lady." He stepped an inch toward the guy. I noticed Black watched with an amused grin on his face. He wasn't one to interfere with his men's quarrels unless it got out of hand. Mace was shorter than Manos' man, but I knew what he was capable of. "Don't lay a hand on me again unless you want to lose it."

"Who the fuck do you think you're talking to?" the guy said.

"Bill, that's enough." The booming voice snapped all of us to attention. The no nonsense voice had to belong to none other than Christopher Manos. Bill took a step back, but Mace had his undivided attention.

"If you're going to threaten anyone in this house, you can be escorted to an undisclosed location. Mace, is it?" Christopher quirked an eyebrow. He seemed somewhat amused, but I had no doubt he was serious.

"Your guy threatened my guy first, he was defending himself. We may have come here for assistance, but that doesn't mean I'll tolerate my guys being harmed." Black was standing on the other side of Mace, his words precise and directed at Christopher.

"Yes, I'm Mace. This is Riordan, and the blond over there is our boss, Black." Mace spoke fast, likely trying to defuse the tense situation.

It looked very much like Christopher was going to say something to Black and Black was ready for it, But Teddy's indignant voice interrupted.

"And I'm Teddy, by the way. In case it was worth mentioning." Teddy narrowed his eyes at Mace and probably wanted to shoot him the bird. Christopher must have welcomed the distraction because he laughed and made his way toward him.

"Ah yes, Teddy. Snow talks about you a lot. Great to meet you." He shook Teddy's hand, something he didn't do to the rest of us. "Snow will be in shortly. He's just helping my nephew with something. Make yourself at home."

Christopher's expression turned icy when he faced the three of us. He stood straighter, and from the devilish glare he was giving Black, he wasn't impressed with the man.

"You three. You seem to have a serious situation on your hands, so I'm told." He was at his bar, pouring four tumblers of Jack and coke as he spoke. "Teddy, did you want a drink?"

"No, sir, thank you. I'll stick to tea."

"You may call me Christopher, Teddy. You're a friend of my husband's."

That one sentence put the entire situation into perspective. Teddy was not included in any decision

Christopher made about the three of us. Teddy would be welcomed back here as long as Snow wanted him to be. I released a breath and felt some of the tension lift from my shoulders. I'd been worried Teddy would pay the price if Christopher thought us a threat.

"My husband never asks me for anything. It's like pulling teeth getting him to tell me he needs a new toothbrush, for Christ's sake. So when he came to me yesterday asking me to meet with you gentleman, it took me by surprise." He took a moment and handed each of us a drink before settling in his chair. "I don't surprise easily." He cocked his head in the direction of where Bill was standing. "Bill told me what Teddy said to Snow about you." We weren't sure who Christopher was talking about until his attention went to Teddy.

"You discussed Riordan with strangers?" Black's words were venomous.

Teddy held his hands up defensively. "Calm down. I didn't know anything. I was worried about him. Snow and Poe are my friends. Bill was with them, and he was the one that put two and two together."

Hug It Out

"Do you have any idea who could have overheard you?" Black was angry and I understood but this wasn't the place.

"Back off, Black." I didn't often snap at Black, but I was oddly protective of Teddy. Black's silver eyes were on me in a second and I was sure he was about to give me a tongue lashing, but Christopher cleared his throat, breaking the impending blow up.

"While I agree talking to a stranger about this situation isn't wise, I also believe had Teddy been told that the den he had walked into was full of lions, this would have gone differently." Christopher placed his drink on a coaster and began typing something on his computer. A slight scowl flickered across his face.

"Sorry I'm late." Snow breezed in, going straight to Christopher and giving him an intense kiss, which wiped the scowl from the crime boss's face. When he saw Teddy, he smiled brightly and fluidly went to sit beside him.

"Snow, meet Black, Mace, and Riordan," Christopher said with a smile. There was no denying he adored his husband.

"I know who Riordan is, we met." When he winked, it wasn't at all seductive, it was like he knew something I didn't. "I didn't know the others, but now I do."

"Good." Christopher glanced at his computer one last time before picking up his tablet and joining us. He sat close to Snow and while he absently caressed his husband's knee, he gave us all a grave look. "You have a very serious problem, Black. And my helping you puts me in a difficult spot."

"How?" Black asked.

"I won't pretend that I haven't used your organization a time or two. I'm aware of the heavy hitters who also use you to rid themselves of their issues. I'm on good terms with many of them. If I get involved in this mess and it gets out that I helped, I'll be looked at differently. Some would see me as disloyal, untrustworthy." He had a slight frown, and the press of his lips conveyed he wasn't having any of it. "I can't have that."

"Nobody would know you were involved," Mace answered.

Christopher shot him a look. "You have a mole in your organization that is leaking so much of your information, if you were a boat, you'd be on the seafloor. Don't sit there and make me promises you have no way to keep."

"What information?" I asked. We knew there was information being leaked, but Black was having trouble getting into some of his systems lately, likely because of the mole. I could tell easily Christopher had obtained quite a bit.

Christopher gestured to Snow. "My husband did most of the information gathering on this shitstorm, so I'll have him tell you."

Snow smiled lovingly at his husband. "Sure thing." He got up and stood in front of all of us. I didn't see a tablet or pad or anything that would be filled with notes about what he had found, so I was optimistic it wasn't too bad.

"We didn't have a whole lot of time to dig,

seeing as I spoke with Teddy last night. But we were able to gather some things that were alarming." He narrowed his eyes as he gave Black his attention. "You have at least five agents working for you that are playing both sides." From his back pocket, he pulled out a small piece of paper and handed it to Black, who readily took it.

"You have a hit that didn't die but fled to Switzerland, and another of your guys hopped a plane to go to meet him." He rolled his eyes as if he couldn't believe the craziness, and I was inclined to agree.

"We weren't able to figure out who or why, but the FBI seems to have a nice sized file on you and your organization, and I'm guessing it wasn't one of you who gave them those deets?" He eyed us suspiciously, and I saw a serious fire in those eyes. "Don't even get me started on the fact you have a mole in your organization who is selling off not just your assassins' information, but some of your clients as well."

"How do you know that?" Black was grinding his teeth, barely holding it together.

Hug It Out

"Because for shits and giggles, I contacted one of those guys on the list I just gave you, asking for information on an assassin who did me wrong, to deal with him myself for a price, and would you believe he gave it to me?" Snow mocked surprise, but this wasn't a joking matter, it was very serious.

"Based on what we could gather and feel out, I think it's your mole who's the one in charge here, not Vincent Abano. And that mole doesn't want to take over your organization, they want to destroy it and build their own." His eyes met Christopher's and there was a fierce protectiveness there. "Not something my guy should be touching with a ten-foot pole, by the way."

"Aren't you full of knowledge?" Mace joked.

Bill let out a growl and his face was beet red as he stared Mace down.

"My husband is astoundingly smart. And as usual, I agree with him. I can't get involved in this." Christopher placed his tablet on the table in a final gesture that this discussion was over. I knew Black wanted to argue, but since Snow had handed him that paper and unloaded all that information, his face had turned ashen. No doubt, his mind was spinning with thoughts of what he was going to do.

"Then why are we even here?" Teddy asked. "I get you don't want to help because it will hurt your oh-so-clean standing. But you could have told us on the phone. Do you have any idea how difficult it was to leave Riordan's house? It was hard." Teddy huffed. The look of defeat on his face bothered me. He flinched and pulled away when I tried to take his hand.

"Christopher," Teddy said. "I have a grandmother, friends, and a job. I want to go back to all of them. I had a pretty okay life. I thought I was going to have a boyfriend, but that is a lost cause."

His words felt like a stab to my heart and I wanted to argue with Teddy, say I was sorry and beg him to forgive me. I wanted to hold him and relish in the heat of his skin as we made love. I wanted to kiss his pouting lips and wash away the frown.

"I'm sympathetic, Teddy, but you have to

understand. You have family and friends. So do I. If I involve my name, take out the issue of my reputation, I will have every assassin that this mole has been able to infiltrate at my door. I can't risk this house," Christopher explained.

Teddy nodded. "I do understand that. I unknowingly put my grandmother and friends in jeopardy. I just want to be able to go back to what I love and forget I ever took this job. I don't want to ruin my whole life. I had no control over where I am right now, and I don't want to spend my whole life running from monsters."

The room was silent, aside from our breathing. Snow took Christopher's hand in his and they smiled at each other, something passing between them in silent conversation.

"I can't involve myself. I won't. But…" That "but" had all of us looking at Christopher hopefully. The huge smile on Snow's face told me we were getting Manos' backing. "I will give you men. These men will have access to me. My name is never to be mentioned, not once."

Black was just as speechless as the rest of us, and the horrified look he had a few minutes ago began to diminish.

I was about to thank him when Christopher walked over to Bill. "You take point on this. You know how to access my files, and you abort if it becomes impossible or your life or my men's lives are in danger." Black stood as Christopher approached him, composed and stoic. "Never contact me again. If you need me, you talk to Bill. Our business relationship ends here. Bill speaks for me, so I suggest you treat him how you'd treat me."

"Absolutely." Two powerful monsters both with abilities to destroy lives with a click of the mouse working together. God help whoever this mole was.

Christopher patted Teddy on the shoulder good naturedly. "It was good to meet you. Perhaps when this shitstorm is over, you'll come by for dinner." Christopher's eyes darted to me and his lips curled at the ends. "Feel free to bring a boyfriend with you."

Hug It Out

Teddy chuckled. "Thank you for everything."

After Christopher and Snow left the room, Bill glared at each of us. He wouldn't tell Christopher he didn't want this job, but it was written all over his face. "You'll need to lead a somewhat normal life. If you change all your patterns, then whomever the mole is will know something is wrong and change their plans. We need them to be all business as usual.

"You kicked Teddy out? Then you have a choice. Either make up with him publicly or say goodbye to him now. He's either with you or he's not. Either way, he will be safe." Bill's expression was practically screaming at me not to be an asshole.

Shit. I wanted people to think we broke up so I could hide him at my place, where I could keep an eye on him. It was all for nothing.

"Can I vote?" Teddy asked.

"No," Bill and I said at the same time.

"I know Teddy hates me right now and it's not that I think you'll do a shit job of it, Bill, but if he's with me, he's safer than if he's not."

The side of Bill's mouth curved up. "I agree." Teddy stood there, mouth gaping as he witnessed Bill and my conversation basically deciding his life. "You two will have to have a public make-up. Maybe at a place you frequented?"

"Quirks and Perks," Mace answered. "We can arrange a meeting. Riordan, Emma, Lee, and me. Teddy can show up and he and Riordan can do their thing in the corner. Word would get out to the organization that the two are back on and it will set it all to rights." Mace was pleased with himself.

"That'll work, I suppose," Bill answered with a sneer.

Black took that moment to speak. "I'll have you both stay at a hotel tonight. By now, my men are sitting in front of your property and think you're inside. Around nine tomorrow, you and Teddy can get back into your house. I'll call around eleven, after Mace has arranged a meet with Emma and Lee." Black stood and adjusted his suit jacket. "Tell them it's an information collection meeting. It won't seem odd that

Hug It Out

way." He pointed at Teddy. "When Riordan leaves, my guys will follow and you'll be able to get out of there. Your car is in his garage, so make sure you're at the coffee shop no later than twelve-thirty."

Teddy didn't have a chance to get a word in. Black left the room, everyone following closely behind. I tried to apologize silently to Teddy, but he looked away fast and stormed out of the room.

Chapter Thirty-One

Teddy

I was not thrilled about having to stay in a hotel with Riordan. Why couldn't we go to Black's or Mace's house? I was in a bad place in my head. The hotel Black chose was The Camille, and I should have been thrilled to be spending a night at the most extravagant and expensive hotel in all of Haven Hart. But I couldn't muster excitement.

While Mace and Riordan got the keys to the room, I took in the lobby of the hotel. Marble floors went on as far as the eyes could see. Golden accents and vases of great opulence filled with exotic flowers made the whole space smell heavenly.

I knew the Hart family practically owned this town, but I didn't know much about them. Camille Hart was the grandmother of the heir to the Hart dynasty, from what I'd heard. The heir wasn't often seen in the public eye. Some say because no one knows what he looks like, he sometimes mingles with the crowds without anyone knowing. Poe said he did some paintings for the family and had seen him once. Said he was enchanting.

"Okay, here's your key. Check out is at eleven, but you'll be leaving earlier." Mace handed me my key with a wink and a nudge like we were best friends. "Be civil."

Riordan and I didn't talk on the ride up in the elevator. I stood on the opposite side of the box and kept my eyes downcast to not see his reflection in the mirrors. When the doors opened, I followed the signs that lead me to my room, my body aware of Riordan's proximity the entire time.

When I slid the key into the door, I was expecting Riordan to walk past me to the next room but he just stood beside me, waiting.

"What are you doing?" I asked.

He seemed confused for a moment, then his features softened. "We are sharing the room, Teddy."

"Sharing? Black couldn't afford two rooms?"

Riordan shrugged and went to push the door open, but I held the nob. "I'm sure he could, but it's easier to protect you if I'm actually in the same fucking room."

"An adjoining room wouldn't have worked?" I knew if Riordan wanted in, he could barrel past me, but that didn't stop me from attempting to block his path.

"You don't know how this organization works. You don't know how we think and what we find normal versus suspicious. You want to be all pissy at me, that's fine, I deserve it, but if you're going to challenge every choice made, then we're going to have a serious problem." Riordan's face was an inch from mine; red, angry, and his words were seething. The muscles in his arms were rippling like he was seconds away from losing it.

"Teddy, I hate you're in this and I'm sorry. But please, you have to do as I say. After this is over, I promise I'll respect your wishes and stay far away

Hug It Out

from you. You'll be safe and I'll do whatever I can to give you back your life." His body began to uncoil and the sincerity in Riordan's eyes was breaking my heart. I wanted to wrap my arms around him and tell him it was okay, we'd figure it out. But I didn't. I opened the door and went into the room.

I made a bee-line for the bathroom and when the door shut, I closed my eyes to calm myself. I didn't have a change of clothes, and I realized I'd be sleeping in my boxers. After washing my hands, face, and body, I wrapped myself in one of the plush hotel robes and went back out. Riordan was stripped down to his boxers. His huge tattoo was on full display, and I practically tripped on air when I saw him.

"Riordan?" I whispered, hoping I didn't startle him. He looked over his shoulder, a placid look on his face. "What's it mean?" I pointed to his back. "I know tattoos are personal and many people don't like talking about them, but it feels poignant. Am I right?"

"I got it five years into doing what I do." He went to sit on the couch and gestured to the seat beside him.

"Why?" Intrigued, I opted for the seat across from him instead.

"It was around that time when what I did started to weigh on me." His eyes were looking everywhere but at me as he spoke. "I never wanted to be this, you know?"

I didn't know. "What did you want to be?"

"Don't know, really. Just not this. But Death needed a hand, so this became my fate." His voice was filled with sadness and regret. I suddenly wanted to know it all.

"Tell me your story, Riordan. All of it." I thought he'd tell me to fuck off, but he didn't. He took a deep breath and started at the beginning.

He told me how a bar fight got him here. How he killed a man who was clearly a piece of shit. Black cornered him and he was forced in. When he told me he had stipulations on his hits, it surprised me. A hitman with a conscience?

"What constitutes a Riordan-worthy hit?"

Hug It Out

"They have to deserve death. Their loss has to be the better choice than their living."

"So, like rapists, murders?"

"Yeah, I was able to sleep at night when they were off the streets." He rubbed his eyes and the exhaustion he was carrying was palpable. "What I do isn't like the movies. Sometimes it's not just a straight kill. We get people who are hurting and want vengeance. I can't say no to every one even though I want to. So when a mother says she wants her son's killer to die slowly and the hit falls under my moral code, I give that mom her pound of flesh."

Made sense to me in a dark way. "If you were okay with their deaths, how was it weighing you down? Was it the slowness, the torture you had to do?"

"Killing is the most intimate thing next to sex." My cheeks heated when his gravelly voice spoke almost passionately about both. "Watching light leave anyone's eyes isn't easy. No matter how bad they are, I decided to play God on Death's coattails. What gave me that right?" He wasn't really asking.

"So you got the tattoo?"

"Yeah. I can only see it when I look in the mirror. I don't like looking in the mirror and seeing what I am. So he's there, I can feel his weight, and when I do see him, I remember no matter how hard I try to forget what I am, it's always there."

I could see the exhaustion in Riordan's posture, but I had more questions. Things I needed to know before I could trust him in this situation.

"Why the headless horseman?"

"Dullahan," he corrected. "When I began killing, Black said we needed a call sign, so to speak. We needed to make the kills our own. In some instances, clients demanded it. I remembered growing up, all the stories my grandmother told me about her little town in Ireland. And the Dullahan was one."

I was still confused, but I sat patiently as Riordan weaved a beautiful and terrifying tale. One that had been inked into his skin and had become a malignant tumor eating away at his very soul.

"He is synonymous with the headless

horseman, but not exactly the same. He carries his head around and where he rides, death follows. It's said he holds his head up high and it screeches the name of his next victim and they will always die." I knew the fond smile had to do with the memory of his grandmother telling him the story and the fantasy of it all. "I was so young and I loved the idea of being feared. So, I chose the Dullahan. When it all became too much, I inked him into my skin."

"You scream your victims' names out before killing them? That's not very stealthy."

Riordan chuckled, and the smile was nice to see. "No. I take their heads and give them to the clients so they know the job is done. When my services were required, Dullahan was what the card would read."

"You took their heads?" It was completely rhetorical. "And what if your services were required but you didn't want to do it?"

"You're so smart, Teddy." He said it with reverence, but it was short-lived. He took a breath and relaxed deeper into the couch. "Black knew my catch, so if one came across that was against my code, he'd inform them I was unavailable. Someone else would take it."

"And this guy. The one who's causing all these problems?"

"Vincent Abano?"

"Yeah, him. You obviously agreed to kill him. What kind of person was he?"

He rubbed over his shaved head and released a breath, his expression thoughtful. "He was the worst of the worst, in my opinion. He had it all but wanted more. Wanted what he couldn't have. The hit for him came anonymously. We know now it was a setup, but looking into this man's background, I'd have done it for free."

"Who… what was he?" I was afraid to know, but at the same time, I needed to.

"He was a frequent flyer on the dark net. He paid a lot of money to watch men, women, children, and animals being tortured and killed. A little girl was recently a victim, and she turned out to be the granddaughter of a Japanese mob boss. I suspected at first, this was who put the hit out on Vincent. New information has shown us that isn't the case. Looks like Vincent put the hit out on himself and is trying to take over Black's organization. But I'm sure that mob boss would love to see Vincent's head on a spike, and that can be arranged. Right now, we need to find him and stop him from destroying Black's business."

"Why, how can he do all this?"

"That is what we are trying to figure out. He orchestrated this whole thing and it cost the lives of his wife and son. He seems fine with that, seeing as he gets a shitload of money because of their deaths."

"He's a horrible man." I could feel bile rising in my throat. "So he's alive?"

Riordan shifted forward and a part of me wanted to push him back, but when he took my hand in his, I felt anchored.

"He won't be forever. It won't matter what a plastic surgeon does to him, I'll find him, get the answers, and end him."

I believed him. "It was the death of his wife and the kid that made you depressed? That's why I was hired?"

His green eyes twinkled with compassion. "Yeah, Teddy."

"Okay. I need to process this, so I'm going to go to bed now." I slipped my hand out of his and immediately missed his warmth.

Riordan didn't argue over me taking the bed.

That night, I had horrific dreams. Nightmares. But right before I woke up, Riordan was there, shielding me from the violent things. I heard him whisper, "Don't let go, Teddy. I got you."

I woke up tired but prepared to do what I had to do to stay safe and help Riordan figure out who was trying to destroy so many lives.

Chapter Thirty-Two

Riordan

The morning went off without a hitch. Teddy and I were able to get back to the house undetected, just as Black had promised. We didn't have much time to talk about last night and all that I'd exposed, but I was happy Teddy was at least looking at me again. I finally left to go to Quirks and Perks, and I felt real good about things when the drones followed me.

I worried about leaving Teddy alone, but my house was a fortress. No one would be able to get to him. The previous night kept playing on a loop in my head. When I told him the whole truth, I felt some of that weight lift. He didn't judge me verbally. I saw some silent words in his eyes, but he had listened.

After this was over and Teddy was no longer chained to me, I wondered if he would stay. Would Black let me out of the organization? If not, would

Mace help as he'd promised? I wanted a normal life; one that made me happy. I wanted to see where Teddy and I could go. I wanted so much, and I couldn't remember the last time I had.

Quirks and Perks came into view and I parked in the first available spot. As I ran across the street, I noticed no one was outside that I knew, so I thought I was the first to arrive. The bells on the door chimed when I entered, and I was about to go to the counter to get a drink when I heard my name.

"Riordan," Mace called out. He was in a corner booth all the way in the back. Emma and Lee were with him and I had no idea why Mace would seat them so far away from the main floor. How were Teddy and I supposed to put on a show for them? And then it hit me. And by the smirk on Mace's face, he'd planned this. He was going to have it right in the middle of the coffee shop. That dick.

"Why are you all over here?" I asked, giving Mace a narrowed look.

"Mace said since the situation was dangerous,

Hug It Out

we shouldn't be outside where flying bullets could get us." Emma was nonchalant and kept on reapplying her lipstick as she spoke. "I guess he has a point." She patted the seat next to her. "Take a load off."

"We ordered a pot," Lee said. There were dark rings under his eyes, his normally styled hair was rumpled, and his clothes were severely wrinkled. Whatever was going on with Jones was really getting to him.

"So, where we at?" Emma asked, breaking the silence.

Mace gave a false story that Emma and Lee bought easily.

"Black trusts these drones who are heading to Switzerland? You think Jones won't decimate them on sight?" Emma scoffed at Mace's story. "I give it twenty-four hours before they are all hanging from Chapel Bridge."

"Black's guys blend in better than we do. If Jones saw us, it would go down a lot worse." I tried to be convincing, but Lee was watching me like a hawk.

"Has Jones gotten a hold of you, Lee?" He just looked at the tabletop, the shake of his head was so slight. "I know he's your friend, but he's—"

"Not his friend," Emma interrupted. "If he's in on this, then he's all in. He broke whatever trust there was. I see him and I'm taking him down."

Lee's eyes widened briefly before he sneered at her. "When did you become so heartless?"

Emma's laugh was like ice. "I lost my heart a long time ago, little boy. Don't act like if it was your life or his, you'd sacrifice yourself. We are assassins. There's no cuddle hour for us."

Mace choked on his coffee at the mention of cuddle hour, and I almost regretted ever telling him about Teddy.

He was mid cleanup of his spilled coffee when something over my shoulder got his attention. Game time.

"That reminds me, didn't you and Teddy part ways?" Mace smiled and sat back, enjoying this far too much.

Hug It Out

"Oh yeah, I heard about that. Had one of Black's men toss him out or something?" Emma turned toward me, a look of disgust on her face. "Couldn't do it yourself? You kill with your bare hands but you can't tell a two-week trick to hit the road?"

"Mind your business, Emma," I snarled. She was always a bitch, but she was almost unbearable lately. Staying with the plan, I gave Mace my attention. "Yeah, we're through, why?"

Mace pointed to something behind me, and with raised eyebrows, he said, "That's why."

"Well, well, well, would you look at that?" Emma shifted in her seat, her smile sinister. "I wish I had popcorn."

Teddy turned and if I wasn't trying to make this believable, I'd have laughed at his mock surprise at seeing me here. He slammed his to-go cup on the counter with dramatic flourish. When it spilled, the barista became flustered and hurried to sop it up. I was having a hard time keeping it together.

"He looks constipated," Emma remarked.

She wasn't wrong. I had to do something before Teddy turned this into a Spanish soap opera. Turning my back on him in a sign of dismissal earned a reaction from Teddy. He let out this high pitched—shriek? Grunt? I didn't know, but I was regretting my choices at that moment. Maybe he wasn't ready for this.

"Riordan Darcy," he shouted across the café, silencing all patrons and drawing them into our spectacle. "Hanging out with your friends, I see. The reason you only ever gave me half of your attention."

We had planned something different, but it looked like he was going off-book. Awesome.

"Hi, Teddy. I'm just having coffee." Looking over my shoulder, hoping to signal that improvising it was dumb, proved to be a horrible idea as he was currently sporting a comical angry face. It was a mistake because he was making it really hard not to laugh.

"Yeah, just sitting there drinking your coffee?"

"Oh, he's terrible at baiting people." Emma

slapped my arm playfully. "He's trying to get a rise out of you. He still likes you. Put him out of his misery."

Taking her advice would only help this horrific display of awful. "Fine," I grumbled.

The scrape of the chair was obnoxious, and intentional. For our audience, I made off like I was aloof. I knew he was out of his league, but faking was something I did well.

"I'm drinking coffee at a coffee shop with my friends. You were always very observant." He swallowed visibly as I stepped closer. "You're the one who wanted nothing to do with me."

He fumbled with his words for a moment, but got a grip. "I said I thought it wasn't working. You didn't have to toss my shit out on the driveway."

A collective gasp was heard throughout the café. Everyone, and I do mean everyone, had their attention on Teddy and me.

"I didn't toss it. I asked a friend to give it to you because you were acting insane."

I could tell he wanted to say something like,

"Fuck you, you lying bastard." Instead, he pushed me. Yep assault. That's improv for you.

"You're a brute."

That gave me a wonderful opening I wasn't passing up for a moment. Taking another step, I was loving the heat coming off Teddy when I was in his space. He may have only been slightly shorter than me, but I was broader, more imposing. Pressing him up against the counter, I wanted to swallow his gasp when my hardening dick grinded against his.

"You seemed to like when I got rough. You begged for it." Brushing my nose against his cheek, I didn't pass up the opportunity to lick the shell of his ear. I relished in his low groan and wanted more. "Liked it when I handled you."

"Riordan," he whispered, and I could feel how affected he was by me.

"Mmmm, Teddy, I miss having my way with you." The taste of his skin on my tongue was addicting. "You're my number one, baby."

"Fuck," Teddy groaned as he flung himself at

me and attacked my mouth. I kissed him with as much intensity as I could, hoping he didn't believe this was for our voyeurs only. It was all teeth, hands, tongue, and would have gotten worse if the barista hadn't stopped us.

"Okay, it's starting to get unsanitary. Can you both move it to a bedroom?" She quirked her brow and laughed, it was then we noticed everyone in the café was pretending they weren't witnessing us dry humping each other on the pastry counter.

"Get out of here, champ," Emma shouted as she fanned herself.

I took Teddy's hand and was thrilled when he didn't protest. I slowed my pace when we were a block away from the café.

"Did it work?" Teddy asked in a whispered tone.

"Oh yeah, it worked." We rounded a corner and I couldn't stop myself. I needed more of Teddy and hoped he wanted more of me. "I want you. Please tell me you want me." I begged, pressing him against the side of a building.

There was so much conflict dancing in his beautiful eyes. He was waging a war. I only hoped his want and need would win out.

"I shouldn't want you, Riordan. I should be angry and disgusted by you. I should fear you and run as far away from you as I can." I was about to pull away, but he gripped my shirt. "But I can't." His head dropped against my shoulder. "I want and need you too."

I didn't realize I had stopped breathing until he admitted he wanted me too.

"Let's go."

I drove as fast as I could to get home, blowing every red light and scaring the shit out of Teddy with the speed at which I drove, but when we pulled into the driveway, I knew he was glad to be there and was as desperate for me as I was for him.

Chapter Thirty-Three

Teddy

I probably would have climbed Riordan like a tree if the barista hadn't stopped us. I was so nervous, and I knew he saw that. We'd rehearsed a little, but when I stepped foot inside the café, I forgot everything.

As Riordan pressed against me, my skin felt like it was going to ignite. I never wanted anything or anyone as much as I wanted this man in that moment. The thought of separating felt like an ache.

I began having second thoughts, but as soon as Riordan cut the engine and turned to me, it came rushing back. I didn't care what he had done. I knew he wasn't heartless. A man didn't send his sister across the world on a cruise or pay insane amounts of money to protect his parents if he was a bad person.

When he told me what Vincent Abano had

done, I wished the man dead. The pain he had caused. Riordan was ridding the world of the most sinister. He wasn't the organization. He was Riordan Darcy, a man creating balance. I had to believe that.

"Teddy," his voice vibrated in the closed space of the car. "If you've changed your mind…"

"I have." I put my hand over the top his when I saw defeat set in. "Not how you think, though. That tattoo weighs you down, reminding you of the darkness of what you do." He watched intently as my hand move to rest over his heart. "Your wings are here." I couldn't tell if his frown was confusion or disbelief. "You're not death, Riordan, you're balance."

"I don't understand."

With his face in my hands and his undivided attention, I did my best to make him understand. "I embrace babies who have survived horrors. Some whose mothers shot up every day and their little bodies are fighting to break free. I hug people who have no one in the world. They are lonely, lost, and forgotten. I can't begin to tell you how many times I wished I could come face-to-face with the ones that hurt those people and made them feel the hurt they do."

In an all too sweet moment, Riordan kissed the palm of my hand. "You do amazing things, Teddy."

"I do, but I'm not balance, Riordan. You face monsters and you make them disappear so they can't hurt the ones I embrace."

"Oh, Teddy." The rest of his words were lost when he kissed me. "Inside."

Riordan's lips were on any piece of skin he could find as he tried clumsily to unlock his front door. As we climbed the stairs, his hand roamed over the curve of my ass, squeezing it in a way that I swore I could've come from right then and there. I was so lost in every feeling, when we fell on his bed, I gasped.

"Just the bed," Riordan said as he began tearing at my clothes.

When the button of Riordan's jeans popped off and slammed against the wall, I was almost lost in a fit of giggles. But then he was stark naked before me and laughing wasn't what I wanted to be doing anymore.

He tenderly stripped me of my clothes in the most erotic and passionate way possible. When his body covered mine, it felt like everything. I couldn't think of one emotion to describe this moment. It felt like everything because it was.

"You need to fuck me, Riordan. I mean it. I need that."

He pushed up and his green eyes sparkled and his grin was wicked. "I'm going to, Teddy."

"I'm sorry," I whispered against his lips. "I said horrible things."

"Shh. No words. We said enough." His hand slid down my thigh and I shivered at the bite of his nails. Lifting my leg and hitching it over his hip had my heart racing with excitement.

"Have we?" I asked, but was having a hard time concentrating.

"Shut up, Teddy." He licked the seam of my mouth, successfully quieting my incessant questions.

We kissed until I turned to putty. Riordan lifted me slightly until my head was on the pillow. Our sweat-slicked skin made every movement a perfect slide.

He kissed and licked his way down my body, making me shiver and moan with wanton need. He took my nipple into his mouth and the hot, wet suction was almost too much to handle. "Jesus, Riordan."

He chuckled as my legs dropped and he went lower and lower. My cock had never been this hard, and when he took it in his mouth, I knew I wouldn't last. I tried. I closed my eyes, thinking of anything to stave off my release. Riordan's touch was everywhere and I was losing my battle. I tried tapping his shoulder, but he didn't let up. He swirled his tongue around the head of my dick, then took it to the root over and over again. One hand was holding my leg up while the other had a perfect grip on my balls. All the sensations were killing me.

"Please, I can't... oh for fuck's sake, Riordan."

My cock slipped out of his mouth and I thought he'd show me mercy, but he didn't. His head dipped down, both of my legs went up to my shoulders, and in one fluid movement, he brushed his tongue over my hole.

"Fuck!" I shouted. No one had ever... "Won't last."

Riordan knew just when to back off, but he always left me on the cusp of want and ecstasy. He lapped my balls as he slid a finger, then two, into me. He lit me up from the inside and I knew in this moment why it was called the little death.

I didn't know how or when Riordan had gotten condoms and lube, because I was floating. He looked like a hungry man and I was happy to be his meal. I reached for him, but he pulled away to put the condom on.

When he lay atop me, I wrapped my legs once again around his waist, holding on for dear life. When he pressed the head of his cock against my entrance, I whimpered, and when he slid inside, I heard myself say, "Finally." I could get lost in this moment with Riordan forever and it wouldn't be long enough.

He trapped my head between his forearms and

Hug It Out

his eyes bore into mine, his gaze never wavering as he thrusted into me. So much was being said without speaking, emotions painted over our skin. He was claiming me. He was telling me this was more than physical. It was us and it was intense.

I came a split second before him. It was like he was waiting for me but didn't want to miss riding the same wave. We stay connected afterward, simply breathing and kissing. Only when we had to part did Riordan go to the bathroom to get a cloth.

Riordan cleaned me off, and when he slipped back into the bed and wrapped his arms around me, I smiled contently. The man who never wanted a single hug and refused to ever cuddle had me snug against him. I was asleep in seconds.

Chapter Thirty-Four

Riordan

Teddy and I spent most of the next three days in bed. We showered, ate, and watched a movie, but we never seemed to be able to finish it. His finger would graze my hand and it was like a magnet to metal. I had never felt like this toward anyone. I couldn't touch him enough or taste him enough. If I wasn't initiating something, he was.

We didn't talk a lot and I wasn't sure if that was good or not. No one ever looked at what I did in the same way Teddy did. I had no doubt my mother and father would never see it like that, and I didn't even want to think about what Aisling would say. I never intended to inform them.

On Thursday, Teddy said he really needed to go over to his place to check his mail. He was getting some new game in that he needed to beta. He tried

Hug It Out

showing me what he did at one point, but when he started playing some hitman game and I told him how unrealistic it was, and then proceeded to explain the best way to stealthily kill a guy, he said he'd play more later. He didn't like backseat players, he said.

This was the first time I'd been to Teddy's and I was curious what kind of place he lived in. We pulled into his complex. No gate, no security. I almost lost it when we got to his door and he just walked right in.

"You didn't lock it?"

Teddy dropped his bag and turned to me with a wide-eyed look. "It's not a dangerous neighborhood, Riordan. We all watch out for each other."

No. Nope. I grabbed the doorknob and checked the deadbolt. "Everything's working, there's no reason to not lock it. It's laziness, Teddy." I knew I was chastising him, but he didn't get it. Even without crazy people trying to kill us, it was foolish to be so nonchalant about safety.

"I know it works. I've lived here for years and we've never had a break-in." He rolled his eyes in dismissal and proceeded down the small hallway.

"What happens when a neighbor falls on hard times and becomes desperate? You think he won't waltz in here, take your games and shit, and sell them to buy what he needs?" He was so naive. "You have too much faith in humanity, Teddy."

He tossed all his dirty clothes in a bin and carried it across the way to a small closet that housed a washer and dryer. He angrily threw his clothes in the washer as he shot me looks that told me how upset he was at my hounding.

"And maybe you have too little. You have forgotten that not all people are horrible, there are some that are good. You balance things, but perhaps you should realize there are a few decent people."

He put his detergent and fabric softener in and when he hit the button, I spun him around, fire and brimstone in his eyes. Was it weird I found him sexy like this?

"Teddy, no one is completely and inherently good. Anyone can flip that switch and be a monster."

His features softened, and he cupped his small hand on my cheek. "Okay, Riordan, I'll lock my door. You're right, I trust too easily."

"Thank you." I kissed his forehead and pulled him to me. "Why didn't you do your clothes at my house?"

He chuckled, his breath ghosting over my neck making me shiver. "I'm still in the mindset that you're my client, I guess."

I kissed him until he was moaning. "I think it's safe to say I'm not a client anymore. You can wash your clothes at my house."

"M'kay."

I helped him clean and gather things he needed while his laundry washed. He tossed the wet clothes in the dryer and said we could go since he'd get them out when he came back.

"I'm starving." Teddy rubbed his flat belly. "Can we stop somewhere?"

Looking out my rearview mirror, I saw Black's drones were tailing us as usual, but I had talked to

Mace the previous night. No word on Jones or Vincent. They were both obviously in Switzerland and the story that drones were headed that way either hadn't made it to them, or Jones was just so good, he had eluded them or they were already dead.

"Sure, we can go to the diner by my place."

Teddy seemed fine with that and he checked his phone as I drove. I glanced at him a time or two. He was scowling at his device like it offended him.

"Everything okay?"

"Hmm? Oh, yeah. My grandmother texted me, asking if I was stopping by this week." His eyes were hopeful, and I knew what was coming. "I need to go see her."

"Where's she live?"

Teddy looked out the window, answering me after we passed a sign. "We're too far out. Maybe tomorrow?"

That wasn't going to work for me. "I have to meet Black and Mace smack in the middle of the day. How about Saturday?"

Teddy shook his head. "I have to work on these games this weekend. I can go to my grandmother's by myself."

"No. I don't want you going alone."

Teddy huffed, slapping his phone against his leg. "Riordan, I have responsibilities. I have to go to my grandmother, and then how about I go to the hospital to see the babies and stay there until you're free to get me? You can follow me back to the house and everything."

A hospital was fairly safe for him. I didn't like him going to his grandmother's alone.

"Will you call or text me when you are at your grandmother's and when you leave? And then when you get to the hospital?"

He smiled and I couldn't remember if anyone ever smiled like that for me before. "I can do that."

We drove to the diner and ate greasy burgers and crispy fries like regular people. We each had chocolate milkshakes and it was so normal, so domestic. I loved the feeling of just being out with

Teddy and having a date. I knew there was dread looming. I knew this would end with dead bodies. But in that moment with burgers, fries, and Teddy, my life felt pretty damned good.

We ended our day with a Jaws marathon and Chinese takeout. That evening as we lay in bed, sweaty and sated, my eyes lingered on the painting Teddy had given me. I felt like I didn't deserve him but there he was, sleeping beside me blissfully. I walked a path not of my choosing for years. I was ready to step away and follow Teddy wherever he went.

My only hope was to figure out who was behind all this, end it, and finally start living my life.

Chapter Thirty-Five

Teddy

Riordan was already working in his office when I headed out to my grandmother's. He made me take his car because he said, and I quote, "If assassins don't kill you, your car will."

I had to admit the car was sweet. It drove like butter, had that new car smell, and the most important part… air conditioning.

My grandmother whistled when she opened her front door. "Snazzy vehicle. Did you finally get rid of your deathtrap?" She gave me a cheeky smile.

"You got jokes, huh, old lady." I kissed her cheek, loving the familiar smell of Shalimar, and followed her inside. The scent of apple pie filled the house. And the mix of the aromas calmed my nerves. It had been a wonderful week with Riordan, but I'd be lying if I said I wasn't worried all the time.

"I'm glad you bought a new car. I worried about you driving that thing." She took the pie out of the oven and poured two glasses of milk.

"It's not mine. It's my maybe-boyfriend Riordan's car."

She paused to give me her what-in-the-name-of-God look.

"I don't know what we are, Gram. Just leave it. He's different." I waved her away before she asked more. "How are you? Did Mr. David finally ask you out?"

She brought the milk over and I was glad to see her moving well today. "That old coot? He wrote me a poem."

My heart fluttered. Who said you couldn't find love at any age? "That's sweet, Gram. You should give the guy a break." She sat across from me and slid my pie over, rolling her eyes the entire time.

"Oh, I'll give him a break, all right. What I didn't tell ya was he wrapped that poem around a rock and threw it at my car, shattering my back window."

Hug It Out

I burst out laughing. "Wow. Good luck with that one, Gram."

She didn't hound me about the car or Riordan. One thing I loved about my grandmother was how she let me live my life. She was a hand on my back, guiding me in the right direction. Only if she saw me headed toward rough waters would she toss me a life vest. A lot like my friend Delly. Probably why they were the most important ladies in my life.

I left her place around noon. Even though the pie was delicious, I was starving. I didn't have to be at the hospital until two, so I figured I'd stop at Quirks and Perks for a sandwich croissant and coffee.

There was heavy traffic, so I parked by the hospital garage and walked the few blocks to the café. A barista greeted me and I ordered a tuna melt sandwich and an iced hazelnut coffee. I was in the pickup line when I heard a familiar voice. I peered over my shoulder and saw Emma at a table near the ordering line. She was speaking to an elderly man. It didn't look like she knew him, just making idle conversation in line.

I waved when her eyes met mine. She bade the man farewell and walked over to me.

"Hey, Teddy, good to see you. You're looking a little less lascivious then the last time I saw you."

I knew she was referring to the scene between Riordan and myself. I thought about that when I entered the café, but no one seemed to remember me so it was fine.

"Oh, yeah… That. Sorry if it made you uncomfortable." I wasn't really sorry. It led Riordan and me to discover what we meant to each other and I wouldn't apologize for that.

She patted my arm softly and her smile was genuine. Kindness was a good look on her. "No, it was lovely. I'm glad you two worked it out." She eyed the growing order line. "I'll be here forever."

I knew she was right, so I grabbed the barista's attention. "I forgot an order, is it okay if I add something super quick?"

The barista didn't seem happy about it, but said

fine.

"Thank you, Teddy." Emma ordered and the barista hurried to make it. "Do you have a few minutes? Maybe we can chat while we eat?"

I had a little bit of time and Emma was pleasant company, so I agreed.

"Great, grab us a table. I'll get our orders."

I managed to snag a window table when a couple left and didn't wait long before Emma was placing our coffees and food down.

It seemed when Emma was away from the others, she was almost sweet. Like the girl next door. We talked and she told me how much she loved animals and how she sent money to her grandfather in Florida. She laughed and I realized how much she reminded me of Delly.

"Thank you for your company, Emma. I need to run. I don't want to be late."

She looked at her watch and her eyes widened. "Oh, you're right. I have a meeting to get to. I feel bad you hardly drank your coffee and it's all watered down. It's going to taste horrible."

Shrugging, I took a huge sip. It did taste gross, but it was coffee and you didn't throw coffee away.

"It's fine. I'll chug it. I just really needed the caffeine. Have a great day, Emma."

She waved at me through the window as I rushed by to get to the hospital.

I entered the hospital five minutes later, gasping for breath. I practically sprinted the entire way and the heat didn't make it easier.

"You okay, Teddy?" Lacey, the security guard, asked.

"Yeah. It's hot out there and I ran because I promised Jules upstairs I'd be here so she could go out to eat with her boyfriend. I'm out of shape."

She chuckled and waved me over to the desk. I downed the rest of my iced coffee and chucked the cup in the pail. Signing in quickly, I only relaxed when I got into the elevator and rested my head against the cool wall. I needed to join a gym or something.

When the doors opened to my floor, I was still

Hug It Out

having trouble breathing. My mouth felt dry and a wave of dizziness came over me. Maybe I should have opted for water instead.

"Teddy, you okay?" Jules asked when I entered the sterilization room.

"Too much caffeine, not enough water or exercise." I tried joking, but as the seconds passed, I was finding it almost impossible to swallow.

"Teddy?" Jules grabbed my arm. "What is it?"

I went to speak, but my throat was closing. I wheezed, gurgled, then there was no sound at all.

"Jesus, Teddy."

I fell to the floor, trying to grip the sink but failing. My vision started to darken and I heard Jules screaming for a doctor. I couldn't breathe, my lungs felt like they were on fire. Oh God, was I dying?

It wasn't until I crashed to the floor that I felt nothing.

Chapter Thirty-Six

Riordan

Teddy didn't text me when he got to the hospital, so naturally, I called. A security guard said she saw him enter and would give him a message. I declined, just happy he had arrived. Maybe his phone died or something. I knew where he was and that he was safe. Now I had to concentrate on the information Bill was about to give Black, Mace, and myself.

"Jones was seen flying out of Switzerland last night. Unfortunately, I didn't get this information until a few hours ago, so he's likely either here or at his next location by now."

Black looked at his watch, grimacing. "Any clue where?"

"No, but here's the other interesting thing I found."

He didn't get a chance to tell us because Mace

Hug It Out

ripped the paper out of his hand and began reading, much to Bill's disgust.

"Lee was seen at the airport a few hours ago. He dropped something off at a locker and left."

"Do we think Lee is working with Jones? That the two are in on it?" I asked.

"If I had been given a chance to speak, I could have answered that." Bill narrowed his eyes at Mace, who smiled cockily at him. "One of my guys retrieved the stuff from the locker. It was a few thumb drives and one hundred thousand dollars."

"And have your band of merry men seen what's on those thumb drives?" Mace asked.

"Look, you piece of shit—" Bill advanced, but I intercepted quickly. I wanted to go to the hospital later to get Teddy, not to drop these idiots off.

"Okay, guys, come on. We don't have time for this love-fest. Just continue, Bill." I pointed at Mace with a raised brow. He put his hands up in surrender, and luckily shut up.

"We are trying to break the codes, but this Lee

guy is good. Everything is encrypted. We replaced the thumb drives with dummies and left the money. We have eyes on the locker, but no one has taken anything."

Weird. "Maybe someone saw you go in there," Black said as he began to pace.

I had never seen him so upset. His organization was crumbling, he couldn't trust anyone, and there were deals going around that could kill us all.

"Do we have any eyes on Emma?" Black asked suddenly.

"Why her?" Mace asked. "She's so uninterested in this. I gave her a task to entice some drones and she came up empty."

"She could be in danger. Obviously Jones and Lee are working with Abano. They will remove each of us, especially now that Lee knows we're on to Jones." Black slammed his hand against his desk, rattling everything on it.

"Calm down." Bill handed some papers to Black. "Two of Christopher's men have been following her. Her day has been boring. She got her hair done, had coffee, went to some meeting, and as far as I know, is still there."

Black scrolled through his phone, likely checking his calendar. "She has a meeting with a CEO. Aki Kato, he arrived a few weeks ago. He has numerous hits to be dealt with and Emma is perfect for what he requires. It's on the schedule."

"So she's safe and we will watch her." Bill sat on one of the chairs.

"So that's it?" Mace asked. "We just wait until Jones comes for each of us?"

Bill huffed and if he could blow up Mace's head with his glare, he would. "No, we watch our backs. I have no doubt that he's going to take each of you out one at a time. At least, that's his hope. You're in the way of his giant takeover. None of you are to live. We need to get to him before he gets to any of you."

"Okay, I'm going to go pick Teddy up at the hospital. Keep me informed and watch your backs."

When I arrived at the hospital, I was greeted by a security guard who directed me to the information desk. Another woman in uniform sat there answering calls and directing people where to go.

"Hi, I'm Riordan Darcy. I'm meeting Teddy Harris here. I don't know what floors he's on. Can you let him know I'm down here by any chance?"

She nodded and started looking at her computer.

"That's odd. He was supposed to punch in to the NICU but he never did. I saw him go up, though. Let me call up there, he probably forgot." She smiled and I leaned against the counter and waited.

"Hey, Donna, you see Teddy up there? He has a visitor." The smile on the woman's face went from happy to worried as she listened.

"When did this happen?" She began typing frantically. "No, I see. Okay. Did you call his next of kin?"

Next of kin, what the fuck? "What's going on?" I asked.

Hug It Out

She waved her hand at me. "Okay. I have a Riordan Darcy here."

"I'm his boyfriend." It was the first time I'd said that, and I wished it felt good, but panic was taking over.

"He says he's his boyfriend. Uh-huh. Okay. Thanks." She hung up and her eyes met mine. "Teddy had some sort of reaction, I don't know much, but he's in the Emergency Room. I'll inform them that you're coming. His grandmother was called and will be there shortly. It will be up to her if you can see him."

I couldn't speak. What kind of reaction? I knew nothing. I think I thanked her, I couldn't be sure. I was running toward the emergency room, nearly colliding with people who were in my way.

"I'm Riordan Darcy, my boyfriend Teddy Harris was brought in here. I know nothing about how or why, but I need to know if he's okay."

The nurse at the desk offered me a small smile. "All I can tell you, Mr. Darcy, is that Mr. Harris is currently with the doctors. If you have a seat in the waiting area, as soon as the doctor has something to report, you can ask him."

I couldn't argue with her and I couldn't start barging into rooms and behind curtains, so I sat. And I waited. I left Mace a message and he said he and Bill would see what they could find out.

An hour into my excruciating wait, an older woman walked in and asked about Teddy.

"I'm Anne Harris, I was called about my grandson, Theodore Harris." She clutched a handkerchief in one hand and it looked like she was holding the counter for support with the other.

"Mrs. Harris. He is still with the doctors. I will let him know you're here and get some information for you. His boyfriend is right over there." The nurse pointed, and Anne turned toward me. She thanked the nurse and came to sit beside me.

She didn't say anything for a moment, just sat and took her time. "I asked him this morning about his fancy new car. He didn't want to talk about it or you, but I knew."

Hug It Out

I didn't know what to say. She looked a lot like Teddy, and even though there was fear in her eyes and tears danced along the edges, she still smiled.

"I don't know anything," I whispered. "No one is telling me anything. All I know is he had a reaction."

Her brows furrowed in confusion. "Reaction? Teddy isn't allergic to anything other than—"

"Penicillin," I interrupted. Sweet Jesus.

"Exactly. I doubt Teddy has been taking shots or popping pills full of it, so maybe he's reacting to something else. Allergies happen overnight." Of course, she wouldn't see why knowing Teddy's allergy was so dangerous when we were in the middle of an assassin organization being infiltrated.

"Does he have anything on him telling the doctors he's allergic to penicillin?"

Shrugging, she said, "He has a card. No bracelet or anything, because it's not really something you worry about all that much. It's on file though, I'm sure."

I walked over to the nurse to let her know, but

she said they were aware and were treating him for anaphylactic shock. I didn't know if she meant to let me know, but I took it back to his grandmother.

"How odd," she said. "Are they sure it was penicillin?"

"I don't know."

We waited what felt like forever before a doctor walked in. "Mrs. Harris?"

I helped her stand and she gripped my arm with a force I didn't think she was capable of.

"I'm she."

"I'm Dr. Alberts. Your grandson is resting. We had a scare. It was a good thing he was at the hospital when he went into anaphylactic shock."

"I don't understand," she began. "Teddy isn't allergic to anything other than penicillin."

"I'm awaiting blood tests, but from what I can tell by the severity of the attack, this was something he has a serious reaction to. We want to rule out attempted suicide because he was here and Jules, the other volunteer, said he was unaware of what was happening to him. Mrs. Harris, Penicillin is rarely a sole allergy. It's possible Teddy has an allergy he's unaware of and that's what pushed this so fiercely, there's no way to know at this time."

"How does someone get penicillin into their body without knowing it?" Anne asked.

"There are many ways. Most likely in Teddy's case, it was oral and in liquid form. Perhaps he took the wrong thing. I just can't know that until we have spoken to him. He's asleep. I'd like to keep him here for seventy-two hours, even though I'm aware that's excessive for a biphasic reaction, but if he does have another allergy, I really need more time."

"Can we see him?" Anne asked, and I was glad she said we. I was standing there just listening, feeling hopeless and angry.

I knew this had nothing to do with Teddy and everything to do with me.

"You can see him, but only for a short time."

When we walked in, Anne gasped and as fast as she could, she was at Teddy's bedside. He was pale, his hair was damp with sweat, and his skin was covered in red dots. The oxygen mask covering his nose and mouth was almost too much and I could feel my skin crawl. My beast wanted out and I was going to let in rip apart whoever had done this.

Whoever had done this couldn't know Teddy would be at the hospital, they were expecting him to die. They were taking us out, and they started with Teddy because he was the easiest target.

Well, that was their mistake, because I'd show whoever had done this exactly why I was called Dullahan.

CHAPTER THIRTY-SEVEN

Teddy

I woke disoriented, confused, and achy. It only took a minute to remember what was going on. I was talking to Jules, then I couldn't breathe and everything went dark.

"Teddy?" I heard my grandmother's voice. The oxygen mask was hindering my speech and my body felt like it was being weighed down with bricks.

"You can't talk, dear. You have an oxygen mask on. Just lie still. I'll get the doctor."

Someone squeezed my left hand. I tried to look but it wasn't working, so I squeezed back.

"Mr. Harris, I'm so glad to see you're awake. I'm Dr. Alberts. You gave us a scare." I could see the doctor. I recognized him. He was in his late forties, always had a smile. He checked my tubes and vitals.

"I'm going to remove the mask to ask you a

few questions. Would you like your grandmother and boyfriend to leave the room?"

I was about to say no, then I stopped. Boyfriend? It was in that moment when Riordan stood and I saw him. I had never seen him so afraid and angry. The mix was terrifying and yet it warmed my heart. He told them he was my boyfriend. So I shook my head and allowed the doctor to divest me of the mask.

"Here, sweetheart, have some water." My grandmother rested the straw on my lips and I sipped slowly, relishing the coolness sliding down my very raw throat.

"Mr. Harris..." the doctor began.

"Teddy, please." My voice sounded like I had smoked a hundred cigarettes.

"Teddy. Your throat will hurt for a while, we had to intubate you. On top of that, you suffered a serious allergic reaction that forced your airways shut." He sat in the chair to my right, tablet in hand.

"Allergic reaction?" I asked. When I looked at

Hug It Out

Riordan, I could tell he knew something.

"Your tests came back and there was penicillin in your blood. I'm aware you are allergic and I know you're aware also. I tend to believe this was an accident and I'm curious if you could tell me what happened?" He wasn't accusatory, he was genuinely concerned. Who would take penicillin willingly, knowing they were allergic?

One more glance at Riordan told me I needed to get rid of the doctor and my grandmother and ask him what the hell was going on.

"I honestly don't know. I was at the coffee shop, Quirks and Perks. I ate, had coffee, and I reached the NICU. That's all I remember. Perhaps I grabbed the wrong drink and it was someone else's?" The medical tape was starting to itch, so I concentrated on that so as not to make eye contact.

"You wouldn't put that in a drink," my grandmother said.

All I could do was shrug. "I don't know."

The doctor jotted some things down on his

tablet and stood.

"You're going to have to stay for at least another day or two. Your counts aren't where I want them to be and I wouldn't feel comfortable with you wandering around." He gave me a pointed look. "I'd like you to speak with our psychologist."

Great, he thinks I tried to kill myself.

"Whatever gets me out of here, doc." I gave him the best smile I could muster, desperate for him to leave.

"Good. I will be back in a couple of hours. Let me see about getting you something to eat." He left, leaving me with a very skeptical-looking grandmother and Riordan, who seemed to want my grandmother to leave.

"Grandma, why don't you go home or get something to eat. Riordan will stay with me. Won't you?" He nodded. "I'll feel better if I know you're okay."

She watched me for a moment, her eyes shifting to Riordan, then back to me. She didn't want to go and was struggling with this, so I let her take a moment.

"Fine. I'll go home for a little bit. I'll come back later with some things to keep you occupied. I trust Riordan will be here until I get back?"

"Absolutely." It was the first time I'd heard him speak since I woke up, and it sounded like he hadn't spoken in days.

She kissed my forehead and left the room. Riordan walked over to the ICU doors, sliding them shut. He turned and we just looked at each other for a moment, taking the other in. When the distance became too much, I held my arms open and Riordan practically lunged.

"I'm so sorry." His words were muffled in my neck.

"It's not your fault." I didn't think it was, but I suspected this had something to do with what was happening with his assassinship.

His head shot up, and his green eyes were frantic. "Teddy, no one hates you. You hug people and play video games. Who the fuck would want to do this to you? We both know this is from my end."

"I don't know, last week I stole a whole cavern full of power gems from a player called Russell the Love Muscle… It was ugly." I tried so hard to make him smile. To not be so serious in a moment I knew we had to be.

"I knew I shouldn't have left you alone today." He kissed my forehead, cheeks, and mouth. I jerked my head away before he had a chance to deepen it.

"My mouth feels like level fifty-four of—" Riordan didn't let me finish, he kissed me like he didn't care.

When he pulled away, his eyes showed all the emotions; fear, anger, amazement, all of them.

"I called the hospital when you didn't tell me you were here. They saw you, so I didn't worry." He slid his fingers through my hair, scraping my scalp softly. "Jones is back in the States, Lee's working with him. It's a fucking mess. I don't know how, but Jones has to be behind this, behind what happened to you."

Hug It Out

"How?" It boggled my mind. I hadn't been near any of Black's bodyguard guys, nor had I been near Jones. He certainly had the type of face you'd remember.

"Lee is trained to remote kill, Teddy. I once watched as he took out five French mercenaries with a ceiling fan. Don't ask me how he did it. He can kill in ways you can't imagine. Don't let his tiny stature fool you."

"You're saying he managed to get penicillin into something or injected me without me knowing it within a twenty-minute period?" There was no hiding the disbelief in my tone. Then I suddenly realized something.

"Oh my God, Emma!" I tried to sit up.

"Calm down." Riordan pushed me back down. "We have eyes on her."

"No, you don't understand. She was with me at the coffee shop. She ate and drank with me. What if Lee or Jones did this to her too. Are you sure there are people looking after her?" I really liked Emma, I didn't want anything to happen to her.

"Hold on. You saw Emma today?" Riordan sat up, but didn't leave the bed.

"Yeah. I was at the pickup line and she was in the order line. We started talking, and then I went to the hospital."

"Did anyone know you were going to the hospital today? Anyone at all?" Riordan was asking me and typing on his phone at the same time.

"No, well, my grandmother and you, but that's it." I didn't know where Riordan was going with this.

Then he was talking on the phone. "We need to get eyes on Emma. She was with Teddy today. Whoever did this may have targeted her too." He paused for a moment, listening. "Yeah. Or that. Let me know."

"Who was that?" I asked as a huge yawn broke free.

"Mace. Look, you rest. I'll be here until your grandmother gets back. Then I have to track things down. I'll see if someone can sit with you."

Hug It Out

"I don't need a sitter."

Riordan wasn't having any of what I was selling. "You do, we all do. I will not leave you unguarded for even a moment."

Part of me wanted to argue but I was becoming more tired by the second, so I waved him off and shut my eyes, letting sleep claim me.

Chapter Thirty-Eight

Riordan

I watched Teddy sleep fitfully at first, but in no time, he was sleeping peacefully. Gliding my fingers along his arm, I was happy the redness on his skin had disappeared and aside from the IV and oxygen, he looked like nothing had happened.

"Is he okay?" I was so deep in thought, I hadn't heard Snow enter the room.

"Hi. Yes. He's going to be okay, I think. They want to watch him for something called bi-something reaction. I forgot what it's called."

"Biphasic reaction. It's also known as the second wave in any severe allergic reaction. It can occur anywhere from one to seventy-two hours after the initial attack. Usually between eight-to-ten, but if his was severe, then taking precautions is wise." Snow spoke almost like he was reciting from a text book. It was a little creepy. But Snow was a mystery to most and no one dared question anything that came out of his mouth, lest we would face his husband.

"Has this ever happened to you or something?"

Snow smirked as he read the screens where Teddy's blood pressure and heart rate were broadcast. "My mother was a nurse."

"Then you probably know more about all this." I waved my hand at the IV and gadgets.

He tilted his head and moved from the screens to the charts that hung by his bed. He didn't speak as he read over it all, so I took a moment to watch him. He really was stunning in an ethereal way. Even though he was only in his twenties, his eyes told a story. One that aged your soul.

"How did this happen?" he asked, taking in Teddy's resting frame.

"Someone slipped it in his drink. I'm thinking when he went to the coffee shop."

Snow nodded, a soft scowl was the only indication that he was upset. He tucked Teddy's sheet higher, and then beckoned me to follow him out to the hallway. It was desolate in the ICU. A few nurses were at the station, but other than that, just me and Snow.

"What's up?" I asked. I almost jumped when Snow rounded on me, pointing an accusing finger at me. His eyes were lit like fire. Angry Snow was a little scary.

"He isn't like you. He isn't like Christopher, hell, he isn't even like me. He doesn't have a bad past or a sad story. No karma queen in her right mind would bestow this on him. So, Riordan Darcy. This is absolutely your fault. He may choose to be in your life and own your demons, but this?" He pointed to the room where Teddy slept. "That's not his burden. That right there is on you. Fix it or I swear to God, I will have my army crush your army."

Snow's army was his husband's. And as angry as Snow was, I saw the worry lingering in his expression.

"I will figure this out and I promise Teddy won't get hurt again. I'll do what I can to make it right." I meant that. Snow dropped his hand, but the acrimonious glare wasn't leaving his face anytime soon.

"I don't have a lot of friends. I don't like getting close to people because they seem to disappear. Teddy was safe."

"I get that. I will do what I have to. I promise."

"There's more ways to hurt Teddy than the physical. Don't forget that."

It was such a loaded statement. But I imagined he had seen a lot. He had to have. "Can you stay with him? I want to hunt things down, but I won't leave him alone."

Snow looked at Teddy through the glass doors and then down the hall. It was then I noticed five large men standing there. Two I recognized from Christopher's house. Nothing was getting near Teddy. "Yeah. Okay. I'll stay for a while. You go make this right."

Without another word, he went into Teddy's room. I walked down the hallway past the men, who all had judgment in their eyes. I had to fix this. Snow was right.

I texted Mace to meet me at Quirks and Perks. It was almost nine at night. I knew Snow would stay at the hospital until I returned. Teddy's grandmother informed me she wouldn't be back due to a headache. The café closed at eleven, so we had time.

Mace and Bill were at the café when I arrived. Neither was looking at the other.

"How's Teddy?" Bill asked as we entered the building.

"He'll be okay. Snow is with him. I don't have a lot of time, I need to get back."

I doubted the barista working was the one from earlier, but I figured I may be able to get some answers.

"Hello, my name's Riordan. My boyfriend was in here earlier. He had a severe allergic reaction to something in his drink and I was wondering if I could talk to whoever served around lunch time?" I believed it was lunchtime, anyway.

"Oh my god, that's horrible!" the male barista

said. "I'm working a double, so I was here then, maybe I can help."

He was a little thing with black and blue hair. He had about ten piercings, tattoos, and a lot of bracelets. I didn't judge, he could have the answers I needed.

"Would you sit and talk with us? I'm trying to figure out how this happened. Teddy is really careful about his allergies, so I worry. You understand?" I tried to take a page from Teddy's book and smile, be kind. It felt foreign, but it put the guy at ease.

"Yeah, I get it. If I had a guy, I'd worry if this happened to him too." He sat at a booth with Mace, Bill, and me.

"What's your name?" Mace asked.

"Quill," he said as he played with his bracelets.

"Quill, like the bird?" Bill asked.

"No, you dumbass," Mace snapped. "Quail is the bird. Quill is the pen."

"Fuck you." Bill shoved Mace and Quill started laughing.

"Wow, you two a couple?" Quill asked, much to my amusement.

"No," Mace and Bill answered in unison.

"Enough." My voice was louder than I wanted it to be, but it shut them up. "Quill, do you remember Teddy coming in here?"

"Maybe, I'm not good with names, what's he look like?"

"He's about six feet, curly brown hair, hazel eyes, sort of lanky, black-rimmed glasses."

Quill's eyes widened in recognition. "The gamer guy! Yeah, he comes in a lot. Talks games with me. Great guy. He'll be all right, right?"

"So you saw him today?"

Quill was nodding before I even finished my question.

"Yeah, he was talking with some lady. Real pretty, red hair? You know her?" He eyed us all and when we said yes, he continued. "It was so busy. I know they sat over there." He pointed to a table by the window. "And at some point, they left."

Hug It Out

"Did you see anyone approach their table or was anywhere near Teddy at any time?" I was grasping at straws. Lee and Jones wouldn't be so stupid as to have been here.

"Nah, they kept to themselves." Quill smiled like he found something funny.

"What is it?" Had he remembered something?

"He bought her a drink and got the table, ya know? And she asked where the sugar and stuff was. I told her by the DIY bar. She said they didn't have cream, so I gave her a couple more and she said something about her loving her cream and…" He seemed to realize he was going off on some tangent. "Sorry."

"Thanks, Quill, for all your help." Mace rolled his eyes and exited the booth. He walked over to the DIY bar and began looking things over.

"What was he allergic to that we put in his drink? We have a board behind the counter where we mark our regulars' allergies so we are always aware."

"It's obscure. Nothing you should worry

about." I got up after Quill slid out and walked over to where Mace was looking over the condiments.

"Quill," Mace shouted. "Where's the cream you store here?"

Quill walked over and opened the fridge. Where there was plenty. "We stock them every half hour. Making sure to check more during busy hours."

I scanned the place. It wasn't busy now, but the DIY bar was in the center of the café. A lot of people could see it.

"So, the lady asked for some? Was she standing here?" Mace asked.

"I think so. I offered to just put it in the coffee, but she said she'd like to do it herself."

Bill stepped up to Quill, crowding him. "It was just you and her?"

Quill gave him a look that indicated he thought Bill was crazy. "Yeah, why?"

"Nothing. Thank you," I said as I rushed out of the café, already dialing Black.

"What's up?" he answered.

Hug It Out

"Where's Emma? Did she have any effects like Teddy?" Mace and Bill were at my side watching our surroundings.

"She was fine. Left the meeting and she was followed back to her place. She's been there since."

My gut clenched and my skin tingled. Something was wrong. "Black, get someone into her place."

"Why?"

"If she's in there, she's in trouble. If she's not, than we've been looking the wrong way."

"Stand by," he said, and I stood at the corner. Mace, Bill and I were on guard for anything.

Were Lee and Jones innocent? Did they kill Emma? Was Emma the mole?

"She's gone," Black said. "No trace."

"Fuck," I shouted, why hadn't we seen it? "Black, we need to find Lee or Jones. Preferably both."

"I'll see what I can do. We've been trying. You guys aren't easy to find when you don't want to be found."

He was right, but I had to figure out a way to get ahold of them.

"I'm going back to the hospital to be with Teddy. Mace and Bill will fill you in on what we discovered tonight."

After hanging up, the three of us parted ways. If whoever tried to kill Teddy figured out he wasn't dead, they'd try again. If it was Emma, she'd assume Teddy had accused her. I needed to see him immediately.

Chapter Thirty-Nine

Teddy

Light illuminated behind my lids and the warmth of the sun streaming in the hospital window indicated it was morning. Snow had left late last night, and I remembered Riordan entering the room. The nurses came in a few times, but other than that, I slept.

Opening my eyes, I scanned the room. Riordan was asleep on some sort of lounger. Normally, the hospital didn't allow overnight visitors in ICU, but there had been occasions where they bent the rules. I guessed they were bent here.

My grandmother must have stopped by because there were blankets, magazines, and Tupperware filled with goodies.

"Morning," a nurse said when she entered. She began looking over my tubes. Jotting things down on her tablet. I heard Riordan stir and watched as he woke up.

He stretched and yawned. His bones made a symphony of sounds as he brought himself to his full height. I couldn't help but smile when he noticed me staring.

"How you feeling?" he asked as he sat by my bed and took my hand.

"I feel good, actually." Turning to the nurse, I asked, "Will I be able to go home today?"

"Dr. Alberts is doing rounds right now, so you'll be able to ask him. He's a stickler for the rules. He won't want you leaving after only twenty-four hours. But maybe we can get you into a regular room." She offered me a small, sympathetic smile, which I returned.

"I understand. Thanks."

She finished up and informed me she'd get me something to eat.

"Since they are going to feed me and hopefully I'll be able to bathe, why don't you go down and eat, or better yet, head home for real sleep and real food,"

Hug It Out

I said to Riordan, knowing even as I did so, he wouldn't go.

"No. And I'm not thrilled with you eating their food. I'll see if you're able to eat regular food and when your grandmother arrives, you can eat what she has or I'll get you something." He scowled at the pink pitcher filled with water. He trusted nothing and I understood.

"Maybe you can bring me some iced tea too?" He nodded at my request. "You don't trust the food and that's fine. I won't eat anything from anyone but you or my grandmother right now. Don't worry." I squeezed his hand in an attempt to appease him.

There was so much going on behind those green eyes of his. Flashes of regret whenever he looked at me, deep concentration as he stared out the window. I wanted to ask what was going on, but last night, Snow had told me to choose whether or not I trusted Riordan. I couldn't be considering something that important in the midst of all this mayhem. He told me if I chose to trust Riordan, to let him guide me without question. I thought on it until sleep took over. Seeing Riordan beside me, protective, attentive, and determined, I decided to trust him.

"The doctor won't let me leave until tomorrow at the earliest, you realize that?"

"I'm glad. You're safer here than in most places. And I see there are some men by your door. No doubt that's Snow's doing?" He gestured in the direction of the men in question.

Snow had said Christopher cleared it with the hospital to have someone here at all times. It looked like it was two someones.

"He worries. I don't know his entire story and I don't expect I ever will. But he's afraid of losing people, and it's sweet I mean something to him, so I didn't put up a fuss and I didn't think you would either."

"You're physically safe here. I'm not worried about that." He spoke, but he was a million miles away. "Teddy, you have to promise me something."

This couldn't be good. "I can't promise unless

I know what I'm agreeing to." I chuckled, but there was no amusement from him.

"Unless your grandmother, me, or Snow visits, trust no one." He gripped my hand tighter. "No one, Teddy, you hear me?"

"What about Mace, Bill, or Black?"

He shook his head. "No one. My gut says Mace and Black are good. I don't know Bill, but he's not in this. He's here to stop it, but…" He released a breath and shut his eyes for a moment. "Emma's missing."

"Missing like taken?" Sitting up fast caused a dizzy spell and I tried to calm down.

"Relax. We don't know. Whoever this is, they aren't taking people, they're killing them. It's odd."

Realization dawned on me. "You don't think it's Jones. You think Emma's the mole?"

He brought my hand to his lips, not kissing me, just grazing his lips against the skin. I could feel how tangled up he was inside just from looking at him.

"I don't know, but I suspect, and that's what frustrates me. I need to get one of them in front of me.

I need questions answered." He scooted up and sat on the mattress. "You have to promise me something else."

"I didn't promise you the other thing." When my smile wasn't returned, I put him out of his misery. "I won't trust anyone else. What else do you need me to promise?"

He took my head in his hands, and his thumbs brushed my cheeks reverently. He leaned in so close, he was almost blurry, but the intensity of the moment creeped up my spine.

"If one day I walk out that door and don't come back, promise me you will go to Christopher. Promise me if I don't get out of this, you will let him protect you. Promise me you will hug people forever and wear a stupid bunny suit while you play video games. Promise me, Teddy."

I didn't like any of this, and a dreadful, ominous feeling was making me nauseous. "Riordan, I don't want to promise that."

He rested his forehead against mine, then took

a breath, his thumbs still rubbing my cheeks like he was trying to make his words stick. "I don't like asking."

His scent washed over me, minty and fresh. Being with Riordan was like running through a forest. Exhilarating and terrifying. Was he memorizing me like I was him?

"Teddy," he whispered.

"Okay, Riordan, I promise." Then his lips were on me like a hungry man.

Tears roll down my cheeks as he kissed me with so much desperation, so much finality. It felt like goodbye and I hated that this could be the last time I was with him.

"Riordan." I tried to speak between kisses. He made it near impossible. "Riordan."

He pulled back, taking in every inch of my face. His gaze flitted over every one of my features... He was memorizing me.

"I don't want my last time with you to be in a hospital room. You hear me?" Gripping his arms, I emphasized my point with a shake. "I want you to take me to bed. I want to discover what you love and what you don't. I want to make love to you. I want to find out if we ever fall in love."

Time froze when he smiled and for a brief moment, everything felt fine. No impending doom, no threats. Just us.

"I want all that too." We kissed and held each other until my grandmother arrived.

She had no idea what was going on and never asked. I once asked her why she never questioned the things I did and she said if I wanted her to know, I'd tell her.

Problem here was I did want her to know. I wanted her to hug me and tell me to have faith. But I couldn't.

With one last kiss, Riordan said he had to go. Like any other day. He winked and was gone. I rested my hand where he had sat. It stayed there until the sheets turned cold.

When I wept, my grandmother held me and

told me to have faith.

Chapter Forty

Riordan

I wasn't sure what exactly I was going to do. Maybe go underground with Mace and see if we could track these fuckers. When I reached my truck, my planning was cut short when my phone vibrated.

"Hey, Mace, tell me some good news." I rested my head against the seat and listened.

"Bill got Lee."

Thank fuck. "How did he manage that?"

Mace chuckled, he was giddy. "It shocked me too. I never saw a man run and tackle like that, and I watch a lot of football. It was impressive. It was like he knew the direction Lee was going to go before Lee did. He fucking leaped over two benches and a small statue, Riordan."

"Jesus." I didn't expect that from a man like Bill, but looks were often deceiving. "Where is Lee now?"

"Bill and I are on our way to the cave." I heard an engine in the background and a muffled voice.

"Lee is with you?"

"Yeah. We didn't trust anyone else."

"Okay, I'm on my way."

I drove as fast as I could to the cave while keeping an eye on my surroundings. I lived a life most people didn't. Most people, the light would turn green and they would go. Not me. I once watched Mace take out three men by driving a cement truck through an intersection, smashing into them and pancaking them against a brick building.

Every opening was an opportunity for someone like me. Someone like this mole.

Bill must have driven because when I arrived, the car was on the lawn. Guy may be fast, but he was on the crazy side.

Black, Mace, and Bill were standing in the living room when I opened the door. Lee was tied to a chair, duct tape over his mouth and anger in his eyes.

I had no doubt he was imagining how each of us would die if he got a chance.

"Where did you find him?" I asked Bill as I knelt in front of Lee, staring through him, hoping to get even a flinch of nervousness.

"Train station."

I ripped the tape from Lee's mouth, enjoying his scream that came with it.

"Fuck, Riordan!" He narrowed his eyes, but the venomous glare just made me smirk. He was harmless without his gadgets.

"Yeah? Teddy had it a lot worse. I don't want to hear it." Standing, I tossed the duct tape at him. "What was you and Jones's plan? Kill each of us off one-by-one?"

Lee actually had the nerve to scoff. "How are you, any of you, still alive in this business?"

"How about we ask the fucking questions?" Black gripped Lee's hair and pulled his head back. I knew that hurt, but Lee didn't react. "What was your plan?"

Hug It Out

"It wasn't the type of plan you think."

"Oh for fuck's sake." Bill grabbed Lee's chair and brought it to the kitchen. Lee struggled to keep balance, and we all followed, curious as to what he was up to. "I can't listen to this anymore. It's like watching golf. Boring and the victory will come in about twelve hours." He slammed the chair down on the floor forcefully, making a piece of wood splinter off the leg, and opened a drawer.

We watched, transfixed, as Bill removed a couple knives, a corkscrew, and a handful of toothpicks. Seeing how determined Bill was made me wonder what his story was.

"You're going to torture me?" Lee screeched. "You don't understand."

Bill turned with a steak knife in his hand. He pressed the flat side against Lee's lips. "I want to get back to my life and I'm stuck with you until this is over, so can you stop with the smoke and mirrors, the play on words, or whatever the fuck you're doing? Either tell us everything in one go or we will see how well you work with no fingers."

Lee nodded nervously, and knowing what Lee had stared down in his time, to be scared of Bill proved whatever emotion he saw in his honey brown gaze made him believe in the promise of pain. Bill moved the knife from his lips to Lee's knee. We all followed the movement.

"Start singing," Bill said, his knife just waiting for Lee to fuck up.

"That night at the bar when Jones left me there, I really didn't know what was going on. I was as much in the dark as all of you." He cleared his throat and licked his dry lips. "Then he called me. Said he was in Switzerland. I knew that, we all did." Lee hissed.

"He found Abano."

"Found? You mean he went to him, they're working together," Mace argued.

Bill pointed at him with his other hand that was gripping a corkscrew. "Fucking shut it, Mace. No side talk. Keep going, Lee."

Mace's glare was venomous, but Bill didn't

seem to give two fucks. Lee's voice shook as he continued. "He found Abano. He had to get to him without anyone knowing because he didn't know how deep it all went. He knew his disappearing was going to get a price on his head, but he had to. See, Jones isn't some asshole like you all think. He is fiercely loyal to Black. Ouch!"

Blood began to blossom on Lee's jeans and the tip of the knife was slightly imbedded right above the kneecap "I don't want a profile on Jones, Lee. Keep going." Bill smirked. Was he enjoying this?

"Fine. The guy who picked him up at the bar was some mercenary that Jones had worked with years ago. He found Abano and they had to go right then. He had no time. He called me when he was there." He took a deep breath, either to calm himself or center himself from the pain. "Abano was never running anything. Sure, he thought he was, but it was what he told Jones before he died that explained everything."

"Abano's dead?" I asked.

Lee nodded. "Yeah, and painfully. Abano

needed money, we knew that. But even the money from his wife and kid's deaths wasn't going to sustain his lifestyle forever. He ended up falling in love. She promised him the world. Said she had a way to not only make him richer than he could ever imagine, but to have some of the world's most vicious hitmen protecting him. She said she had money set aside to get people on board, but would need more. He agreed." Lee shook his head, grimacing in disgust. "She's been planning this for over two years."

We all knew who "she" was, but we needed to hear it.

"Who is she?" I asked.

Lee locked eyes with Black, the look of betrayal in Lee's eyes matched all of ours when he uttered her name. "Emma."

"So it was her who tried to kill Teddy?" It felt like acid was dancing through my veins, mocking me and taunting me to react.

"Yeah," Lee whispered as he stared at the knife still in his leg.

Hug It Out

"He was the weakest link. Knew he'd make you vulnerable. She knows what she's doing." He eyed Bill, who lifted the knife from his leg.

"What was with the thumb drives and hundred thousand dollars?" Mace asked.

"That was why Jones needed me. He wanted me to do some digging. Had to go into the dark net. It was there I found how Emma was communicating with Abano." His eyes shifted to Black, whose rage was so apparent, it had him shaking. "And about thirty of your men, Black."

"And the money?" Bill tossed the knife in the sink.

"Jones needed the money to flee if it all went south, and the thumb drives were the proof that Emma was the mole."

Black kneeled in front of Lee, he still was shaking, but I could see he was doing everything in his power to rein it in. "You could have been killed. You would have died for Jones? Why didn't you trust me enough to tell me?"

Lee didn't take his eyes off Black. He didn't even blink. "Jones is the only person I'd ever die for. And it wasn't that we couldn't trust you, it was better if you didn't know at the time. Emma didn't know you all knew that she was working with Abano. If she figured out that Jones and I knew she'd split her reinforcements, then we'd have her."

"You should have told us," Black rasped.

Lee chuckled, but it was devoid of humor. "You might be amazing hitmen, but actors you are not." Lee looked over at me. "Your make-up with Teddy was only convincing because you have great chemistry."

He had a point. If I had known at the time she was the mole, I probably would've tipped my hand.

"Do you know where she is now?" Bill asked.

Lee eyed each of us, I knew before he spoke that our actions, while providing us with information, likely screwed things up. "She knows you're all aware. The second Sasquatch here grabbed me, she knew you'd get it out of me. She's watching all of us. Let me call Jones. We have to draw her out."

We all looked to Black for a decision, which came a few moments later.

"Call him in."

Chapter Forty-One

Teddy

Monday was busy. My grandmother came by, and Delly visited for a few hours. Even Poe stopped over to keep me company. Holding my cellphone to my chest, I wished for a message, anything from Riordan. Nothing came. I loved how my family and friends cared so much about me and spent time with me, but I was so worried about Riordan, I had a hard time being appreciative.

The huge men guarding my room were still there, they barely moved and never spoke to me. Delly asked about them and I told her that until the hospital was sure my poisoning wasn't malicious, they were taking precautions. I knew she didn't believe me, but it was the most she was going to get.

I was glad to at least be in another room. I had no doubt someone pulled strings to get me the private room. I didn't argue, I enjoyed the peace... until it became insufferable.

I read gamer magazines, watched dumb television, and did far too many crossword puzzles to pass the time and try to calm my paranoid mind. The only time I smiled was when the nurse informed me I'd be discharged the next day. I wasn't sure where I was going to go. It was too dangerous to go to Riordan's. I didn't want to go to Christopher's like I had promised. So I called Delly and asked if I could crash on her couch for a day or two. Explaining that it was better if I wasn't alone just yet. She was glad to help. I hoped I'd hear from Riordan or have a chance to contact Snow before I wore out my welcome.

Tuesday morning brought rain. It had been so hot out that with the rain came thunderstorms. It was the type of day where cuddling on the couch would be perfect. I wondered if I'd ever get to do that with Riordan again.

"Okay, I'm here to take you to my humble abode." Delly came into the room with a wheelchair, grinning like a fool.

"A wheelchair? I'm fine to walk out of here."

"No can do. Get dressed. I saw the nurse and she's headed this way with discharge papers. Maybe we can stop and get you some horrible, greasy fast food on the way back." She waggled her eyebrows, garnering a laugh from me.

"Sure, Del. Gimme a few." Slipping into the bathroom, I divested myself of the gown and got dressed as fast as possible. I wanted a shower and I was desperate to get lost in my games.

On the way to Delly's place, she let me be and my mind began to wander. The men guarding my room said nothing as I rolled out, so there was no worry there. I hoped Riordan wouldn't be mad that I went to Delly's. Surely, he wasn't referring to her as someone he couldn't trust. I dropped a text to him, telling him where I was so he wouldn't worry. No response came. And with each passing disregard, my heart ached more and the reality of the situation was hammered home.

"Maybe we can get some of your games and

stuff over here while you recuperate. Are they at Riordan's?" Delly asked as she opened the door to her apartment.

"Some are. I have consoles at my place too."

Delly's place was exactly like her. Tiny, bright, colorful, and chaotic. She had a kitchen that was styled with sunflowers and rainbows, a bathroom that made you feel like you were lost in the clouds, a small living area that was all mismatched and quirky, and a bedroom that she always said was her sanctuary. Her pullout couch was really comfortable, so staying for a couple of days wasn't a hardship.

"If it's better for you, you can take my bed," Delly shouted from the kitchen.

"I'm good." I wasn't really. I was sad, but this was an emotion I tried to avoid at all costs. I was always able to see the positive in everything. I was worried about Riordan. The last time I saw him, it was so final. My grandmother didn't poke for information, but she was upset for me and of course me being me, I hated making her worry.

"I'm going to make some spaghetti and meatballs, sound good?" Delly smiled warmly. It was my favorite comfort food. She was such an amazing friend.

"Sounds perfect."

I was getting situated when there was a knock on the door. Without a care in the world, she went to answer it, but I stopped her. This confused Delly, and rightly so. She had no idea of the possibilities behind that door.

"Go cook for me, woman, I'm starved. I'll get it." My joke sort of fell flat, but she let me answer it.

Bill was standing on the other side and he was angry. I didn't need to be a genius to see that.

"Explain something to me, Teddy." He pushed his sunglasses up on top of his head, his expression unhappy. "At what point did you think staying at your friend's apartment was a good idea?" His eyebrows rose and I knew it was a rhetorical question. "Because from what I can see, there's zero security, you have no self-preservation, and though I'm sure your friend is a capable person, I highly doubt she can take on Emma and about thirty of Black's men."

My eyes widened at the mention of Emma. "So it's confirmed? She's the mole?"

For a moment, Bill's angry face faltered. "Yeah. I thought you knew. Shit's getting real serious, Teddy, and you can't be here." He looked behind him, checking things out. "Christopher is expecting you, so please get your stuff and come on."

"Who's at the door?" Delly's voice got louder as she came toward me. "Oh, hey." She smiled at the hulking man, her eyes taking him in from head to toe. "Are you Teddy's friend or something?"

"Or something," Bill deadpanned.

There was a silent showdown between Bill and Delly. It was like she knew Bill was here to take me from her and she wasn't letting me go without a fight. The sudden thought made me laugh, and it felt amazing.

"Would your friend like to stay for dinner?" Delly asked as she watched my hysterics in amusement.

"No," Bill said matter-of-factly. "I came to pick Teddy up."

"Up?" Her hands went to her hips and her attitude was front and center.

"Yeah, I said up. It's not a difficult word to understand." Bill had zero patience, so I decided to step in before Delly ripped his eyes out.

"Okay, okay, let's chill," I chuckled, desperate to defuse the situation. "Del, Bill is Riordan's friend and he came to take me to his place. I guess Riordan is indisposed and because I left the hospital so abruptly, he was worried." I was getting too good at lying.

She nodded, buying my story. "Oh. I see. So no spaghetti?"

Without thought, I pulled her into a hug. "You're an awesome friend, Del. I can stay to eat since you started, and then after food, we'll go."

"Yeah, no, we go now, Teddy," Bill argued.

"Go if you want, I promised Delly I'd stay." Narrowing my eyes in an attempt to be scary was futile

Hug It Out

with Bill. He rolled his and stormed inside, plopping himself on the couch.

The next couple of hours were tense. Bill ate faster than any man I'd ever seen and when he was done, he actually gestured for me to hurry up.

After nearly choking eleven times, I grabbed my belongings, said goodbye to Delly, and followed Bill to his car.

Bill didn't look like he wanted to talk much on the way to Christopher's, so I sat there watching the world go by. I wanted to ask him so many questions about what he knew and how Riordan was, but Bill didn't have a very welcoming face.

Christopher's house looked just as daunting as the last time. It didn't look like a place someone like Snow would live in, but knowing Snow, he didn't care where he lived. It was all material.

Speak of the devil. The front door swung open and the man in question skipped down the steps with a huge smile. I had just grabbed my bag when he embraced me in a strong hug.

"Wow, thanks." I hugged him back, then pushed away when I heard a throat clear.

Christopher Manos stood atop the steps, a look of strength and power, and while I didn't fear for my life, I got the impression many who came face to face with him wanted to run or pee themselves. Possibly both.

"I was standing in this exact spot the first time I saw Christopher," Snow said. "He had that same look on his face, too." When Snow smiled at his brooding husband, Christopher softened immediately. "Come on, let's get you settled."

Snow took my bag and hopped, yes hopped, up the stairs. He placed a quick kiss on his husband's lips and disappeared inside.

"Thank you for letting me stay here, Mr. Uhm, Christopher." He laughed when I held my hand out.

"Don't be afraid of me. You are no threat. I'm happy to help you. Snow set you up in one of the guest rooms, so if you'd like to go on up, it's the third door on the right. I'm sure after that, he will keep you

Hug It Out

occupied until you're ready to pass out." He gestured to the steps.

I took the stairs, noting how ridiculously wide and long they were. The Rockettes could perform on them. The room I was staying in was extravagant with its emerald-green silk sheets, honey-gold carpeting, floor to ceiling windows with embroidered curtains, and what looked like an ensuite. After visiting the last time, I'd come to expect nothing less from this house. Snow sat on the mattress, waiting for me.

"So, I was thinking we could watch a movie in the theater room, eat some popcorn and candy?" He twisted onto his stomach on the mattress, chin in his hands, with an expectant look on his face.

"Sure. Whatever you want."

"I wish I could have introduced you to Simon, Chris's nephew, but he's at a sleepover tonight. Snow rolled his eyes in exaggeration. "This is something he's never done before. Christopher spent the entire day running surveillance on that poor family, and then he put a tracker on Simon. He will be staring at the monitor all night, so I need you to entertain me."

I couldn't tell if he was joking or not and I decided I didn't want to ask, so I agreed to spend the evening with him after taking a shower.

He left me to it and I enjoyed the peace and quiet. I didn't enjoy my mind running on a loop watching Riordan walk out of my hospital room. I just had to have faith, like my grandmother said. I would certainly try.

Chapter Forty-Two

Riordan

We all wanted to trust Lee that he and Jones were innocent and had the organization's best interests at heart, but it was hard.

Teddy had texted that he was leaving the hospital and staying at his friend's about the same time Christopher's men texted Bill, telling him the same. It was a bad idea, so Bill said he'd take Teddy back to Christopher's. Outside of Mace, Black, Jones, and myself, Bill was the only one who would be in the loop about what was happening with Emma.

"Does Emma know Abano's dead?" Black asked as we all sat around the kitchen table.

"I suspect so. If she doesn't, she'll get word soon enough." Jones' smile was sinister.

"You hung him, didn't you?" Mace shook his head.

Jones didn't deny it, but he didn't elaborate, he merely shrugged and went back to polishing his knife.

We were still trying to figure out a way to draw Emma out, either on her own or with a small amount of men. Lee's thumb drives named all of the men on Black's payroll that were Pro-Emma.

According to the conversations Lee was able to pull from the dark net's chat rooms, Emma wanted to dismantle Black's organization and take over. She was wrangling as many guys as possible and would go for a hostile takeover. In one chat, Emma explained to Abano and a few of Black's drones why they needed to remove major issues and heavy hitters before wiping out the rest. All in all, Emma was looking at a huge body count. I hoped she had a lot of money to start because with Abano confirmed dead, soon there would be no way Emma was getting his money.

Black knew that once she managed to take him down, she'd go after his competition and make herself the only available resource for people to hire hitmen. It all pointed to money and power, but something wasn't sitting right with me. Emma had been here longer than any of us, except for Black. She likely made more than each of us, so why do this?

No one else seemed to know her motives, but everyone agreed that money and power were enough to mark her as a hit. She had to go, and we had to take down the insurgents.

"Do we have a plan at all?" Mace smacked the table, the sound snapping us all out of our head. "We can't sit here staring at each other."

Again, Jones smiled at each of us. "Actually, that's exactly what we're going to do."

"What the hell, Jones?" Black snapped. He didn't like being the one not in control. "What are you playing at?"

"Look, Emma is coming for us. She knows about this place. She's going to find out from a little birdie that we are all at the cave. She'll come and she'll take us out. She won't get a better opportunity to have us all together than this." He was so nonchalant about it, he simply wiped the polish off his knife and slid it back in the sheath.

"I'm not fucking dying!" Mace stood suddenly, jolting the table into Jones.

"Sit down, you fuckwit." Jones pushed the blueprint we had spread out on the table toward us. "Under this house are tunnels. Emma doesn't know. Only Black and I do because I was the one that came up with the idea."

"Why would you think that was a good idea?" Mace asked.

"We fucking need it now, don't we? So shut up." He pointed to the area marked "kitchen." "Under this table is a door. That's where we will be. She's gonna rig this place to blow. We just need to get to the tunnels before they do. She won't chance losing her men. She needs them, so it's a bit like playing Russian roulette, but I'm hoping they don't check in the house."

Lee placed his hand on Jones's arm and it was amazing how much softer Jones looked at Lee, never yelling or speaking down to him. "But why are we doing this?"

"If she thinks we're dead, we aren't a risk." Jones sharp eyes focused on me. "Teddy will be a thorn in her side. We wait till she gets him where she wants him, then we strike."

"Fuck no." I pounded the table. "He's been through enough."

"Bill will know all this and won't be far from him. It's the only way," Jones argued.

"Hold on," Black intervened. "How can you be sure that these shits are going to rig the place to blow and not check inside first? That's not how I've trained you all."

Jones stood, holding a finger up to signal us to hold on, and stepped outside for a moment. We all looked at each other, wondering what the hell was going on. I was about to follow when the back door slammed and Jones walked in, dragging one of Black's men. He was beat to shit and had his arms and legs tied. I was about to ask where the hell he was hiding him, but Jones' booming voice halted my questions.

"This here is Jimmy." Jones kicked Jimmy's side, making him grunt. He reached in his back pocket and pulled out a cell phone. "Lee was able to do some digging and found out that Jimmy has been Emma's number two through all of this." He pulled Jimmy off the floor and slammed him against the fridge. "He's going to call Emma and tell her that tonight, they hit us all. He will state he's watching and had checked inside first. She won't question him."

"I'm not doing shit." Jimmy spat in Jones's face, earning a knee to the groin.

"You'll do it or that precious little girl of yours that your sister watches for you will have a really bad day at the playground tomorrow." Jones jiggled the phone in front of Jimmy's face. "Riordan'll tell ya how dumb it is to show anyone in this organization that someone matters to you."

I saw the resignation on Jimmy's face. He knew he was dead no matter what, but one road led to his daughter's life, the other to her death.

"What button?" Jones asked.

Hug It Out

"One."

Jones dialed it and put it on speaker. "Be convincing."

"Jimmy?" The second I heard her voice, a wave of anger slammed me in the face.

"Hey, Em. I got some news for you."

She chuckled and I could practically see her hands clapping in glee. "I knew you'd come through for me. What do you have?"

"There's some safe house on Rooster Ave, been staking it out all day. All of them are there. Inside now. Looks like they're lying low for a while. We can wait till they're asleep, ya know? What are the chances we'll get them all together again? I'm keeping watch, so I'll make sure to do a sweep beforehand and blow this fucker up." He sounded convincing, even though the look on his face was sorrowful.

"Oh, that is fantastic news. Hank here is an explosives expert. If we wait till they're asleep, he can stage it like a gas leak or something." She sounded thrilled and it made me want to scream.

"I'll stay here to let you know if anything changes."

"Wonderful. You're one of a kind, Jimmy. When I rule all this, I'll do it with you by my side." If I didn't know better, I'd say she meant that.

"I'll stand there happily," Jimmy's voice cracked, but he covered it up by clearing his throat. "Text when Hank's on the way."

When they disconnected, Jones hit him over the head, knocking him out.

"As soon as that phone pings, we hit the tunnels," I said. "He won't come in on Jimmy's word and risk waking us, they aren't completely stupid."

Everyone was in agreement. We sat around that table for an hour, then two. Long after the sun set, the text came through.

It was showtime.

We fit in the tunnels perfectly. We walked far enough so we weren't on the property anymore, but we'd know when the place went up. Jimmy was tied up on the ground at Jones's feet. If looks could kill,

Hug It Out

we'd all be dead men.

I wasn't sure how long we had waited, but we felt the vibration, the ground shook, and small clouds of dust danced through the tube.

"It's done," Black said, and he turned to me. "We need to let Bill know. Teddy needs to think all of us are dead or it won't work. She will come for him, and if she smells a ruse, she will change her plans and I don't want her in the wind."

My heart felt heavy. Teddy wouldn't know that I was okay. I hated having to hurt him.

We walked for a mile until Jones climbed up a wall ladder and opened a manhole. We came out a few streets over. We could see the smoke from the cave. Sirens blared in the distance.

I dialed Bill with a heavy heart. It wouldn't matter that I lived, the chances of Teddy ever forgiving me were nonexistent.

"Hey," Bill said.

"Be sure to turn on the news. There was an explosion on Rooster Ave. Teddy needs to think we all died. In an hour, Christopher will say he has a phone call and will take it in his study. You'll go with him and when you come out, you better pull off an Oscar-worthy performance." I choked on my words several times.

"Okay. I'll let him know." He hung up.

Please forgive me, Teddy.

Chapter Forty-Three

Teddy

Snow and I were talking in the living room when Bill stormed in, followed by Christopher and a few of his guys. Snow and I were bewildered by the rush and I was about to say something when Bill grabbed the remote and turned on the TV.

A female reporter was talking about an explosion. Behind her, there were firetrucks, ambulances, and police cars. Smoke was all around, but she was a fair distance away.

"I'm being told this quiet neighborhood was rocked awake when an explosion came from the house behind me at around 9:00 P.M. this evening. The Fire Chief said he was unable to explain the cause of the explosion and the identities of any people who may have been inside." She looked down at a piece of paper. "The house was owned by an organization in the city. Neighbors say there isn't anyone who lives there consistently, and it seems to be a place for visits and vacations."

"Is that?" Christopher asked, and Snow gripped my hand.

"Is that what?" I asked, that feeling of dread starting to form in the pit of my stomach.

"Are we sure?" Christopher was talking to Bill, who simply nodded.

"What is it?" My voice rose and Snow wrapped his arm around me. Whether to support me or stop me from lurching at them, I didn't know.

"I was there a couple days ago with Mace. I'm positive." Bill turned and the expression on his face told me something horrible had happened.

"No," I said.

"Let's not jump to any conclusions," Snow spoke up. "We wait. We don't panic. Assuming will get us nowhere." He squeezed me and gave me a smile that almost made me believe everything would be okay.

Hug It Out

It didn't take long for that thought to come crashing down. An hour later, Christopher was summoned by Frank to take a phone call. We all sat flipping through the channels, hoping to find more information on the explosion but all stations were reporting other things, so Bill put it on mute. He was usually a quiet guy, but now his stare was vacant.

After long minutes, Christopher came in. Bill, Snow, and I turned when he didn't speak. He was looking directly at me. That look would stay with me forever.

"Who was on the phone?" Snow asked.

"Teddy." Christopher pinched the bridge of his nose. "I know some people downtown."

"How nice for you." I knew I sounded like an asshole, but if he had to tell me what I thought he did, then he needed to just say it.

Christopher stood in front of me. He lifted me off the couch and pulled me into a bone crushing hug.

"I'm so sorry, Teddy. Riordan was in that house. His body is downtown." He didn't let me pull away when I tried, he just held me tighter. When I wet his shirt with my tears, he didn't budge. When my legs gave up, he scooped me up and let me sit on his lap while I cried.

I must have passed out, because I woke up some time later in the night and I was in bed. What shocked me was Snow was lying beside me. His hand in mine, facing me. I wanted to get up, but his grip was solid. He'd wake if I hiccupped.

My mind wandered as I lay there. I hadn't known Riordan very long, but when he opened his door a month ago, he lit a spark inside me. I knew the second I saw him, my life was about to change. I had no idea that in such a short a time, I'd get so attached.

His goodbye in the hospital kept playing over and over again in my head. He knew he likely wasn't making it out alive. He'd made peace with it. I had seen it in his eyes.

When I last saw him, I told him I wanted to find out if we'd ever fall in love, and as I lay there befriending the darkness, I realized I already had.

Hug It Out

A sudden thought hit me, causing me to sit up. Snow jerked awake.

"Teddy?" He began rubbing my back.

"His family. His parents. His sister is on a cruise. They have to know. Oh god. This will kill them." The ache in my heart grew more painful.

"Oh, Teddy." Suddenly I was covered with Snow. He cried with me and when it felt like my chest was going to tear open, he grabbed my face, forcing me to look at him.

"You're allowed to crumble a little right now, Teddy, but you will not shatter. You hear me? We are going to get through this. No matter what, you're never alone." The seriousness and sincerity in his eyes lessened the pain.

"Okay, Snow."

He gave me a small smile and we laid back down. He hugged me like I had done so many times for people like me in this moment. He was good at it. It was the embrace from someone who gave a shit.

The next few days were numbing. It felt like I

was standing in the eye of a storm. But I could see its destruction all around me.

They weren't releasing any of the bodies, and Christopher assured me he was taking care of Riordan's family. I felt like I should be talking to them, but to say what? I let everyone move around me. I begged for time to speed up so the painful shredding inside me would turn into a dull ache. I didn't even care if I was in danger anymore. All of it felt insane. Maybe if Emma came for me next and killed me, it would all end.

My phone vibrated in my pocket. Absently, I looked and saw it was my grandmother. I wanted to ignore it, but it could be serious, so I answered.

"Hey, Gram." I cleared my throat, realizing I hadn't spoken in hours. It was raw.

"Hello, Teddy." That wasn't my grandmother's voice. I knew that voice.

"Emma," I grit out.

"Oh, you sound angry, Teddy." Her laugh was menacing. "Surely you aren't shocked."

"What did you do to my grandmother?"

"You should be nicer to me. Your dear old grandmother has been very kind to me and my people. We would just love it if you could join us."

"If you want to talk to me, why don't you come on over here?"

Her laugh was like ice and I felt its unwelcomed caress. "I haven't gotten this far by being stupid. One doesn't simply waltz into Christopher Manos' house. That's one war I don't need right now. So you can either come to me, alone, or you can bury her right alongside your dear boyfriend."

I was not a violent person, but I wanted to rip her eyes out. I welcomed the anger over pain.

"It won't be easy getting out of here. It's locked up tight. Give me some time." I searched the room. Bill was far enough away, he couldn't hear me, but he was watching.

"You have two hours. Traffic is light. Hurry up, Teddy bear." The call ended and I slipped the phone into my pocket.

I had to think of something. I had to get off this property. Once I did, I could break free and make it to my grandmother's in plenty of time.

"Bill?" He kept his eyes on his phone, but jerked his chin. "Can you drive me to my place to get some things?"

"Now?" He seemed surprised, but took his keys out of his pocket like he wasn't going to argue with me.

"Yeah. I need things to distract me. My things."

We stared each other down for a minute, then he gestured for me to follow. He walked into the study and I heard him telling Christopher he was taking me to get a few things.

If Snow wasn't off picking Simon up from something, he'd likely have offered to come, so I was grateful he wasn't here.

In the car, Bill had the music on low. I waited until we were really close to my grandmother's and near a convenient store.

"Hey, pull in here. I want to grab some candy

Hug It Out

too. Chocolate cures all, right?"

Bill furrowed his brows. He was suspicious, I could tell, but I didn't care in that moment. My grandmother was in danger.

"I'll go in, you stay here. What candy bar?" he asked as he pulled into a spot.

"Anything with nuts and chocolate."

He nodded and slipped out. I waited until he was inside, and then I got out of the car and ran. I was a mile and a half from my grandmother's. If I ran, I'd make it in plenty of time. The sun pounded on my head and sweat poured down my back, but I just kept going. I slowed when I saw her house in the distance.

Closing my eyes, I said a silent prayer that she was okay and if Emma got what she wanted from me, she'd have mercy on her. Just have this end quickly. Please.

My foot had just landed on her property when the front door opened and three huge guys stepped out. One gestured for me to enter. The others didn't give me a chance to run. Like I was going to.

I realized my mistake the second I entered the house. Emma stood in the middle of the living room. Eight guys were around her. Three more were behind me and my grandmother was nowhere in sight. Emma gave me a pleased smile.

"I don't kill bingo loving grandmothers, Teddy." She lifted her gun, pointing it right at me. "I do, however, kill stupid little boys."

Chapter Forty-Four

Riordan

I checked in with Bill as often as I could to get updates on Teddy. I knew he was annoyed with the constant texts and phone calls, but I didn't care. I doubted Teddy would ever forgive me when he realized what I'd done.

When Bill said he barely came out of the bedroom and wasn't even playing any video games, I was about ready to call it quits, sneak into Christopher's place, and beg him to forgive me.

Of course, Jones threatened to knock me out and tie me to a tree if I even thought about it. It was Black, surprisingly, that comforted me. We were hiding out in a house close to Christopher's. I was flipping through the channels on the TV, not really watching, when Black sat beside me. Neither of us spoke for a few minutes. It wasn't awkward, it was surprisingly nice.

Then Black took the remote from my hands and spoke. "I give you a lot of shit for having people in your life that mean something to you. I've told you a million times it's what will be your end."

At first, I thought he was rehashing the same lecture. I was ready to walk away because I didn't need to hear this shit. But his next words halted me.

"I think I was jealous."

I jerked my head toward him. He had a faraway look on his face.

"All those years ago when I forced you into this life, I was a different man. I felt very little and cared about nothing but the mountain of money I sat on and the power that ran through my veins." He released a sigh. "It gets lonely at the top, Riordan, when you have no one to share it with."

When he looked at me, there was a softness I'd never seen from the man adorning his features.

"It's one of those very people that you care so much about who will save us all. There's irony in that

Hug It Out

somewhere." He patted my leg before standing. He towered over me, silver eyes staring almost through me. "When this is all over, when Emma has been taken down and I've regained control of my organization, you're free, Riordan."

"What?" I couldn't hide my surprise. He had told me there was never a way out.

He shrugged. "Between myself and Christopher, I'm sure we can erase your fingerprints, your life as Dullahan, all of it. If Teddy forgives you and loves you like I think only he can, I want you to die old with him in your arms. I want you to enjoy your family. I want you to live the life I never will."

I wanted to say so many things in that moment, but Lee came running in. "We got her!"

Black and I followed Lee as he ran back to his den.

"That guy, Jimmy, he told me the last place Emma was at. It was close to the cave, so I accessed all the street cams. She's good though, I didn't pick her up at first. After the explosion, no mad dashes or anything. It was weird. So I started to hack into the underground cameras. The city has subways and such, but nothing in the 'burbs."

Black rubbed his eyes. "Please get to the point, Lee."

"I am," Lee snapped. "Back in the Twenties, Hart's grandfather built these passageways with rooms during prohibition. Remembering how Jones built the tunnels, it got me thinking, so I looked into the town's history. Sure enough, there was this house with passageways. One in particular leads to an old factory."

"She's using old tunnels?" Mace asked, leaning against the doorframe.

"Yes. But here's the interesting part. It's smack in the middle of everything. It's the only large structure in this area close to Teddy's apartment, his friend Delly, and his grandmother."

"Well, we know he wouldn't go to his apartment if Emma tried to lure him there. He'd see it for what it was," I argued, knowing Teddy would never

Hug It Out

go somewhere because he was told to for no reason.

"I agree." Lee smiled. "Which tells me she will lure Teddy to either his best friend's house or his grandmother's."

Black spoke to Mace, ever the leader. "Text Bill, tell him the two locations Teddy might have been sent to. We need to have eyes on both."

Jones lit a cigarette like none of this was huge news and we needed to get moving. "She won't give him a lot of warning. Emma isn't some dumb bitch. She's one of the smartest people I know. She'll move quickly. We will only have hours. We can't set anything up in advance."

Lee chuckled and Jones' brows shot up. "I don't need hours, Jones." When Lee winked, it was strange. I rarely saw a playful side to either of those guys. "I'll begin preparing now. When we figure out where she's taking him, we will be ready."

Black nodded, already working on his phone, organizing. "Okay, we all need to suit up and be ready to move the second we get word."

We all moved like the machines we'd been trained to be. Bill was able to get us some firepower and some gadgets Lee had asked for before we'd hunkered down here. We dressed and packed.

Mace got his hands on a .308 bolt-action sniper rifle with a variable range adjustable scope and laser range finder. Depending on how many men Emma had, I could take out a few from a distance before busting in and raising hell.

On top of the sniper riffle, I had my .22 caliber, five throwing knives, and garrote. One could never be too careful.

"We want to take as many from afar as possible. I can get close to wherever she is going to work some magic." Lee was shoving gadgets into a black duffle and clipping stuff to his vest. "The more we get before we enter, the better our odds."

We didn't argue. This was Lee's specialty. He was called Whisper for a reason.

We sat, ready to go when Mace's phone beeped.

Hug It Out

"Bill texted. Said Teddy suddenly wanted to go back to his place for something."

That was bad, we hadn't predicted Teddy would go home.

"He got to a convenience store, Bill watched from the window as Teddy ran north. Not the direction of his place."

We looked at the map. Fingers traveling the path north.

"His grandmother's place is the only one north from there." Lee slapped the map, we had a location.

"Let's move," I said. My only worry was we'd be too late. I couldn't lose Teddy. Not when for the first time since that fateful day in a bar, I had a chance to really live and do that with him.

CHAPTER FORTY-FIVE

Teddy

"Do you know what they call me, Teddy?" Emma was sitting on my grandmother's hunter-green lounge chair. I'd been forced to sit on the couch in front of her. Two of her men were on both sides of me, and there was an army behind her.

"I don't. Where's my grandmother?"

"They call me Hemlock." Her smile was wide and victorious. "My specialty is poison." She rested her gun on her lap. She radiated confidence, and even though I was afraid to die, I was a realist too. The chances of me getting out of here were slim. She wanted to torture me with the waiting game, and I was defenseless to stop her.

"Medical files aren't sealed well. I was able to get into yours and noticed you have a rather aggressive allergy to penicillin." Of course, that made sense.

"Had I known you were going to the hospital right after our encounter, I would have chosen something else. But penicillin was your poison and to die from it wouldn't have raised as many flags as cyanide, belladonna, polonium, or something else."

"And now you're going to kill me with a bullet because you weren't smart enough to use your skills to see the places I worked?" Knowing one's fate gave them a second wind, so to speak. Foolish or not, I didn't care. This woman had killed the man I loved, and has done god only knows what to my grandmother.

Her smile faltered for a moment. "I can see why you're angry with me. I will ease your mind. Your grandmother is at church playing bingo for the next hour." She sighed and comically pouted. "You have no one to fault but Riordan, and maybe his sister for hiring you." She tapped the side of her head. "I know why you were staying at Riordan's. You broke the contract by sleeping with him, by the way."

She was joking and laughing. She was a

sociopath. But my grandmother was safe, I hoped.

"Why are you doing any of this? I thought they were your friends. I thought…" I didn't really think anything. I didn't even know why I kept her talking. If death was here for me, I wanted it done already.

"You couldn't possibly understand why." Her face morphed into disgusted anger. "Years, I gave everything I had to Black's organization. I have been there the longest and do you know the thanks I get?" Her question was rhetorical.

"None. No thanks at all. Black is all equal rights for equal fights. I'm worth more than all of them. I'm smarter, more experienced. Better than any man working there. I'd run that company better than Black ever did." Her fingers dug into the upholstery. "I wanted it all. So, I decided to take it. Then they fuck up my entire plan, forcing me to change everything I had worked years to build."

"Ever think that you may be fucking insane?" My voice was raised and I was awarded with a punch to the face from the man to my left. This caused my

Hug It Out

lens to crack and the throb to my temple was immediate.

"You put on your big boy pants today, didn't you, Teddy bear?" Emma stood and stalked toward me. Her moves were feline. "I think I've had enough playtime."

This was it then. I only hoped my grandmother wouldn't be the one to find me and that no one mourned me for too long. I hoped this brought an end to all of it and Emma left Riordan's and my families alone.

Something over Emma's shoulder caught my attention. Four red dots on the foreheads of the men behind her. I didn't have much time to think and no one had any time to react, because it all happened in seconds. One of the windows shattered, the men went down. The men beside me and in back of me barely got time to draw their weapons when the front door burst open. Like dominos, they fell, leaving just the men next to me.

"What the fuck?" Emma shouted, aiming

toward the door. Her shot made me jump because of her proximity.

The window beside her shattered. She didn't know where to turn and she didn't have enough time to make a choice. It was then I realized who was breaking into my grandmother's house.

Lee kicked the gun out of Emma's hand and the two men beside me held their necks as blood poured out of them. I was frozen, watching as the man I thought was dead grabbed Emma by the throat and threw her against my grandmother's chair.

She tried to get up, but Mace came from behind her and held her down while Black and Jones tied her to the chair.

"How are you all alive? Jimmy told me…" Then Riordan interrupted.

"Jimmy told you what we told him to." He looked over at me briefly. A flicker of tenderness and then a mask of fury as he leaned into Emma. "You fucked up, Hemlock."

"Fuck you. Fuck all of you," she screeched. I

had to cover my ears. She began thrashing, her perfectly styled hair was a mess, her eyes rabid, and the snarl she gave Black was threatening.

"I can't listen to this," Black said as he took a syringe out of his pocket, tapped it twice, and then jabbed it into her arm.

The silence was almost as bad as the screeching. No one seemed to move. My grandmother's house was in chaos. Blood covered the couch and carpet. How was I going to explain this to her? How was Riordan alive?

At the sound of crunching, I looked over my shoulder, and my eyes widened when Bill stepped in. It was that moment something inside me snapped.

"You knew?" I shouted, then stood, marching over to him with purpose. "You sat there and watched me fall apart and you knew?"

Bill didn't move, didn't even flinch. He was a wall and he let me beat him down. "I thought you were my friend. How could you?"

"Teddy." Riordan's voice hit me like a ton of

bricks. I'd longed to hear him say my name again. Wished for another minute with him. Yearned to touch him, smell him, and taste him. Now I wanted to throw up.

"No," I whispered. "You died." Spinning around, I took in each of them. Most remorseful. Jones leaned against a wall and lit a cigar. "All of you died." My throat was dry and my stomach churned. "Christopher, he got…" Realization dawned. "All of you knew?"

"You don't understand." Riordan took a step toward me, but I held my hand up to stop him.

"It's like every time I decide to try with you, you hurt me. I mourned you, Riordan." My voice cracked on his name. The mere thought of ever saying it again was a distant hope.

"I hated this, Teddy, you have to know that."

My eyes roamed over the mess, the anger that covered the home I grew up in. The woman in the chair slumped over.

"Is she dead?"

Black shook his head. "No. Asleep. She will be dealt with."

I didn't want to hear it. "I can't." Riordan's green eyes nearly broke me. "I wanted to fall in love with you so badly. But I can't live in this world. I can't be in your orbit, wondering if I'm sleeping with lies or living with ghosts."

"Please," Riordan whispered, taking another step toward me.

"I have to go." My hand swept over the room. "Make this right before my grandmother gets home from bingo in the next thirty minutes." Bill moved out of the way as I passed.

The air outside gave me no reprieve. There was no car to speed off in. I just knew I had to run. I had to get as far away from all this as possible. I didn't know where to go or who to trust. I had blood on my clothes, so Delly's was out of the question. Even though I knew I'd be found, I had to go home. I needed to start over, I needed to rewind an entire month and try to forget ever laying eyes on Riordan Darcy.

Chapter Forty-Six

Riordan

Two weeks. I groveled, sent flowers, emailed, snail mailed, and tried knocking on his door. Lee even offered to help kidnap him and force him to listen. I declined. I couldn't get Teddy to even speak to me. He returned the mail, changed his email, and refused any and all deliveries.

Black called in expert cleaners to take care of Teddy's grandmother's place. She was told someone threw something through her window so it had to be replaced, and she blamed someone called Mr. David. Black said she didn't understand how glass getting on the furniture meant new everything, but she seemed okay with it when one of the men said her grandson wanted it for her. She was also too happy to accept a week at The Camille where she'd be pampered while the renovations were completed.

Hug It Out

Black kept his word and I was officially out of the business. He was cleaning house and said he had things under control. This gave me too much free time.

Aisling came back from her cruise and yelled at me for about a full hour when I told her I'd upset Teddy and he was no longer talking to me. I went to Sunday dinner at my parents' house, but was horrible company. My life was a series of mundane tasks and I walked through it all like I was in a dream.

I was sitting on my couch one Friday in September when there was a buzz at the gate. I was perplexed to see my father's car idling at the entrance. I'd tried to give them the codes when I changed it, but they got tired of remembering them.

I tried to give him my best smile, but my father was no fool. Sometimes, I wondered if he was a spy or assassin in his past given he just knew what lay beneath a person's skin.

"Your mother and I pride ourselves on letting our children grown into who they want to be. Happiness and health were all we wanted for both of you." His fatherly gaze met my nervous one. What was this about?

"I know whatever life you've been living the last fifteen plus years is not one you've wanted. Through the years, your smile dimmed more and more. Health-wise you looked good, but your light was gone." He leaned across the kitchen table and gripped my hand.

"Teddy lit you up. When we were at that barbeque, I saw how you watched every move he made. You smiled when he did even if you couldn't hear what he was saying. You did it subconsciously." His smile was wistful like he had remembered something. "I fell in love with your mother six seconds after I met her."

I knew they met near a café in Ireland. She was visiting her grandmother and he was studying abroad. She had tripped on some broken cobblestones and her shoe got stuck in a hole. My father pried it out, falling into a puddle. Her shoe had flown up in the air and hit him in the head.

Hug It Out

"She looked me dead in the eye, utterly amused with my clumsy heroics, and said, 'Shoes go on your feet, eejit, and red is not your color.' I fell hard for her right then and there."

The smile that formed felt foreign and good. I envied the love my parents had.

"You looked at Teddy how I did, and still do, look at your mother. It doesn't have to make sense, the how or when it happens. Love is a force that no living thing can fight. Love conquers all, son." He released my hand when I got up to fix us coffee.

"I fucked up, Dad." When I handed him the coffee, he was laughing.

"I fuck up a lot, son. Once, I slept in my car for two nights. Then the couch for a week. In all that time, I groveled. I did everything. One night, your mother came into the living room and held her hand out to me and said I'd done my time." He shook his head. "That woman is a firecracker."

"I've been trying. He won't take my calls, my visits, anything." Talking about Teddy made the pain unbearable.

"How long you been at it?" he asked with concern.

"Two weeks, almost three."

My dad knuckled the table. The action made me peek up at his mirth-filled eyes.

"Keep at it."

"How?" I was exasperated.

Shrugging, he answered, "I don't know what you did. I'm guessing it's almost unforgivable. But if you love him, you'll push aside the fact that this is all about you. Who is Teddy? You need to put yourself in his shoes. Be ridiculous if you have to. Embarrass yourself. Show him that no matter how badly you fuck up, you will sacrifice everything to make sure he never forgets how much you love him."

My father was a brilliant man. I'd seen him do the dumbest things to make my mother laugh. He was my hero and I knew he was right. I had been selfish with my apologies. Everything I did to get Teddy to forgive me were things I thought were good. But material things meant nothing to Teddy.

"Thanks, Dad. I know what I have to do."

"I know you do." He smiled and finished his coffee.

After he left, I made a bunch of phone calls and put my plan to work. I needed help and I happened to know a bunch of guys who were clever and had the resources to pull this off.

When everything was set, I called the person I needed to make sure Teddy was where I needed him to be.

"Hello?" The angry greeting told me Snow knew who was calling.

"Don't hang up. I need your help."

He chuckled darkly. "I'm not even speaking to my husband fully. What makes you think I'd talk to you? What you all did was fucked up. Christopher kept it from me and I'm debating divorce. You can go jump off a cliff for all I care." He hung up.

I called back.

"I love him," I said. There was silence. I

thought he had hung up until he spoke.

"I fucking hate you, Riordan." It didn't sound like he really did.

"Yeah, there's a line forming for that."

He hummed as if he believed that to be true. "What do you need me to do?"

And just like that, Operation Get Teddy To Forgive Me was in full effect.

The next morning as I sat in a van at Fredrick's Park with Mace, Lee, and Jones, looking like a fucking idiot, I was nervous. Would Snow keep his word and make sure Teddy came to meditate today?

I could see Black across the way, speaking with the instructor, letting her know what was going to happen. Her head fell back and she was laughing. Yeah, it was absolutely embarrassing.

"Speakers are hooked up," Lee said through his laughter.

"He better fucking forgive me."

Mace patted my shoulder. "If not, we can have a kickass Halloween party this year and you can wear that."

"He's here," Jones grumbled.

Snow, Teddy, and Poe had their blankets in hand and were walking toward the site. Black had darted behind a tree. Snow was looking all around, eyes settling on the van briefly before bumping Teddy's shoulder when he said something.

I hadn't seen Teddy in weeks and the man walking toward the grass wasn't the Teddy I knew. He looked exhausted, he'd cut his hair, taking the curls with him, and his posture sagged.

"Hop to it," Mace joked. I flipped him the bird. He laughed louder and opened the back so I could get out. "Don't forget your prop."

"You're a true friend," I deadpanned.

The door shut and I walked toward the meditation site, waiting for the music to start. God, I just knew this was going to end up on YouTube.

Chapter Forty-Seven

Teddy

I wasn't feeling much like going out, but Snow wasn't accepting no as an answer. Blankets in hand, the three of us strode to our spot. Everyone was stretching, so we settled in and joined.

"What the hell is that?" someone close by said. Tilting my head, I saw the world's biggest, pinkest bunny rabbit carrying an umbrella.

"Oh my god." Snow laughed.

"Is that—?" Poe asked.

Suddenly, Rihanna's "Umbrella" began to play from a van nearby and to my absolute horror, the pink bunny opened the umbrella and began hideously dancing.

"What is he doing?" I asked, unable to look away.

"That, sweet Teddy, is a man with nothing to

Hug It Out

lose but you. He's apologizing by embarrassing himself." Snow slapped my back. "You may want to rescue him before he's arrested for something."

I was so mad at him, the past weeks had been spent doing everything to forget him and trying not to die as I suffocated on the memories of everything. But as I watched him try to move in that bunny suit, I couldn't stop the laugh that erupted.

"That's so romantic," Poe practically swooned.

"How can I forgive him?"

Snow shrugged. "We love men who live in the dark, Teddy." His blue eyes met mine with all seriousness. "We need to be their light."

Love. The song was coming to an end and Riordan was tiring. If I didn't know better, it looked like defeat was settling in. Did I love him?

The other day as I sat with my grandmother, I asked her the same question, and she told me it wouldn't hurt this bad if I didn't love him.

The song ended and the park was quiet. Only the breeze and the birds sang now. Riordan's shoulders slumped and he clumsily walked toward me. I waited.

"I wish there was a more meaningful apology than I'm sorry." He was so close to me. I could smell mint, the scent that reminded me of him. "You told me in that hospital room you wanted to find out if we ever got a chance to fall in love."

"I remember."

"I already fell in love with you, Teddy, and I'll spend every second of the rest of my life proving it if you give me a chance. I won't ask you to forgive me. That will take time. Trusting me again will as well. I get that, I just—" He took a deep breath and his green eyes, full of hope and heartache, met mine. "I want you to let me love you."

I knew everyone in the park was watching and waiting. This man dressed like a fool had killed god knew how many people. Lied to me, hurt me, but they all wanted a storybook ending.

"You hurt me more than anyone ever has," I whispered so only he could hear.

I didn't stop him when his large pink paws

cupped my face. "I did. And I'd do it all again because it was through that pain that you are standing here right now, alive and hating me."

Oh fuck, I was so screwed.

"I want to hate you, Riordan." I really did. "But I can't."

"My father told me that love is a force that conquers all." The side of his mouth curled up.

"Did he also tell you to dress like an oversized rabbit?"

Chuckling, he answered, "He told me to stop making it about me. I realized I knew so very little about you. But it was a moment a month ago when I walked in on you wearing a bunny suit, listening to that song, which changed everything."

I could feel tears pricking my eyes. "Did I look as ridiculous as you do right now?"

Shaking his head and laughing, he only got out the word, "No." Then my lips were crashing against his.

I could hear people clapping, cheering, and

whistling. But I was too busy kissing my huge, pink, assassin rabbit man in the middle of the park.

When we pulled away, I took a peek around, noticing Black, Mace, Jones, and Lee were there clapping with everyone else. These merry murdering men with hearts of gold. What insane world had I fallen into?

"Can I take you home?" Riordan asked, and I didn't have to think about it.

"Absolutely."

I didn't know what my life had in store, but I knew I'd be mad at Riordan a million times and we'd make up. I knew what Snow said was right, I had to be his light. What Snow didn't realize was Riordan was also the light I never knew I needed.

Epilogue

Riordan

Nine Months Later

"Oh God, is that normal?" I asked Teddy as I watched Aisling's belly transform. "It looks like there's an MMA championship going on in there."

Teddy was hysterically laughing. "She's about to give birth, the baby is active. It's totally normal." His eyes widened when he looked at me. "Are you going to pass out?"

"He better not fucking pass out!" Aisling shouted. Sweat dripped down her face, her eyeliner was flowing down her cheeks. She never looked more beautiful than she did in that moment.

"I won't I promise." I took her hand, Robert took her other. Teddy wiped her forehead. My mother was counting while Aisling gave her a look like she wanted to murder her. My father was pacing outside the delivery room. He said he couldn't see his daughter that way. We all had our jobs it seemed, and I didn't want mine. She was my sister. I didn't want to see things come out of her body.

"Maybe I should go wait with Dad, there's already too many people in here and the nurse is gonna kick some of us out soon. I'm sure of it."

Aisling made some unladylike noise and waved me away. I was free and I fled like dogs were snapping at my feet. When I opened the door, my father looked at me expectantly.

"Nothing yet. Sorry."

He nodded and I paced alongside him. We watched as nurses went in and out of the room.

A nurse poked her head out of the delivery room. "Doctor, she's ready to push," the nurse said, and suddenly I was terrified. Of all the things I had faced in my life, nothing was scarier than the thought of losing someone I loved.

My father wrapped an arm around my shoulder. "She's a warrior. She'll be fine."

Hug It Out

Of course, my father was right and less than thirty minutes later, the sound of a baby crying filled the corridor. My father and I hugged, and yeah, cried.

After a couple of minutes, Teddy came out, smiling brightly.

"It's a boy," he said.

My father didn't wait, he ran into the room, much to Teddy's amusement. When he looked at me, I saw all the love he had for me in those hazel eyes.

"You're amazing," I told him as I held out my hand.

"So are you, Uncle Riordan." He wrapped his arms around me. Best hugger in the world.

"I love you so much, Teddy Harris."

He chuckled and pressed his lips against mine. "I love you so much too, Riordan Darcy."

It had been a difficult nine months. Teddy had a hard time trusting me. He questioned every time I went out and everything I said. I snapped at him, he snapped back. We made love and we fucked. He walked out, I went after him. Finally, one night when

I lay in bed watching him sleep, I realized even though he was putting me through hell, I loved every second of it.

Tonight I had asked him to go with me to dinner. I was going to ask him to be a part of my family forever. We'd just sat down to eat when my phone rang. Robert was uncharacteristically frantic. He didn't say hello, he just shouted, "Baby coming now," and hung up. Our night was cut short but there was a new addition to our family.

The ring felt heavy in my pocket. "Take a walk with me?" I asked, and Teddy agreed.

There was a garden on the ground floor. It was after midnight, so only a few people lingered. The fragrant smells likely a balm for so many receiving bad news. Tonight, it would see some joy…. I hoped.

"I wanted to ask you something, Teddy." Sitting at the fountain, I patted the seat next to me. Smiling, Teddy took it.

"Oh? And what did you want to ask me?" He had a knowing smile, but he wasn't going to take this moment from me.

I reached into my pocket and pulled out the Claddagh ring that had been my grandfather's. Teddy noticed it, but he wouldn't look away from my face.

"Teddy Harris, you've changed my life. You've given me a life I never thought I'd have. To think of living without you tears my heart to pieces and I never want that."

"Sounds painful." He chuckled.

"Yeah. So, I was wondering. Maybe." When I got to one knee, the few people who were there started noticing. "I seem to like making a spectacle of myself for you."

"You're very romantic," Teddy said through his tears.

"Teddy, would you do me the honor of hugging me till death do us part?"

His tears turned to laughter. He said yes through his blubbering. I was grateful he let me stand before attacking my face with kisses.

I would never know how safe I was. I had

enemies out there, people I had pissed off. Black said I was safe, but that wasn't a promise he could keep. I refused to let that fear control me. I chose to love. I chose to wrap myself around this man for as long as fate allowed. No matter how bad life got or how horrible I felt, all I had to do was look at those hazel eyes and know he'd make it okay.

In the words of this amazing man, we'd hug it out.

THE END

Author's Note

Thank you for reading Hug It Out. Riordan and Teddy hugged my heart fiercely while I wrote this, and I hope you loved them just As much as I did.
I love talking with readers so find me on social media or shoot me an email at davidsonkingauthor@yahoo.com
Facebook:
www.facebook.com/DavidsonKingAuthor
Twitter:
www.twitter.com/DavidsonKing11
Instagram
www.instagram.com/davidsonkingauthor/?hl=en

Acknowledgements

With each passing book I learn more and appreciate more. I'm creating a universe and loving every second of it. But, it's more than just me doing it. There are so many people to thank for making these books possible.

My children and husband for being patient with me when I'm freaking out over deadlines and editing. They give me strength and remind me to breathe.

To Annabella, Luna, and Morningstar, for being my unpaid therapists and helping me make Hug It Out all it could possibly be.

Heidi Ryan for believing in me and pushing me every day to trust myself and dig deep to make this world spectacular.

Kate Aaron never fails to teach me with each book I write. She encourages and loves and settles for nothing less than my best.

Jenn Gibson for wanting all the darkness to

pour from my characters. She scares me, but I love her so much.

Jami Dabney, every time I think I've broken her she dusts herself off and comes back for more. She may be just as crazy as I am, but I love her for it.

Michelle Slagan, my extraordinary cheerleader. Never fails to remind me I can do this.

And of course, Nutter. AKA TC Orton. He's my best friend and I adore his insane chicken loving, mayo obsessed brain.

This book wouldn't have come to fruition without this team of people and I can't thank them enough or tell them enough how amazing they are to me.

The support I receive from all my readers means more to me than words will ever express. Thank you so much. I love you!

About the Author

Davidson King always had a hope that someday her daydreams would become real-life stories. As a child, you would often find her in her own world, thinking up the most insane situations. It may have taken her awhile, but she made her dream come true with her first published work, Snow Falling.

When she's not writing you can find her blogging away on Diverse Reader, her review and promotional site. She managed to wrangle herself a husband who matched her crazy and they hatched three wonderful children.

If you were to ask her what gave her the courage to finally publish, she'd tell you it was her amazing family and friends. Support is vital in all things and when you're afraid of your dreams, it will be your cheering section that will lift you up.

Readers May Also Like

Found (Hamilton Heroes Book 1)

As a former USAF pararescueman, Jeremy O'Brien is used to following orders, no questions asked. So, when Micah, his boss at Hamilton Security, asks him to take on a special case, he readily accepts. Micah's instructions are simple, find the man in the picture and bring him back to Chicago.

Seven years ago, Zane Wilkinson left the hospital against doctor's orders, only to suffer a final, devastating blow that left him with no choice but to leave the only place he'd called home. Feeling heartbroken and empty, Zane moved from town to town just trying to survive, while never letting anyone get too close.

In a chance encounter, Jeremy finds himself crossing paths with a man who fits Zane's description. His instincts tell him that he's on to something, but Micah warns him that he needs to be absolutely sure. Jeremy sets a plan in motion that will allow him to get closer to the man he believes to be Zane. However, the closer he gets, the more he likes the man and begins to question why he was sent to find him.

Will Jeremy be able to follow through with his orders without becoming too attached? Or will he realize that in his search for Zane, he's found so much more than he bargained for?

A Different Light (A Begin Again Novel Book 1)

Bennett Cole had lived next door to Mitchell "Mac" Campbell, III for eighteen years of his life, in the small town of White Acre. They'd never gotten along, never seen eye to eye, and never understood one another…not that they'd ever cared to try.

But when Bennett's so-called buddies ditched him at a party in the woods where he was assaulted and left for dead, Bennett pulled through. The emotional scars rendered him too terrified to go back to school and face his "friends" or his attackers. With little choice, his family packed up and left town.

Ten years later—at the request of his mother—

Bennett returned to the place he'd grown up and the home he'd once felt safe, to oversee the repairs before his childhood house was sold. The contractor? None other than Mac, the once annoying boy next door, who still lives there in the home his parents gifted him.

Being in such close proximity—working together every day, to repair the Coles' family home—Bennett and Mac's contentious relationship goes from bad to worse as their personalities continue to clash. But their heated exchanges may not be as antagonistic as they seem. And when new information is revealed, can the men begin to see each other in a different light?

Let Me In (The Boys Club Book 1)

Twenty-year-old Liam Cavanagh works three dead-end-jobs to take care of his family. He's been the sole breadwinner since he was fifteen and yearns for a life of his own. Forced to grow up too fast, he carries the burdens of responsibilities that shouldn't be his, and it's slowly destroying him. The more he tries to control, the more out of control he feels.

When he gets a hit on a personal ad he placed

on The Boys Club app, he shrugs it off as impossible. With nearly 600 miles between him and "Boston Daddy" he knew the odds were against them. Until Boston Daddy's current boy convinces him otherwise and persuades Liam to take on the role of Daddy's new boy.

Saying forty-year-old entrepreneur Cash Moreau is having a bad week is an understatement. The man he's been with for years leaves him for a new job, his own company is in crisis, and to top it all off, a young stranger shows up on his doorstep with all his worldly possessions, claiming to be his new boy. Liam wants a Daddy to depend on, and Cash refuses to believe he's what's best for Liam.

Despite their powerful connection, Cash finally pushes Liam away, and the beautiful boy who stole his heart disappears. Soon, Cash realizes what he's let slip through his fingers. The elusive thing he's been searching for is Liam, it's only ever been Liam, and suddenly Cash will move heaven and earth to find what he's lost. Will he find his boy in time to make things right, or is it too late to let him in?

Printed in Great Britain
by Amazon